PRAISE FOR ⸃
THE LIFE S

"The glamorous cast of characters in Anita Abriel's *The Life She Wanted* captivated me from the start, while the unforgettable setting had me dreaming about stepping inside every mansion in wealthy 1920s New York. But I adored Pandora most, the novel's plucky heroine whose single father works at one of the region's grand estates, giving Pandora entrée into a world of glittery formal balls and suitors with deep pockets. And while Pandora seems like she's on a path to good fortune, her story shows us it's rare that life turns out as planned—no matter how much money you have. For anyone who loves a sweeping rags-to-riches tale, Anita Abriel's novel delights!"

—Brooke Lea Foster, author of *On Gin Lane*

"A compulsively readable coming-of-age story set against a dazzling Roaring Twenties backdrop, *The Life She Wanted* had me flipping pages late into the night. Full of intricately researched history and characters you'll root for, Anita Abriel's latest proves it might be a long and winding road, but true love always finds a way. Fans of *The Gilded Age* will devour this treat of a novel!"

—Kristy Woodson Harvey, *New York Times* bestselling author of *The Wedding Veil*

"This is a fast-paced historical read that examines the roles of men and women in the 1920s, what was accepted and what was not, and the idea that sometimes what you are looking for is right in front of you."

—*Booklist*

The PHILADELPHIA HEIRESS

ALSO BY ANITA ABRIEL

The Life She Wanted
A Girl During the War
Lana's War
The Light After the War

The PHILADELPHIA HEIRESS

ANITA ABRIEL

LAKE UNION
PUBLISHING

Text copyright © 2024 by Anita Hughes
All rights reserved.

Published by Lake Union Publishing, Seattle

www.apub.com

Amazon, the Amazon logo, and Lake Union Publishing are trademarks of Amazon.com, Inc., or its affiliates.

ISBN-13: 9781662509841 (paperback)
ISBN-13: 9781662509834 (digital)

Cover design by Faceout Studio, Elisha Zepeda
Cover images: © Anneka / Shutterstock; © Arelix / Shutterstock;
© Everett Collection / Shutterstock; © Lana Nikova / Shutterstock;
© Retan / Shutterstock

Printed in the United States of America

To my mother

Chapter One

The Main Line, Philadelphia, May 1927

If only nineteen-year-old Helen Montgomery hadn't seen her father across the restaurant at the Plaza Hotel in New York, it would have been the best birthday she could have imagined.

The day started with her eighteen-year-old sister, Daisy, coming into her bedroom at their parents' estate, Dumfries on the Main Line in Philadelphia, and heaping the bed with presents. A book on Ayrshire cows and the new Al Jolson record for the gramophone their parents bought last Christmas.

Breakfast was waiting for them in the morning room downstairs. Sunny-side-up eggs that the cook, Mary, prepared just the way Helen liked them—runny in the middle, served blissfully hot on whole-wheat toast with lots of butter. Helen's mother, Charlotte, poured the morning coffee from the silver coffeepot on the sideboard. Helen felt so grown up and mature, sipping coffee with milk and sugar.

Her mother's presents had been what she expected: a new dress from Wanamaker's department store and a bottle of Chanel's Gardénia perfume. Helen loved the perfume's pretty glass bottle and the golden liquid inside, but she wasn't much interested in fragrances. She would have preferred a pair of sensible boots she could wear when she visited her father's cows and some lotion to rub on her hands after a day spent working on the farm.

But Charlotte didn't approve of the hours Helen spent with the cows. Her mother felt she should be preparing for the debutante balls that would be held that summer. Helen loved her mother and didn't want to disappoint her, so she rubbed the perfume on her wrists and declared she'd wear it every day.

Then Uncle Jack appeared, rakishly dressed in a pin-striped suit with suspenders and pleated slacks. A boater hat was perched on his head, and he didn't wear a vest or waistcoat.

Their excursion to New York was the real birthday treat. A two-hour drive in Jack's bright red Packard Twin 6 Roadster. Lunch in the Palm Court of the Plaza Hotel, followed by an afternoon at the Natural History Museum and a Broadway show at night. They were going to see *No, No, Nanette*. "Tea for Two" and "I Want to Be Happy" were already hits on the radio, and Helen had been looking forward to it for weeks.

Except now the day was ruined, as if the weather forecast had promised nothing but sunshine and instead the sky was filled with ominous rain clouds. The man in the booth couldn't be her father. Robert was at his office in Rittenhouse Square or lunching with clients at his private club. He couldn't be sitting across from that woman, a girl really, with a sleek dark bob, kohl under her large brown eyes, and a slash of red lipstick for a mouth.

"We'll start with oysters Rockefeller, and I suggest the pork chop with mashed potatoes and green beans," Jack was saying. "I already asked Jacques, the maître d', for two champagne cocktails. It's a pity we have to drink them in coffee cups; the best part of champagne is watching it fizz." He sighed, putting down the menu. "Prohibition is getting so tedious; I'm tempted to visit President Coolidge and ask him to put a stop to it."

Helen pulled her gaze away from her father and turned to Jack. Jack was her mother's younger brother. He was thirty, and even if Helen had known him for too long to be impressed by his good looks, she would still be aware of what an attractive man he was. Wherever they went, women stopped and stared at Jack. His eyes were the color of aquamarines, and he had blond hair and a long, lean physique. The best part about Jack was his smile. It was wide and genuine and accompanied by a twinkle in his eye.

Helen laughed. "You don't know the president."

"No, I don't," Jack admitted. "The country can't go on like this forever. The bootleggers are getting rich, and the rest of us behave like criminals. I had to slip Jacques a twenty-dollar bill for the champagne. I don't mind paying extra; it's the underhandedness of the thing."

Helen glanced again at the booth across the room. She had seen only the man's profile; she must be mistaken. Her parents had been happily married for twenty years. They might not be demonstrative toward each other, but they weren't characters in the Georgette Heyer romance novels her mother read by the swimming pool.

If her father was passionate about anything besides his family, it was his cows. Robert loved the Ayrshire cows as much as Helen did—it was one of the bonds between them. Together they named every calf when it was born, and he kept photos of his favorite cows over the years on a table in his study.

"Thank you for bringing me." Helen determinedly fixed her attention on the silver saltshaker on their table. "Lunch at the Palm Court and a whole afternoon in New York. I'm the luckiest girl there is."

"I'm the lucky one," Jack returned. "I get to spend the day with one of my two favorite nieces."

Helen smiled. "You only have two nieces," she said.

"That's because they're the loveliest young ladies anywhere. What would be the point of having more?"

Helen wasn't sure what Jack did with his days. He didn't go to an office like her father, who managed Montgomery Investments, the financial firm started by Robert's grandfather. Helen's mother's family was even older than her father's—a female member of the Tyler family made her debut at the inaugural Philadelphia Assemblies ball in 1748.

When the railroad line pushed west from Philadelphia in the 1830s, Charlotte's great-grandfather bought a plot of land in Ardmore along the stretch of green countryside that would become the Main Line. Helen imagined what it must have looked like then: just paddocks and creeks and fields.

Now the winding roads were lined with maple trees and studded with grand estates. The Wideners' neoclassical-style mansion, Lynnewood Hall, had 110 rooms and its own art museum, and Cheswold Manor, which was built in the 1870s for the stockbroker Alexander Cassatt, was a Queen Anne–style villa with stained-glass windows and more bedrooms than Helen could count. When Helen and Daisy were young, they used to love playing hide-and-go-seek in the woods that adjoined the two properties.

Jack probably lived off his inheritance and the pieces he sold as an artist. He had attended the Pennsylvania Academy of the Fine Arts. His teachers thought he was gifted, but it wasn't a suitable profession for someone of his social status. Instead, he showed his work only at small galleries or sold them to friends.

Jack interrupted her thoughts. "Your mother asked us to pick up the dresses for your season at Lord & Taylor."

Helen flinched. She didn't want to be reminded of the parties that would take up so much of her summer.

Jack noticed her disappointed expression. "Don't look so crestfallen," he said. "Most girls would be thrilled to have their gowns made in New York."

"The only reason debutante balls exist is to find a husband, and I don't want to get married."

"Of course you do. Everyone wants to fall in love and get married."

"You're not married," Helen pointed out. "And you're already thirty."

"You mustn't remind anyone over twenty-five of their age." Jack grimaced. "And I'm happier being the doting uncle."

"Didn't you ever want to get married?" Helen asked curiously.

Jack's face, which was usually as bright and welcoming as the sun on a summer day, closed up. He hunched forward and fiddled with the silverware.

"It's easy to believe you're in love when you're young," he said non-committally. "Then you wake up the next morning and realize it was actually a reaction to a particularly fine bottle of wine. By the time you've recovered from the hangover, the feeling is gone as well." He turned to the menu. "Now, let's move on to the important things. Will you have the pork chop or lobster?"

Helen looked up and caught sight of her father again. He was talking to a waiter, and this time she could see his whole face. It was definitely him.

She glanced down quickly and noticed her hands were shaking. If only they could leave, but it would be too embarrassing. The maître d' had seated them at a table in the middle of the room, and everyone would see them.

"The pork chop, please." Her voice was tight, and she tried to ignore the tears that sprung to her eyes. "Without the mashed potatoes. I'm not that hungry."

They ate oysters Rockefeller sprinkled with parsley and talked about the new stables in Central Park. Helen adored horses almost as much as her beloved cows. She had her first pony when she was four and won her first ribbon at the Devon Horse Show at the age of ten.

"You've barely touched your pork chop," Jack said, eating the last bite of his lobster.

Helen wished she had ordered the lobster instead. Lobster was soft and pink; it practically melted in her mouth. The lamb chop was delicious, but it required chewing. Helen was too upset to make the effort, and she had completely lost her appetite.

"We can send it back if you don't like it." Jack turned around to signal the waiter.

His gaze fell on the booth where her father and the girl were sitting.

Jack dropped his arm and turned back to Helen. His cheeks were ashen, and lines formed on his forehead.

"Oh, I see."

Helen put down her fork. Her voice was as light and airy as when she and Daisy ate fairy floss at the Devon Country Fair.

"She must be one of my father's clients," she said. "He's probably advising her on whether she should invest her money in real estate or the stock market."

Helen knew it wasn't true. The girl wasn't wearing gloves like most of the wives of Robert's clients, and her handbag looked like it came from Woolworth's. Even her eyebrows were different from the women Helen knew. They were thick and arched, like the back of a caterpillar.

"Why don't we get the check and go somewhere else," Jack suggested.

Helen glanced once more at the two figures across the room. Her father was forty, but he was still handsome. He had thick, dark hair and angular cheekbones. Helen had inherited his brown eyes and long patrician nose. Helen thought her nose made her look like a schoolteacher, but on her father, it made him resemble a Roman statue. And he dressed beautifully. Today he was wearing a herringbone suit from his tailor in Philadelphia and a Gieves & Hawkes shirt that Charlotte brought back from her latest shopping trip to London.

Jack had already dropped a few bills on the table. Helen gathered her purse and followed him into the lobby.

Helen had visited the Plaza only a few times. The last time was when she was sixteen and her parents brought her and Daisy to see the Christmas windows in the department stores.

Afterward, they had sat in the deep velvet sofas of the Plaza's lobby. Helen and Daisy wore their new holiday dresses, and other guests commented they were a beautiful family.

Now, Jack sat on an upholstered armchair in the lobby and took out his cigarette case.

"Can I have a cigarette, please?" Helen held out her hand.

Jack raised his eyebrows. "Since when do you smoke?"

He gave her a cigarette and held up his lighter.

"Since now," Helen said grimly, leaning forward to light the cigarette.

The cigarette tasted terrible, like molasses mixed with cough syrup. But the sharpness of the smoke hitting her lungs, the stinging in her eyes, somehow numbed the pain in her chest.

Helen may not have had a boyfriend or been properly kissed, but she knew all about sex. She had helped her father birth cows since she was a child. How could he put his marriage in jeopardy for a fling with some showgirl?

"We don't have to stay in New York," Jack offered. "I'll ask the valet to bring around the car, and we'll drive back to Philadelphia."

Helen didn't know what she wanted to do. She remembered her first day at boarding school, at Foxcroft School in Virginia. Until she was sixteen, she'd had a governess, and she envied the other girls who loaded their trunks into their parents' roadsters and drove off to some faraway place where twenty girls ate together in the dining hall, and there were games and weekend excursions.

But when her parents allowed her to go to Foxcroft, she was terrified. Sharing a dorm room with six girls who already knew each other was the loneliest feeling in the world. She had the same feeling now, of not belonging anywhere. She didn't want to stay in New York, and she certainly didn't want to see a Broadway musical. But would Dumfries look the same as it had this morning? Or would her father's jacket hanging in the closet, the chess set waiting for him in the living room, make the pain in her chest even sharper?

"I don't want to go home yet," Helen answered.

"What would you like to do?" Jack asked.

They could go riding in Central Park. Nothing was as soothing as being on a horse. But that reminded her that she and her father were supposed to take part in the foxhunt at the Radnor Hunt on Saturday.

Or they could stop at the animal shelter in Bensalem outside Philadelphia and pick up a dog for Tommy, the stable hand. Helen's mother had taught her that doing something nice for someone else was the quickest way to get over one's own disappointments.

The pain in her chest became more pronounced. Helen may have been closer to her father because they had so much in common, but her mother was beautiful and kind, and she loved her fiercely. How could her father do something to hurt her mother?

It was Helen's birthday, and she was supposed to be enjoying herself. She would put it out of her mind and do exactly as they planned. Spending all afternoon at the Natural History Museum would work up her appetite, and she'd make up for not eating lunch by ordering crab cakes at Sardi's, with chocolate ice cream for dessert. And she'd spend some of her birthday money on presents for her mother and Daisy when she picked up her dresses at Lord & Taylor. A bottle of Coty perfume for Daisy and a new pair of gloves for her mother.

She opened her mouth to tell Jack when she noticed her father and the girl entering the lobby. She expected them to walk to the row of elevators, but instead they strolled through the lobby toward the street.

They weren't going up to a room. Perhaps it was perfectly innocent. Her father was investing in a Broadway show. The girl was the star, and Robert had taken her to lunch. Now he was driving her back to the theater.

Suddenly, Helen knew what she had to do.

"Ask the valet to bring the car. I want to follow them," she said to Jack.

"Wouldn't it be better to wait until your father gets home?" Jack pleaded, taking another cigarette from the case.

Helen was already standing up and walking toward the entrance.

"Please, I have to see where they're going."

Jack studied the cigarette, as if it would give him the answer.

"All right, if you insist." He stood up. "But I feel terrible. It's your birthday; it should be the happiest day of the year."

Helen climbed into the passenger seat of Jack's Packard, and he pulled onto Fifth Avenue. Her father's blue Chrysler was ahead of them.

Instead of driving to the theater district, the car drove through to the Queensboro Bridge.

"Are you sure you want to do this?" Jack asked when the Packard was sailing along the bridge.

Helen wished she had brought her scarf. Her light brown hair flew around her cheeks, and the breeze tickled the back of her neck.

She nodded. "Quite sure." She turned to Jack and gave her most winning smile. "You really are the best uncle. You were promised an afternoon of visiting the water buffalo exhibit at the museum, and now you're playing taxi driver."

"I can see the water buffalo anytime." Jack matched her smile with one of his own. "Anyway, I've always enjoyed a good mystery. Sherlock Holmes is one of my favorite literary characters."

They drove in silence for a while. The sky was pale blue, and flocks of seagulls soared above the East River.

"You know, maybe you don't have to hold your debutante ball this summer," Jack said. "You and I could go hiking in the Swiss Alps. There are dozens of dairy farms."

Helen would give anything to miss her season. But she had to come out first—Daisy already had to wait until next summer. And Daisy was looking forward to it. The wall above her sister's dressing table was plastered with illustrations of white satin gowns from Bergdorf's in New York.

Jack was just being kind, as if he knew what she was thinking. That the idea of taking her father's arm in the ballroom of the Bellevue-Stratford Hotel, when she had seen that girl clinging to his wrist, was impossible to imagine.

They drove past a sign welcoming them to Oyster Bay. Mansions facing the Atlantic were painted pale pink like pearls in their shells. One resembled a Scottish castle, and another was the architect's idea of the Taj Mahal. It had a rectangular swimming pool and domed roof and gold-tipped white columns.

All of New York's new money had built summer homes on Long Island. J. P. Morgan; Charles Pratt, who owned Standard Oil; and the department store magnate F. W. Woolworth. It was different in Philadelphia. Everyone on the Main Line knew money alone couldn't buy entrance into society.

Jack's car stopped in front of a four-story mansion built in the French neoclassical style. Gray stone columns flanked the entrance, and three separate wings faced a forecourt. Behind the gates was a park and a formal French garden. Robert's Chrysler was parked in the driveway.

Jack let out a low whistle. "I thought the Main Line had huge estates. Some of these places make them look like matchboxes."

The girl couldn't own one of these palaces. So what were her father and the girl doing here?

"Maybe this wasn't a good idea. Why don't we keep driving," Jack suggested. "Buy some oysters to take home."

Helen had always prided herself on being brave. She'd started competing in horse jumping at the age of nine. Whenever she fell off the horse, she brushed herself off and climbed right back on. She had to be brave now; she couldn't turn away.

"You buy the oysters," Helen said. "Come back and pick me up later."

"Helen, please. You're nineteen, and it's none of your business."

"Of course it's my business." Helen opened the car door. "And my great-aunt Alice was a nurse in the Civil War when she was seventeen."

Helen walked briskly through the parklike setting. A sundial was made of roses, and the gravel drive was lined with pink flowering horse chestnuts and pin oaks.

She knocked and waited for someone to answer. To her surprise, a maid didn't open the door. Instead, it was her father.

"Helen! What are you doing here?" he asked in shock.

Robert had taken off his jacket. He held a brandy glass in one hand; in the other there was a cigarette.

Helen felt slightly sick. She put on her most confident tone. "Can I come in?"

"Of course." He ushered her inside. "Why are you here? Did something happen . . ."

The interior was furnished in the French eighteenth-century style, with low-hanging chandeliers and gold mirrors resting against the walls. Reception rooms led off from the entrance, and she caught sight of a dining room with an ornate ceiling and an oval table set with silver candlesticks.

"Jack and I were having lunch at the Plaza." Helen pulled off her gloves and followed her father into the living room.

Robert's cheeks turned pale. He placed the brandy on a coffee table and sat heavily on a chair.

"I can explain—"

"You don't have to," Helen cut him off. "It's perfectly clear."

Until the moment her father's expression changed, she had hoped that it was all a mistake. But now she knew for sure. Anything her father said wouldn't be an explanation, it would be an excuse.

"I suppose it is." Robert sighed.

The lit cigarette glowed in his hand. He took a long drag and flicked the ashes into an ashtray.

"I should go," she said shakily, telling a small white lie. "Jack drove me here; he'll be waiting in the car."

"Helen, wait. We'll drive back to the city together. We'll take my car."

Helen shook her head. "No, thank you." The pain in her chest was so sharp it was hard to breathe. "There's no need for you to go."

She was about to leave when the girl appeared in the hallway. She had changed into a pink satin hostess gown. A bandeau was wrapped around her dark hair, and she wore slippers adorned with silk rosettes.

"I didn't know we had company." She joined them and held out her hand. "I was changing out of my city clothes. I'm Rosalee."

Up close, the girl appeared older than she did at the restaurant. Her cheeks were heavily powdered, and her skin sagged a little around her mouth. She had reapplied her lipstick and wore a diamond bracelet around her wrist.

"You must be a neighbor; we've only been here a month," Rosalee continued before Helen could answer. "Isn't this place divine? It's called Chateau-sur-Mer. I love everything French. See that clock?" She pointed to an antique clock on the sideboard. "It's a Louis XVI musical clock. It was a gift to Marie Antoinette.

"I'll give you a tour if you like," Rosalee prattled on. "There are twelve bathrooms, and each one has a bidet. The designer said they're all the rage in Europe." She leaned forward conspiratorially. "The French don't like to use toilet paper."

"No, thank you. I have to go," Helen said quickly.

"You must at least see the garden." Rosalee took Helen's arm. "It was designed by Carrère and Hastings in New York."

Helen let herself be dragged to the terrace. A fountain stood in the middle of a swimming pool. There was a pavilion and a long walk lined with marble statues.

"The fountain has twelve jets," Rosalee said proudly. "We haven't had any parties yet, but when we do, you have to come."

Robert joined them on the terrace.

"Helen isn't a neighbor," he said to Rosalee. "She's my daughter. It's her birthday, and she was having lunch at the Plaza."

Rosalee's brow furrowed. She took a moment to absorb the information.

"You're Robert's daughter! He's told me so much about you." She beamed. "Why don't we go in and celebrate. I'm sure the cook baked some type of cake. Pineapple upside-down cake is my favorite."

Helen couldn't take another minute. She ran through the house and down the driveway until she reached Crescent Beach Road.

She waited in the hot sun for Jack and wished that it was any day besides her birthday and that she was anywhere besides Oyster Bay.

Chapter Two

On the drive from Oyster Bay to Philadelphia, Jack kept glancing at Helen to make sure she was all right. Helen couldn't look at him. She kept her hands on her hair to stop it from blowing in the breeze and her eyes focused ahead of her.

Helen was grateful that Jack didn't press her. What could she say? That her father had installed this girl in a mansion that rivaled Dumfries. She recalled the glimpses of more reception rooms as she hurried toward the entrance. Rooms with green velvet drapes and petit point Louis XVI love seats. A small army of gardeners had been working outside when she fled down the driveway.

Helen insisted they pick up her dresses at Lord & Taylor. She refused to ignore her responsibilities. At the same time, she bought the gifts for her mother and Daisy. She even selected a scarf for Mary, the cook.

Jack dropped her off in front of Dumfries, and she ran straight up to her room. She threw her gloves on the bed and curled up with her new book on Ayrshire cows.

She had to tell Daisy. Daisy would be so upset; she and their mother were very close. They shared the same classic beauty and the same tastes. Daisy had Charlotte's blue eyes and blonde hair worn in waves to her shoulders.

When her parents took them to France last summer, Charlotte and Daisy stayed in Paris and picked out a new wardrobe at Chanel and Jean

Patou. Helen and her father spent two days driving in a rented Peugeot around the Loire Valley, sampling goat cheese at farms.

The "chèvre," as it was known in France, was soft and sweet, with a thick rind and a center that resembled sponge cake. In the end, they decided not to keep goats at Dumfries. Nothing could compare to the cheese produced by Ayrshire cows. It was as rich as cream and had a taste that was tangy and flavorful at the same time.

"What are you doing home?" Daisy asked, entering the bedroom. "You're supposed to be at the theater."

Helen closed the book. She jumped up and straightened her room, trying to think of what to say.

"I didn't feel like going." She placed her T-strap sandals in the closet. "A birthday dinner at home sounded like more fun."

Daisy arched her eyebrows suspiciously.

"We have family dinners every night, and you've been looking forward to *No, No, Nanette* for weeks. You were going to go backstage and get William Bailey's autograph."

William Bailey was the male lead, and he was incredibly handsome, with brooding eyes under dark eyelashes.

"We'll go together and see a matinee," Helen suggested.

Daisy sat on the bed. She crossed her arms and gazed at Helen steadily.

"Something's wrong. I just saw Father arrive. He and Mother went straight into his study."

Helen ran to the window. Her father's car was parked at an angle in the driveway. He almost never left his car outside; it was kept in the garage.

He must have left Oyster Bay soon after she did. Her heart beat wildly, and she wondered what her parents were saying.

"You better tell me what happened," Daisy insisted.

Helen told Daisy about her birthday lunch and the estate on Long Island. When she finished, Daisy crossed her arms. Her blue eyes were larger than ever.

"Nothing has to be different. Maybe Father won't tell her," Daisy said.

"She has to know! Wouldn't you want to know if Roland was unfaithful?"

Daisy had been seeing Roland for more than a year. They were going to announce their engagement next summer after Daisy's season. Roland was in his third year at Harvard, and they planned to get married after he graduated.

"Roland would never do that," Daisy said. "Mother has been married since she was nineteen. What would she do all alone?"

"She wouldn't be alone. You just started college, and I'm not getting married anytime soon," Helen insisted. "Anyway, nothing is as important as knowing the truth."

Daisy shook her head. "I don't agree. No one is perfect. Husbands have dalliances all the time."

"You sound like the heroine in one of Mother's romance novels," Helen said angrily. "How could Mother respect herself if he carries on under her nose?"

"I'm not saying she should agree with it," Daisy said. "But if he promises not to see the girl again, she should forgive him."

Helen gazed out the window. It was a perfect spring evening. The forests and fields were greenish gold under the setting sun. She and Daisy had so much fun when they were children. Daisy loved riding as much as Helen, and they often packed a picnic and rode across the pastures. Whole days were spent in the swimming hole that was fed by its own spring, and they loved to play tennis.

Had they taken it for granted? That everything in their world would always stay the same.

Helen turned back to Daisy. "It's not up to us."

"Well, I hope he doesn't tell her." Daisy moved to the door. "I'm going to get dressed. Roland is coming for dinner."

"Wait." Helen remembered her present. She picked it up from the pile on the bed. "This is for you."

"But it's your birthday." Daisy frowned, taking the package.

Helen felt foolish. It had seemed like a good idea, but a bottle of new perfume wouldn't ease the pain of what was going to happen to their family.

After Daisy left, Helen washed her face and changed into a blouse and a pair of knickers.

She tugged a brush through her hair and ran down the staircase. She was too restless to sit in her room. An hour on the farm before dinner would help calm her nerves.

The barn was built in the Swiss style. The doors were large enough for a hay truck to drive inside, and the second floor was wider than the first, so there was room to store more hay. At one end was a cooling tank that kept the milk fresh and vats for making cheese and butter.

Helen's father had no interest in selling the dairy products. For him, the farm was a hobby, as it had been for his father and grandfather. Helen was passionate about it. From the time she was allowed to milk her first cow, she knew that's what she wanted to do.

In the two years since she graduated from Foxcroft, she'd been working to develop the tastiest butter and cheeses. One day soon, she hoped to partner with a local creamery and produce enough milk products to sell to supermarkets.

"You wouldn't let a bull treat you the way Father is treating Mother, would you, Nellie?" Helen addressed a brown-and-white spotted cow.

Most people didn't understand cows. They thought they were dumb and lazy. Helen knew differently. Cows were intelligent and sensitive. They loved having their necks stroked. And they could tell if someone really cared for them or was only trying to extract as much milk as possible.

"Of course you wouldn't." Helen petted Nellie's spotted nose. "You have too much self-respect."

A shaft of light came through the entrance and the door opened.

Her mother stood in the doorway. At thirty-nine, Charlotte was still a beautiful woman. Her blonde hair touched her shoulders, and her eyes were wide and blue. She had wanted to be a ballerina when she was young, and she carried herself with grace from years of dance lessons.

Charlotte joined Helen in the stall. "Your father told me everything. He's taking a bath and changing before dinner," she said.

"He's coming to dinner?" Helen repeated, frowning.

Charlotte noticed Helen's puzzled expression. "We talked things through. He's not leaving."

Helen set aside the bucket she had been holding.

"You can't let him stay. How can you face him every day across the breakfast table?"

"I've faced worse things over the breakfast table." Her mother smiled. "Do you remember when you and Daisy both had chicken pox and you had itchy spots all over your faces?"

"You know what I mean. If you'd seen the girl in that house, as if she owned it . . ."

The memory of Rosalee standing proudly on the terrace rushed back to her. She swallowed the lump in her throat.

"I'm not happy about it, of course," Charlotte conceded. "But Robert has been a wonderful husband for over twenty years. He promised to stop seeing her."

"You can't let him get away with it," Helen implored. "Daisy and I will keep you company. You've got your work at the Children's Aid Society and the women at the New Century Club. You can start taking dance lessons again."

"I'm too old for ballet except for watching *Swan Lake* at the opera house." Charlotte shook her head. "I enjoy the company of women, but it's different."

"Because women don't run around with their tongues hanging out like naughty puppies," Helen said, pulling at a piece of hay. "And they don't make fools of themselves in front of half of New York and spoil their daughter's birthday."

Charlotte sat on a stool.

"Do you remember Parents' Day at Foxcroft during your first term? You were the only student who didn't have a picture in the art exhibit. I asked the art teacher why, and she said you didn't think your painting was good enough."

"What does any of that have to do with anything?" Helen inquired.

"You've always demanded perfection," Charlotte answered. "That's fine when you're young; it's more difficult as you get older. Everyone has strengths and weaknesses."

"Please don't tell me that Father said he didn't know what came over him," Helen said desperately. "A single clandestine lunch at the Plaza is one thing; a mansion in Oyster Bay is another. You should have seen it; you could have fit this entire barn into the living room. And the grounds! It probably employs a dozen gardeners."

Charlotte's cheeks paled, and Helen felt sick all over again. But her mother had to know everything. There was no point in hiding it.

"Your father explained it to me," Charlotte said quietly. "It's not quite like you think."

Helen was too upset to listen.

"Father betrayed you," she implored. "Think what you're teaching me and Daisy by letting him get away with it."

"Your father knows he's disappointed you, and Daisy is in love. It doesn't matter what anyone else does—she'd still be certain that she and Roland are different." Charlotte stood up and took Helen's arm. "Let's go back up to the house. Mary made meatloaf for your birthday, and she'll be furious if we let it sit."

Dinner passed more pleasantly than Helen expected. Her father and Roland were dressed in topcoats and tails, and her mother wore one of her latest gowns—a red silk Chanel with butterfly sleeves in honor of Helen's birthday. Daisy looked fresh and lovely in a yellow crepe gown from Jean Patou, and Helen wore a Grecian-style dress from Bergdorf's.

"To my beautiful daughter Helen." Her father stood up and raised his champagne flute. "It's been my privilege to be your father for the last nineteen years. You'll make some man very happy, and I hope that one day you'll raise a toast to your own daughter on her nineteenth birthday."

Helen didn't touch her champagne. It reminded her too much of her lunch at the Plaza.

Her father sat down, and Roland told everyone about the summer course he was going to take in Greece. After dinner, Daisy and Roland went for a drive, and Helen and her parents sat in the living room.

It was one of her favorite rooms at Dumfries. The ceiling was over twenty feet high, and the furniture was light and airy. Pale blue sofas were arranged around a glass coffee table, and an old-fashioned harpsicord stood in the corner. The blue velvet wallpaper had a scalloped design, and there were yellow silk drapes.

Robert poured two brandies. He handed one to Charlotte and one to Helen.

Helen shook her head. "I don't want anything to drink. I have a headache. I'm going to bed."

"Please, take it." Her father held up the glass. "After you hear what I have to say, you might need it."

Helen took the brandy, but she didn't drink it.

"The whole thing started innocently." Robert poured a brandy for himself. "A client took me to see *The Cocoanuts* on Broadway. Rosalee was in the chorus. We ended up at the same party after the show." He glanced at Charlotte. "A few months ago, Rosalee suggested I buy a cottage in Oyster Bay. Her brother was in real estate, and he could get me a good deal. It wasn't a bad idea. The prices are sure to skyrocket.

"I gave her a checkbook to one of my bank accounts and forgot about it." He sipped his brandy. "A month ago, she took me to Oyster Bay and surprised me. I thought she'd choose some little cottage facing the ocean. A sitting room and a couple of bedrooms with a pretty garden. Instead, she led me through that palace.

"I told her I couldn't afford that house and Dumfries. She'd have to sell it and send back the furniture. She dug her heels in. She had quit the

Broadway show and was tired of living in the city." Robert sighed. "Her brother bought the house in Rosalee's name. I couldn't make her sell it."

The air rushed out of Helen's lungs. How could her father, who was so meticulous in his business dealings, let this happen?

"For weeks I tried to persuade her. I even offered her money to buy a smaller house, anywhere she liked. She refused to budge." Robert stopped to sip the brandy.

"Today, I took Rosalee to lunch to tell her our affair was over. She was a lovely young woman, but the whole thing had been a mistake. I loved my wife and daughters. I couldn't keep doing something that could hurt my family." Robert continued, "Rosalee was heartbroken. She's really quite insecure. She grew angry, and now she's even more determined to keep the house in Oyster Bay. I'm afraid I've gotten us in a terrible mess. The monthly upkeep of Dumfries is a fortune. There's the household staff, and gardeners, and everyone that works in the stables and the farm." He walked to the sideboard and topped off his brandy. "I've never worried before, because the firm had a solid roster of clients. But Joseph Widener heard about Rosalee, and the news swept around the Union League."

Joseph Widener was one of her father's wealthiest clients. Joseph's father, Peter Widener, had been a real estate magnate, and his older brother, George, died on the *Titanic*. Joseph bred thoroughbred race-horses and had recently purchased the Belmont Park racetrack in New York.

"I'm sure other men who belong to the Union League have cheated on their wives," Helen said before she could stop herself.

"If only it was that simple," Robert responded. "You see, I brought Rosalee's brother to lunch at the club several times. He became friendly with a few of the other members. Apparently, he set up real estate deals and cheated them out of a great deal of money. Jay Gould's grandson was practically ruined. My membership has been suspended, and several of my clients who were members have taken their money to other firms."

Helen almost felt sorry for her father. His membership at the Union League was one of the things he cherished most. The Union League was the oldest private men's club in Philadelphia. It was started during the Civil War to promote Abraham Lincoln's policies and support the abolitionists.

When Helen was a child, Robert would often take her past the Second Empire–style brownstone on Broad Street. He'd point to the ochre-colored building and say she didn't need to study American history books about the Civil War. All the history she needed to learn was right in front of her.

"I'm sorry you lost your membership, but how does that affect us?" Helen asked briskly.

She pictured Rosalee's brother, in some cheap suit bought for the occasion, lunching with her father in the Union League's paneled dining room. Her father had always been a good judge of character. How had he not seen through him?

Robert looked even more nervous than when he started the conversation. "The thing is, unless something is done, I'll have to sell part of Dumfries."

Helen let out a gasp. Her father couldn't sell part of Dumfries. What if he had to get rid of the farm?

"You can't be serious!" She picked up her glass from the coffee table.

"It's the last thing I want to do." Robert sighed. "Your mother and I came up with an idea. Your season starts next month, your debutante ball is in July. You're lovely and accomplished. Plenty of young men will fall in love with you."

Helen wondered why he was telling her that. She wasn't conventionally pretty like Daisy. She was too tall—most of the young men wouldn't want to dance with her. But she was happy with her looks.

"I doubt that." She traced the rim of her glass. "The men in our social circle fall in love with girls who reek of perfume, not of cow manure. They're looking for wives who'll greet them at the door with an old-fashioned mixed the way they like it and a pair of slippers warmed to the perfect temperature."

"I'll teach you how to make an old-fashioned. It's easier than making cheese or butter."

Helen glanced at her father anxiously. She had been joking, but the expression on his face was deadly serious.

"What are you saying?"

There was an ominous feeling in the air, as if everything was about to change.

"Your father and I discussed it," Charlotte said. "You must get engaged before the end of the season. The only way his clients will come back is if other members of Philadelphia's wealthiest families join the firm first."

"Who am I supposed to get engaged to?" Helen asked in astonishment.

"Someone whose family has money and connections. Preferably members of the Union League and the Philadelphia Club." Robert refilled his glass. "The wedding has to happen by Christmas."

"You want me to get married in six months?" Helen gasped.

"We'll have the reception at the Bellevue-Stratford Hotel," her mother suggested. "It's always beautifully decorated for the holidays."

Helen couldn't believe what she was hearing. She could usually count on her mother to support her. Their financial situation must be precarious.

"Father brings a scandal on the family, and I have to be auctioned off like a racehorse," Helen fumed, trying to squelch the fear bubbling inside her. She couldn't get married yet; no husband would approve of her working on the farm. She'd never realize her dream of seeing their dairy products on supermarket shelves.

Charlotte smoothed the tassels on the armrest.

"It wouldn't hurt you to fall in love and get married," she said carefully.

Helen knew what her mother was thinking. That devoting herself to cows was no life for a young woman. Love might soften her, and she needed a husband to be happy.

Helen stood up and set her glass on the table.

"Well, I think you're both mad." She rushed to the doorway.

Tears threatened to spill down her cheeks, and she brushed them away.

"I'll do it, but I'm not doing it for Father. I'm doing it for you and Daisy. And for Nellie and the other cows, so they don't lose their home."

Chapter Three

During the next few weeks, Helen spent most of her time at the farm. She rose early for the cows' morning feedings and spent the late afternoons cleaning the stalls and giving the cows hay and water. It was only then, when the sky turned different colors outside the barn window and the air was filled with the snuffling of calves, that a peace settled over her.

She was doing the right thing by agreeing to her parents' wishes. She wouldn't let Father sell the farm.

She avoided seeing her father at breakfast and grabbed a piece of toast and cup of coffee to take to the barn instead. And she often skipped dinner altogether and took a tray up to her room.

Jack took her to the South Garden Room at the Hotel Walton to make up for their failed lunch at the Plaza. The minute they sat down, Helen knew it was a mistake. She was too worried that one of her father's former clients would walk in to enjoy the hotel's famous roast pork sandwich.

Charlotte acted as if nothing had happened. Every morning by the time Helen returned from the barn, the house was bustling with activity. Her mother hosted a luncheon for the Children's Aid Society and held a book club tea for the New Century Club. If some of the women came to see if the rumors were true and Robert Montgomery had an affair with a showgirl, they were disappointed. Charlotte talked effusively about her husband, and whenever he came home early, she kissed him in front of her guests.

Helen's debutante ball would take up an entire weekend, with fox-hunting and picnics.

The dance on Saturday night would start with oysters and champagne on the terrace, followed by a five-course sit-down dinner and dancing in a tent constructed on the lawn. There would be a late supper, and the night would end with fireworks set off over Dumfries's private lake.

Every afternoon, Charlotte sat at the walnut desk in her study, surrounded by menus and color swatches for the tablecloths. Helen ached for her. Her mother had been looking forward to Helen's season for ages. She should be splanning it without worrying that if Helen didn't find a husband, a part of Dumfries would have to be sold.

It was a Saturday evening in June, and Helen was at a ball at Fieldstone Manor in Villanova. She didn't know the debutante, Ivy Scott, but the family was very wealthy. Ivy's grandfather, Thomas Scott, had been the first president of Pennsylvania Railroad Company. The moment the engraved invitation arrived in an embossed envelope, Charlotte opened it eagerly and began planning Helen's wardrobe. Daisy helped. Together, they chose a Norman Hartnell gown from the dress salon at Lord & Taylor.

Norman Hartnell was a British designer, famous for dressing young ladies who were being presented at court, as well as actresses like Gladys Cooper and Gertrude Lawrence. The gown had a low-cut V-neck bodice and a gold sash around the waist. The skirt was yards of oyster-colored chiffon over a white satin slip.

The moon was white and full above the lawn, and the stars were the same silver as the orchestra that played "I'll Be With You in Apple Blossom Time" on the terrace. Outdoor tables were covered with white tablecloths and sprinkled with gold confetti. Fluted vases were filled with ostrich feathers, and each table had a diamond mesh band as a table runner. Helen couldn't wait to tell her mother and Daisy about the birdcages that were arranged on a long table. She thought the guests were going to receive canaries as party favors, but instead the birdcages held the place cards.

She had stood on the edge of the dance floor, sipping fruit punch and tapping her shoe to the melody. By the time the orchestra played the fourth song and no one asked her to dance, she began to grow uncomfortable.

What if the same thing happened at her own debutante ball and she didn't get any marriage proposals? Or if the only man who was interested in her couldn't understand her need to work on the farm? How the smell of hay filled her lungs with oxygen, and the sheen of a cow's back felt more luxurious under her hands than the finest silk.

She had a strong desire for a cigarette. But she couldn't smoke in front of the other guests. She refilled her punch glass and walked briskly across the lawn to the stables.

The cigarette tasted smooth and cool in the night air.

Helen knew she shouldn't smoke. But ever since Jack gave her that first cigarette at the Plaza Hotel, it was the only thing that calmed her nerves. She still thought about Rosalee every day. What if her father started seeing her again?

The doors to the stable opened and a young man walked out. He wore baggy slacks and a workman's shirt beneath a brown vest. His boots were caked in dry mud, and he clutched a felt cap.

Helen slipped the lit cigarette behind her back. "I'm sorry, I didn't know anyone was in the stables."

"You shouldn't do that." He motioned to the cigarette. "You'll burn down the stables."

He was handsome in the moonlight. He had light brown hair and a chiseled jaw. His eyes were green, and she couldn't help but notice the muscles under his shirt.

"I'm sorry, I shouldn't be smoking." She opened her cigarette case. "And I'm being rude. Would you like one?"

"Yes, please." He took a cigarette and lit it with his lighter. "Why shouldn't you be smoking?"

"It's not the kind of thing girls in my social set do," she said matter-of-factly. "I needed some time away from the other guests."

He glanced at her ball gown and at her pink T-strap sandals that were embroidered with flowers.

"You don't like the party?" he inquired.

"The party is fine, though I don't know the debutante. The Scotts are friends of my parents."

"Then is it the food you didn't like, or the music?"

He leaned against the stable wall next to her. Helen could smell sweat mixed with the familiar scent of horses.

"I didn't really eat the dinner; I haven't been hungry lately."

"These things will do that for you." He pointed at the cigarette. "My mother swears by them. She sneaks them when my father isn't home. She claims she's dropped a whole dress size."

"It's not that—I don't worry about my weight," Helen said thoughtfully. "It's a family situation."

Helen knew she shouldn't be discussing private matters with a stranger. But the fruit punch mixed with the cigarette was having a strange effect on her.

"Can I have a sip of that?" he asked.

She offered him the glass. "It's only fruit punch, but it's very good."

"Actually, it's a Mary Pickford, rum and pineapple juice with maraschino cherries. No wonder you didn't enjoy the party." He took another sip and handed back the glass. "A few of these and I'm either so happy I start singing or so maudlin I want to throw myself out a window. Why don't you tell me what's wrong."

Helen hadn't told anyone besides Jack about her parents' plan for her to get married. Maybe it would be good to talk to someone. He wasn't part of her social set—he wouldn't tell anyone.

She told him about her father's affair and her need to find a husband.

"I take it if it were up to you, you wouldn't let your father stay," he said when she finished.

"Of course not!" she proclaimed.

"Well, it could be more complicated," he suggested. "These things often are."

"Betrayal isn't complicated, and I can't stand anyone who lies," Helen said stiffly. "It must seem strange to someone like you."

"Someone like me?"

She waved at his work boots. "Someone who labors with their hands. Why does any family need a fifty-room mansion and 850 acres of land? My father's grandfather had nothing when he arrived in Philadelphia from Scotland. He wanted to build an estate that would be in the family for generations. Now it's all going to disappear."

"It might not, if you find the right man."

Helen thought of the young men at the party who ignored her. Instead, they danced with girls who were the right height or wore more risqué dresses.

"It doesn't seem very hopeful. Not a single boy asked me to dance." She sighed. "I should go back. But I feel like the chickens at the market when no one wants to buy their eggs."

The ball would be over soon, and everyone would go to bed. The Sunday festivities consisted only of brunch followed by a game of croquet. There was hardly any time to meet a suitable man.

She slipped the cigarette case into her purse.

"You're lucky you work in the stables. My favorite thing at Dumfries is the farm and the stables. That's why I can't bear to lose it." She held out her hand. "You've been very kind. I'm Helen Montgomery."

"Edgar." He shook her hand. A smile came to his lips, and his eyes were warm. "It's not every day that a stable hand gets to share a cigarette with a young society woman in distress. The pleasure was all mine."

When Helen returned to the lawn, dessert was being served. Icebox cakes made with ice cream and whipped cream and graham crackers. The slices of cake looked cold and delicious served on fine white china, but Helen didn't dare sit at a table. She still smelled like cigarettes. It was better to stand near the dance floor.

She almost envied Edgar. He could smoke and drink without worrying what anyone would think. And he got paid to work with horses. At night, he probably took a hot bath and went to bed with just enough ache in his muscles to know he had done a good day's work.

Helen had never wanted to be born a man, and she accepted her place in society. But at this moment, with couples twirling around the dance floor, the night air thick with perfume and cigar smoke, she wondered if a different life was possible. One where she could wear riding breeches instead of changing for dinner. Where she could work in the barn without worrying about getting hay in her hair before a society luncheon. And where if a husband cheated on his wife, he wasn't kept around for the sake of appearances.

A young man stood beside her. He had bright red hair, and his eyes were small and set close together.

"I'm Clarence. Would you like to dance?" he asked.

No one else was coming to ask her, and the orchestra would stop playing soon. She set her glass on a table and followed him onto the dance floor.

～

The next morning, Helen took a long walk around Fieldstone's grounds before she went to the dining room for brunch. There was a row of greenhouses and a pond shaded by maple trees.

The main house was built in the Italianate style. Overhanging eves were supported by decorative brackets, and the roof had a square belvedere where one could stand and admire the view. Behind the stables was a long wooden house where Helen guessed the stable hands lived, and there were stone cottages for the maids and gardeners. She walked all the way to the gatehouse before turning back and hiking up the driveway. When she had driven up in the car, she hadn't noticed how the oak trees met in the middle of the road or that the drive was built on an incline so that when you reached the entrance, the whole valley—verdant green and dotted with paddocks—stretched out below.

She took deep breaths, willing the headache from too many Mary Pickfords to disappear. She only had to get through brunch and games on the lawn before she could go home. Her mother and Daisy would want a full report. She'd tell a small fib and say she danced with half a dozen men; she couldn't remember their names.

The dining room had tall, arched windows facing the terrace. A mural was painted on the ceiling, and the walls were covered by land-scape paintings in gold frames. The floor was a polished parquet, and a sideboard was covered with a white lace tablecloth and arranged with silver platters of scrambled eggs, crumpets, and bacon.

The room was empty except for a man seated at one end of the oak table. His open newspaper hid his face, and there was a coffeepot and a plate of fresh scones on the table next to him.

The man folded the newspaper and set it down beside him. Helen recognized him immediately. It was Edgar, the stable hand she had shared a cigarette with at the stables.

"What are you doing here?" she asked in surprise.

He didn't look anything like he had last night, when his work shirt had been rumpled and his boots were caked in mud. This morning, he wore a crisp white shirt under a yellow V-neck sweater. A watch with a leather band was strapped around his wrist, and his light brown hair was slicked over his forehead.

"Eating breakfast." He waved at the sideboard. "I'll make you a plate. The scrambled eggs are delicious."

Helen frowned. "I don't understand."

"You mean why aren't I eating with the other stable hands?" he asked cheerfully. There was a glint of humor in his eyes. "Well, because I'm Edgar Scott, Ivy's older brother."

Helen's mouth dropped open. She recalled in horror everything she had told him last night.

"You lied to me!" she exclaimed. "You let me make a fool of myself."

"I didn't lie exactly. You thought I was a stable hand and I didn't correct you," he said smoothly. "I don't see how it would have made a difference if you knew I wasn't a stable hand."

Helen was so humiliated; she was tempted to storm out. But what if Edgar told his sister or his parents? She had to make him promise not to say anything.

"Of course it would have." Helen waved her hand angrily. "I was smoking, and I said horrible things about my family. You must think we're awful."

Edgar motioned for her to sit down. He went to the sideboard, piled a plate with eggs and bacon, and set it in front of her.

"What you need is a good breakfast." He poured a cup of coffee from the silver coffeepot. "I feel the same whenever I wake up with a hangover. I recommend the scones with honey."

Helen glanced from the plate of eggs to the coffee. Even though she was hungry, her stomach wasn't ready for eggs. She spread honey on a scone.

Edgar smiled at her expectantly.

"You'll feel better in no time." He sat down. "Now, let's address last night. You didn't give me a chance to explain. You assumed I worked in the stables."

"It was too late to go riding. Anyway, you weren't wearing breeches and riding boots. You were dressed in work clothes."

"One of the mares had trouble giving birth. I was checking up on the foal," he answered. "I don't think there's anything wrong with a woman having a cigarette."

Helen flushed even harder. She gulped her coffee so quickly that it burned her throat.

She set down her cup and stood up. "Look, Mr. Scott, you've had your fun. I shouldn't have said anything last night. I was tipsy and upset. I'll find your mother and thank her for a lovely weekend. Please don't repeat anything I told you."

He stopped her. "You can't leave; you'll miss the croquet. And I wasn't having fun. On the contrary." His voice softened. She noticed he was even more handsome when he was serious. The cocky smile disappeared, and his green eyes seemed clearer. "I thought you were the bravest woman I've ever met."

"You thought I was brave?" she repeated.

"Sacrificing yourself for the good of your family is one of the noblest things I've ever heard."

Helen sat back down. She picked up her coffee cup.

"I shouldn't have come to the ball. I don't even know your sister. I'm only here to find a husband," she said glumly.

"That's the whole point of a girl's season. Half the young women are doing the same thing."

"Why weren't you at the dance last night?" she asked.

"I'm four years older than Ivy. I've escorted plenty of girls to debutante balls." He looked at Helen thoughtfully. "I would never tell anyone about your situation, but maybe I can help."

Helen wondered if he was offering himself as a husband.

"Don't worry, I'm not proposing," he said, as if he could read her mind. "I'm already spoken for, and I don't meet all your criteria. My father belongs to the Union League, and my family is wealthy, but I'm a bit of a black sheep. I promised my father I'd work at the railroad company for a year. Then, if it's not a good fit, I can quit and concentrate on writing."

"What do you write?" Helen asked.

"I studied journalism at Harvard, but I'd like to write a novel." He leaned forward, his voice bright and eager. "For a long time, I believed a writer had to come from poverty to produce anything worthwhile. But look at F. Scott Fitzgerald. His novels are about privilege, and they're a huge success. Not that I'd be doing it for the money. There's really nothing I want to do besides write."

That's how Helen felt about working on the farm. It's where she belonged.

"How does the girl you're engaged to feel about your career?" she asked.

"We're not engaged yet, but I quite like her." He smoothed his napkin. "She's pretty and has a lot of friends to keep her busy. As long as I send flowers and take her to dinner once a week, she's happy."

"That doesn't sound like a strong basis for a marriage."

"No marriage is perfect, but one can't stay single forever." He shrugged. "I have a little black book of names from Harvard. I can introduce you to suitable young men."

Edgar was kind, but he was only trying to help because he felt sorry for her. And what if he told anyone that she needed to get married to save her father's company?

"I don't need help, thank you," she said stiffly. "I'll manage by myself."

"You didn't sound sure of it last night," he reminded her.

Helen pushed back her chair. She stood up and faced him.

"My great-grandfather landed in New York with ten Scottish shillings in his pocket and ended up owning one of the grandest estates on the Main Line. And even if I haven't been to finishing school and spend most of my time at Lord & Taylor's dress salon, I'll still make someone an excellent wife." She turned to the door. "If you'll excuse me, there's a young man waiting for me on the lawn. We danced last night, and he's already claimed me as a croquet partner."

Helen strode onto the terrace. The lawn was set up for croquet, and there was a badminton net and a pile of badminton rackets. She noticed Clarence, the boy she had danced with last night.

She turned around to see if Edgar was watching. Then she waved to Clarence and walked toward him.

Chapter Four

The following Thursday, Helen stretched out on a chaise longue next to Dumfries's swimming pool. She would rather spend the afternoon making cheese in the barn, but Daisy said that sitting in the sun would lighten her hair. The next dance—to be held at Knollbrook, the home of Howard Pew, the president of Sun Oil Company—was two weeks away, and she wanted to look her best.

Clarence had called and sent flowers every day. Each afternoon at 5:00 p.m., Helen held the phone to her ear and paced around the living room hoping to find something they had in common. Clarence had been thrown from a horse as a child and hated riding. Helen told herself it didn't matter. She was happy to ride by herself or with Daisy if she needed company.

There were other things on her mind.

A few days ago, she had come across one of her mother's gossip magazines, *Town Topics*, which wrote about society in New York. There was an article about the influx of wealthy New Yorkers to Oyster Bay on Long Island.

Underneath the second paragraph was a photo of Rosalee in front of her oceanfront mansion. She wore a red cloche hat over her dark, wavy hair, and she was beaming proudly at the photographer.

Helen hid the magazine before her mother saw it. Now it sat on the little table next to her, with a glass of lemonade.

The back door opened, and Jack entered the garden. He wore a boater hat with a blue-and-white striped band. His suspenders were fastened over a white button-down shirt, and he wore navy slacks and two-tone oxford shoes.

"I was hoping I'd find you," he greeted her. "Is anyone else home?"

Helen slipped a robe over her swimsuit and sat up.

"Mother and Daisy are shopping, Father is at his office," she replied. "Would you like a glass of lemonade? There's a pitcher on the table."

Jack poured the lemonade and sat beside her.

"I have some news about Rosalee," he said.

Helen handed him the magazine.

"Is it this?"

Jack scanned it quickly. He closed it and let out a low whistle.

"I hadn't seen that. What did your mother say?"

"I hid it," Helen said. "I'm not going to show it to her."

Helen didn't want to hurt her mother. For now, she'd keep the magazine article to herself.

"That's wise," Jack agreed. "A friend of mine received this."

He took an envelope from his pocket. Inside was an invitation.

Ms. Rosalee Watson requests your presence at a house-warming party.

Chateau-Sur-Mer, Oyster Bay, July 3rd at 4 pm.

295 Crescent Beach Road, Long Island.

"Where did you get this?" Helen gasped.

"From a friend who's a theater critic in New York," Jack answered. "It was a coincidence. He asked if I wanted to join him."

Jack had many friends in the arts world in New York. He kept a small apartment in Greenwich Village for when he attended gallery openings.

"I hope you told him that you wouldn't go," Helen said.

"Of course I did," Jack assured her. "But it's bound to be attended by people from Philadelphia. The Coes just built an estate in Oyster Bay. And the Phippses own a summer home at Old Westbury Gardens. It won't take long for gossip about the party to reach the Main Line."

The Coes were in oil like the Pews. Helen often saw Margaret Coe at the Merion Cricket Club. John Phipps's father, Henry, had been Andrew Carnegie's business partner before he quit the steel company to devote his time to philanthropy.

Jack was right. Philadelphia and New York society were intertwined. Robert had begged Rosalee to sell the mansion and move away, and she hadn't listened. He wouldn't be able to stop her from having the party.

Helen's gaze settled on the cover of *Town Topics*. Suddenly she had an idea. If she told Jack, he might try to stop her. It was better to handle it herself.

He interrupted her thoughts. "Perhaps there's another way to address the situation. Your father could make a public apology, set up a plan to pay his clients back. It isn't his fault; he didn't know that Rosalee's brother was a crook."

"He'd ruin his reputation for good." Helen shook her head. "Anyway, I've already met someone to marry. His name is Clarence—we danced at the ball last weekend. He sends flowers every day. His family owns a shipping company."

Jack's eyes narrowed. He studied her closely, as if he were trying to read her mind.

"Dumfries has rose gardens; you don't need flowers delivered daily. How does he feel about horses and cows, and a wife who wants to work on a farm?"

"None of that matters. What's important is that I find a husband."

Jack sipped his glass of lemonade. He turned his straw hat over in his hand.

"Your parents are asking a lot from you. You shouldn't have to marry someone you're not in love with."

"Everyone has an opinion on what I'm doing," she said sharply. "My mother thinks being married will soften me, and Daisy would do anything to be in my position. She can't wait to marry Roland. I have to do what my parents asked. I can't bear the thought of losing Dumfries."

Jack stuffed the invitation in his pocket. He stood up and put on his hat.

"You have to think about yourself, Helen," he said. He had never seemed so serious. "When you're young, you believe you have your whole life ahead of you to change things. But some mistakes last forever."

After Jack left, Helen went inside to change for dinner. A new bouquet of flowers was sitting in the entry. She was about to read the card when the phone rang.

She answered it. "The flowers are beautiful," she said, taking the phone into the living room. "You shouldn't send roses. They're expensive, and we grow roses at Dumfries. Daisies will do perfectly."

"Roses are the only flower worth sending," the male voice said over the line. "This is a special kind of rose. It's called the Scotch briar rose; it was imported from Scotland in the eighteenth century. You were going on about your Scottish ancestors, so I thought you'd appreciate them."

The roses were different than the ones Clarence had sent before. These were white with a yellow center. She pressed the phone closer to her ear.

"Who is this?" she asked.

"Didn't you read the card?" The voice became impatient. "It's Edgar Scott. We met at the ball."

Helen took the card from the envelope.

"Dear Miss Montgomery," she read out loud. "Please accept these as a token of my apologies if I offended you. Sincerely, Edgar Scott.

"They're beautiful," she said, glad that Edgar wasn't there to see her embarrassment. "You didn't need to apologize for anything."

"I made you feel bad," he replied. There was a pause, and his voice took on its familiar light tone. "Who did you think the roses were from?"

Helen tucked the card in the envelope.

"It doesn't matter. Yours are lovely. You still shouldn't have sent them." She matched his light tone. "What will Jane say?"

"Jane helped me pick them out," Edgar said. "That's the other reason I called. Jane has a friend who went to Yale. Apparently, he's good-looking, and his family owns half the buildings on Rittenhouse Square. His name is Harold Barclay, and he wants to take you out."

"He's never met me."

"He met Daisy somewhere; he thought she was lovely," Edgar explained. "We'll make it a double date. The Warwick Hotel on Saturday night."

Clarence hadn't officially asked her out yet. And it was nice of Edgar to send roses. Perhaps he could help her with Rosalee.

"I'll consider it, if you do a favor for me."

"What kind of favor?" Edgar inquired.

"You studied journalism at Harvard. Do you know anyone who works at *Town Topics*?"

"The society magazine in New York?" he asked. "My old classmate Philip Barry published a few pieces with them."

"Could he publish one more if I asked him to write it?"

"Doubtful at the moment," Edgar answered. "He's in Argentina; he won't be back for months."

"Could you write it?"

Edgar chuckled. "This is getting interesting. What did you have in mind?"

"I'll explain on Saturday night. Tell Harold not to worry about picking me up. I'll meet everyone at the Warwick at seven thirty."

~

The Warwick Hotel had only been open for a few months, but already it was very popular. It was built by the architect Frank Hahn in the English Renaissance style. The exterior had large square windows and a steeply pitched roof. Doormen wearing green uniforms greeted guests at one end of a long red carpet. Young men holding walking sticks and women wearing bandeaus stitched with peacock feathers climbed the front steps.

Helen had dressed carefully in a sleeveless crepe evening gown. She wore a rope of her mother's pearls around her neck and a diamond bracelet. Daisy had done her makeup, and her hair lay sleekly at her shoulders.

Harold and Edgar and Jane arrived together in Harold's late-model Ford. The minute Harold greeted her—taking Helen's hand and saying he heard so much about her—she was glad she made the extra effort. Harold was good-looking. His sandy blond hair flopped over deep blue eyes. His arms were muscular from rowing crew at Yale, and he was obviously wealthy. His topcoat and tails fit perfectly; they must have been made by a personal tailor. Helen recognized his top hat as being from Christys' in London. Christys' was the Prince of Wales's personal hat maker; her father had a top hat just like it.

Helen had been afraid that Harold would be disappointed that she wasn't classically pretty like Daisy. If he was, he didn't show it. He complimented her dress and perfume. When they were seated at the table, he asked what she wanted to eat and drink and enthusiastically agreed with her choices.

Harold ordered shrimp cocktails for both of them, and Edgar and Jane started the meal with oysters Rockefeller. There was a pitcher of gin rickeys and a silver bread basket.

"Would you like an oyster?" Edgar asked Helen.

Helen couldn't look at the oysters tucked into their shells without remembering her birthday lunch at the Plaza.

She shook her head and turned to Harold. "Daisy said you met at a Harvard-Yale football game."

"We all sat together. My parents have known Roland's family for years. Our mothers are members of the Acorn Club. After the game, the whole group grabbed a bite in New Haven." Harold dipped his shrimp in cocktail sauce. "Roland said that he's going to join his father's real estate company, and Daisy wants to start an interior design firm."

Daisy often talked about designing the interiors of mansions on the Main Line after she graduated from Bryn Mawr. She had wonderful taste in decor. Helen could imagine her creating light-filled reception rooms with pastel-colored furniture and elegantly textured walls.

Harold had given her the perfect opportunity to ask how he felt about women working after they get married.

"I'm all for it," Harold said. "My mother runs a charity store, and she's always telling interesting stories. She'd be bored if she spent all her time at home."

"Would it depend what the woman does?" Helen peeled apart her shrimp. "For instance, would you approve of a wife who owned a dress boutique but not one who worked with horses?"

"It's up to the woman." Harold shrugged. "My aunt is a lawyer, and I have a female cousin at medical school. As long as a woman puts her family first, it would be the same to me."

Helen took a sip of her gin rickey. Harold was educated and charming. If they got married, he would support her in whatever she did.

"That's very noble," Edgar addressed Harold. "I've told Jane that I don't mind if she works. But she's only interested in shopping and going to nightclubs."

Helen stole a glance at Jane. She really was beautiful. Her auburn bob was covered by a silk turban, and she had large hazel eyes. She wore a gold lamé dress with a fringed hem. She had been carrying a pearl cigarette holder, and now it sat on the table next to her mesh evening bag.

Jane defended herself. "Men expect women to look pretty," she said. "And everyone goes to nightclubs. Edgar's just old-fashioned. He'd rather sit at home and listen to Chopin on the phonograph than listen to live jazz."

Jazz was becoming hugely popular. A couple of months ago, Jack had taken Helen and Daisy to a nightclub to hear Louis Jordan and the

Rabbit Foot Minstrels. Helen had thought she preferred classical music, but she couldn't help tapping her feet.

"Nightclubs are too crowded." Edgar slurped his oyster. "When I smoke cigarettes, I want to enjoy the smell of my own brand, not everyone else's. And jazz music stays in my head too long. It makes it impossible to write."

"What have you written?" Harold inquired.

"Nothing important yet." Edgar shrugged. "It takes a while to know what I want to say."

"Writing is a good excuse to avoid the mundane parts of life," Jane said airily. "You don't know how many times I had to stock Edgar's kitchen at Harvard because he forgot to buy milk. But he does have good qualities. No one writes nicer cards; I have a drawerful of them."

Helen felt anxious. She wasn't used to meeting new people. At Foxcroft, she had avoided the dances held with neighboring boys' schools. And one reason she didn't go to college was that she didn't want to make new friends. All the social activity she needed occurred at the Devon Horse Show and the Radnor Hunt.

She'd give anything to be in Nellie's stall at the barn. Instead, she had to get through dinner and dancing. If she was lucky, Harold would offer to drive her home. They'd sit in his convertible, talking about the Phillies' baseball season. She wouldn't go inside right away, because she'd miss the possibility of him inviting her out again.

If all went well, by the end of the summer he'd ask her to marry him. Only then would Dumfries and her father's business be safe.

She finished her cocktail and asked Harold for another. It might take a few gin rickeys and several trips to the powder room to refresh her makeup, but she was determined to come across as fun and sophisticated.

The rest of the evening passed easily. She learned that Harold was going to spend September in Italy and then join his father's real estate firm. He liked skiing and tennis, and his parents were members of the

Merion Cricket Club. Helen wondered why she hadn't seen him there. Perhaps she had and hadn't noticed him.

By the time she got home, it was close to midnight. Her parents were in the living room, but she didn't feel like answering their questions. She slipped out the side door, to the swimming pool.

The sky was a dark stretch of velvet, and the moon was brighter than the floodlights of the cars in front of the Warwick Hotel. Helen felt lucky to live in the countryside. She couldn't bear breathing the smell of gasoline or hearing the whistle of the tram when she was trying to sleep at night.

"Well, look at you," a male voice said when she stepped out of the changing room. "I didn't guess you owned a bathing suit, let alone one that was so revealing."

Edgar stood next to the swimming pool. He still wore his topcoat and tails, and he held a shiny object in his hand.

Helen walked back to the changing room and grabbed a robe.

"What are you doing here?" she asked, tying the sash around her waist.

"You left your cigarette case in Harold's car." He handed it to her.

"Why didn't you give it to me before?" She glanced at him suspiciously. "You deliberately kept it! You were curious what happened between Harold and me after we dropped you and Jane off."

Edgar stuffed his hands in his pockets.

"I am the one who set you up. I don't know Harold that well," he replied. "What if he's one of those ax murderers you read about in the newspapers who go after society girls? I'd never forgive myself if I didn't check that you were all right."

"Harold is taking me to the Sapphire Room at the Bellevue-Stratford next Friday night."

"That's all right, then. I'm glad it worked out." Edgar nodded, sitting on the chaise longue.

He took out his cigarette case and offered her a cigarette. This time, Helen declined. The night air was too sweet and warm.

"Jane is stunning," Helen said. "I can see why you're in love with her."

"I never said I'm in love. I said we're probably getting married," he corrected. "There is another reason I came. You said you needed a favor."

Helen told Edgar about the photo of Rosalee in *Town Topics* and the invitation to the housewarming party.

She had it all planned out. They'd drive to the mansion in Oyster Bay. Helen would introduce Edgar as a reporter for *Town Topics*. She'd say that Edgar was going to publish a scandalous story about Rosalee unless she canceled the party.

"I can't make up stories about someone in print. They'd sue me and the magazine for libel," Edgar said when she finished.

"You wouldn't write anything specific," Helen replied. "Just the sort of thing one reads in gossip magazines."

Edgar studied the orange glow of his cigarette.

"It could be done," he said thoughtfully. "But it's a big favor to ask," he mused. "Her brother is a crook; he could come after me."

Helen hadn't thought of that. There had to be a way around it.

"If Rosalee agrees to cancel the party, you'll write a piece instead saying she inherited her money from a rich aunt. She'll be the new society queen of Oyster Bay."

Edgar looked at Helen approvingly.

"I should pay you to think up my plots. That's quite good."

"So, you'll do it?"

His green eyes were bright, and a smile played around his mouth.

"No writer can pass up the opportunity to have a byline. I'll cable Philip and ask him to put in a good word with the editor."

Helen took a deep breath. Her father's name wouldn't be dragged through the gossip magazines.

"We'll go to Oyster Bay next week," she said. "I don't know how to thank you."

"You could invite me to go swimming."

The swimming pool was so tempting. But her mother might come outside and wonder what she was doing with Edgar.

Edgar was different from other men. When she was with Clarence or Harold, she felt like one of the dolls that she and Daisy played with as children. They would dress the dolls in different outfits and pretend they were attending afternoon teas and dinner parties.

When she was with Edgar, she was completely herself. But Edgar was involved with Jane. And she couldn't marry a writer. She needed someone who could save Dumfries. Someone who spent his free time at private clubs or on the tennis court, not sitting at a typewriter.

Edgar looked handsome, stretched out on the chaise longue in his formal wear. His white shirt was beautifully pressed, and his pearl cuff links glimmered in the moonlight. She couldn't let herself fall for him.

"Another time," she said. "I've changed my mind. It's too late to go swimming."

Chapter Five

Harold arrived at Dumfries on Friday evening dressed in a pin-striped suit and wing-tipped shoes. He presented Helen with a yellow tiger lily corsage that matched her chiffon evening gown and gave her mother a bouquet of daffodils.

Helen wondered how he knew what color corsage to buy, and he admitted he'd called the house and asked Daisy. She hadn't known a man could be so thoughtful.

They had cocktails in the living room with her parents before going to the hotel. Robert and Harold discovered they both attended the horse races in Saratoga Springs every summer, and Charlotte shared a great-aunt with Harold's mother. Afterward, Helen gave him a tour of Dumfries. She even took him to the farm. He wasn't interested in the cows, but he was impressed by the horses. His family had their own stables at their estate, and he was an accomplished rider.

The Bellevue-Stratford Hotel was on Broad Street, around the corner from Rittenhouse Square. They arrived early so they could take a stroll before dinner. They toured a new collection of antique books at the Philadelphia Museum of Art and admired the bronze statues in Rittenhouse Square Park.

Dinner was a delightful few hours of delicious food and conversation and dancing. The first course was tomato soup, followed by a Waldorf salad and broiled chicken. There was devil's food cake for dessert and a bottle of champagne. For the first time since Helen's birthday lunch, the champagne didn't give her a headache. Instead, it made her feel light-headed and giddy. She laughed at everything Harold said. When he took her in his arms to dance, she rested her head on his shoulder and felt almost happy.

The next day, Harold sent chocolates and flowers and called to make another date. Helen accepted and then poured all her energy into the farm. For the first time, she took a sample of her cheese to a creamery.

The creamery was in Haverford, and the owner's name was Thomas Danforth. He was in his midforties, with a broad face and wispy hair combed over his forehead. He gave Helen a tour of the operations. She watched in fascination as the milk was bottled and loaded onto a truck to take to the train station. Farmers from all over the Lehigh Valley brought their milk, and the creamery delivered it to grocery stores in Boston and New York.

He showed her the butter churn, which was bigger and more efficient than the old-fashioned churn at Dumfries's barn. There was a giant cooler where milk could be stored overnight and separating stations where the cream and the milk were separated.

After the tour, Helen gave Mr. Danforth a wedge of cheese and told him her plans.

"I've heard of Dumfries's Ayrshire cows," he said. "They're the envy of farmers all over the Lehigh Valley." He flipped through a large ledger. "I can't take on any new customers at present, but I'd be happy to talk again in the fall."

Helen left the creamery with a spring in her step. She was one step closer to achieving her goal.

Now it was lunchtime, and she walked down Broad Street carrying a Wanamaker's shopping bag. She had spent the morning shopping for a new hat to wear for her meeting with Rosalee. She was about to get on the tram when Daisy appeared on the front steps of the bank.

Daisy wore a floral day dress with white gloves and a yellow cloche hat.

Helen approached her. "Daisy, what are you doing here?"

Daisy glanced at Helen's bag. "What are you doing? Don't tell me you've been shopping. You only go to Wanamaker's when mother drags you there."

Helen couldn't tell Daisy about her plan to confront Rosalee. Daisy would tell her to stay away.

"I wanted something new to wear for my date with Harold this Saturday," Helen said instead. "We're going to have a picnic in the botanical gardens."

"Roland said Harold is very taken with you." Daisy nodded. "You'll be engaged by the end of the summer."

"It's too soon to think about that. He hasn't even kissed me," Helen replied. "What were you doing in the bank?"

Daisy's eyes dropped to the ground. She pulled at her gloves.

"It's not important."

"Of course it's important," Helen persisted. "If you're in trouble, I want to know."

"All right, I'll tell you," Daisy relented, "but you have to keep it a secret. First, let's sit down. It's hot—I need something cool to drink."

Helen and Daisy walked to the drugstore on the corner. One wall was taken up by a long white counter. There was a large mirror and a soda fountain with bottles of flavoring and bowls of whipped cream.

Their father used to take them to the soda fountain when they were children. The first bite of banana split—bananas and ice cream smothered in chocolate sauce—tasted even better than any dessert Mary made at Dumfries. It wasn't the banana split itself that was so delicious. It was the joy of being out with their father—his humorous stories and the way he boasted proudly about Helen and Daisy to the waitress.

Helen ordered two root beers and a turkey sandwich for them to split.

She turned to Daisy. "Does Mother know you're here?"

Anita Abriel

Daisy shook her head. "She was gone before I left. Roland is going to pick me up; he had to run an errand."

Daisy reached into her purse, and a small black book fell out.

It was Daisy's bankbook. When Helen was eleven and Daisy was ten, their father took them to the bank to open bank accounts. They sat at the wide oak desk while the bank manager wrote their names in the little black books.

"The important thing is not to touch it," he'd instructed them. "As long as you don't take money out, it will keep growing."

Helen had pictured her bank account like the chickens sitting on their eggs at Dumfries's farm. She had followed his advice. Every year, she and Daisy deposited some of their Christmas and birthday money, and the numbers kept growing.

Daisy looked at Helen guiltily.

"If you must know, I withdrew some money. I lent it to Roland."

Roland's father owned a steel company, and they lived in a neoclassical mansion in Haverford. Roland was the third generation in his family to attend Harvard. They wintered in Palm Beach and spent their summers as guests of the Vanderbilts in Newport.

"Why did Roland need money, and why didn't he ask his parents?" Helen inquired.

"His father is very strict; Roland isn't allowed a penny more than his allowance." Daisy sighed. "He attended a bachelor party and bet on the horses. All the young men were doing it; he would have spoiled the fun if he didn't join in."

"He shouldn't have bet more than what he had in his pocket," Helen said briskly.

"He won the first three races; he was going to quit. Then he bet everything on the last race and lost." Daisy poked at her half of the sandwich.

"You still shouldn't have taken it out of your account. He could have found it somewhere else."

Daisy's eyes were bright, and her mouth formed a small pout.

48

"He didn't want his parents to know. Anyway, it's my money, I can do with it whatever I like," she pointed out. "You spent your birthday money on presents."

"That's different—the money wasn't in the bank," Helen said. "What if Roland gambles again?"

"He promised he wouldn't. And what difference does it make? We'll be married in a year; then the money will belong to both of us."

Helen knew marriage wasn't like that. Her father gave her mother a monthly household allowance, but he made all the financial decisions.

Daisy kept talking. "We can't all marry perfect people. I love Roland—that's all that's important."

"I don't know what you mean," Helen snapped. She took half the turkey sandwich.

"If you didn't have to get married, you'd never find anyone who was good enough," Daisy said.

"You sound like Mother." Helen was angry despite herself. "There's nothing wrong with having standards."

"As long as they don't interfere with love." Daisy sucked on her straw. Her large blue eyes were thoughtful. "One day you'll experience love yourself, then you'll see what I mean. It's like nothing I've felt before."

Helen wanted to answer honestly. That you could love different things: The view from her bedroom window in the early morning when the grass was dewy and soft as a magic carpet. Rubbing Nellie's back in her stall at the barn. Swimming in the pool and lying on the chaise longue at night and gazing up at the stars.

She had too much ambition to depend on a man to make her happy. She wanted to accomplish things for herself. To become one of the biggest producers of dairy products on the East Coast. To one day start a foundation to help young girls achieve their dreams. But her mother was right. Daisy was hopelessly in love; nothing would change her mind.

"I don't want to talk about it anymore." Daisy pushed away her plate. "You promised you won't say anything. It has to stay our secret."

"Of course I won't say anything." Helen took a long sip of her root beer. There was no point in arguing. Daisy was her sister. Aside from her parents, Helen loved her more than anyone in the world. "I gave you my word, and I'd never break it."

After lunch, Helen took the tram to the Warwick Hotel. Edgar was waiting for her in the lobby. He sat in an armchair, flipping through a magazine.

"There you are." He jumped up. He was dressed in a V-neck sweater and white pleated slacks. He carried a boater hat with a wide green sash and was wearing a watch with a leather strap.

Helen started laughing. She put her hand over her mouth, but the laughter wouldn't stop.

"What's so funny?" Edgar wondered.

"The way you're dressed. You're supposed to be a gossip magazine writer. You look like you're lunching at the yacht club."

"I put a lot of thought into this outfit," Edgar said indignantly. "Rosalee obviously loves money. She's going to have more respect for a man wearing expensive clothes than she would for a struggling writer."

Helen nodded. "That's quite clever. I hadn't thought of it."

"I'm glad I'm able to surprise you." Edgar took her arm. "We should go. There's so much traffic these days, it could take ages to get to Long Island."

They were quiet on the drive. Helen recalled her last visit to Chateau-sur-Mer. Rosalee pointing out the fountain in the swimming pool. The way she had offered Helen a piece of cake as if they were close friends celebrating Helen's birthday.

What would it be like to see Rosalee again? To watch Rosalee swan around that great, elegant mansion when it was because of her that they might lose Dumfries.

"One has to be careful of the police out here," Edgar was saying. "The last time I drove through Nassau County, I got a ticket."

"You won't get a ticket if you don't speed." Helen knotted a scarf around her neck.

"Actually, I was driving too slowly. The cop said I was obstructing traffic." Edgar glanced over at her. "A family of ducks was crossing the road. One duckling got separated from its mother. I couldn't leave him there, so I stopped my car."

Helen did the same thing whenever a herd of cows or sheep crossed the road.

"I didn't know you were an animal lover," she said. "Besides horses, of course."

"I learned to ride a horse before I had a bicycle," Edgar mused. "I've always loved animals. When I was a child, my mother complained that I was turning the house into a menagerie. Once, I had a dog and a lizard and a canary at the same time. I spent most of the day making sure they didn't eat each other."

Helen recalled how she had loved Doctor Dolittle books when she was very young. Years later, she asked her father if they could get llamas for the farm. It was too costly to import them from South America, so she had to settle for visiting the llamas at the Philadelphia Zoo.

They passed the sign welcoming them to Oyster Bay. Edgar turned onto Crescent Beach Road and stopped in front of Rosalee's gate.

Edgar whistled. "I see what you mean. It's as big as a palace." He leaned forward to get a better look at the house. "Rosalee is as likely to give this up as Mark Twain would have been to go without his bourbon."

"I haven't read Mark Twain, and we're not asking Rosalee to give up the house. We just want her to cancel the party."

Somehow, saying Rosalee's name out loud made Helen angry at her father all over again. She shouldn't be lurking at the gate as if she were an intruder. She shouldn't be in Oyster Bay at all. She should be riding with Daisy or working on the farm.

"Are you sure you want to do this?" Edgar inquired. "We could buy oysters and have a picnic on the beach instead."

"Jack said exactly the same thing."

"That's because he was using his common sense." Edgar loosened his collar. "What if Rosalee's brother is here? He might greet us at the door with a pistol."

Helen couldn't worry about that. If Rosalee went through with the party, it would be talked about all over the Main Line.

"Then I'm glad I'm not thinking clearly," she responded. She retied her scarf and stepped out of the car. "Leave the car and we'll walk up the driveway. Every army general knows the best offense is a surprise attack."

This time, a maid answered the door. Helen gave their names, and the woman led them into the living room.

Rosalee was sitting on the sofa, drinking a cup of tea. She wore a flowing silk hostess gown. Her hair was held back by a diamond clip, and her mouth was coated with red lipstick.

She glanced up. "Helen, what a surprise! I see you met Gladys. My brother insisted I hire a live-in maid. He doesn't like me living out here alone."

Rosalee put down the teacup. She motioned for them to sit down. "Did Robert send you?" she asked. "I haven't heard from him in weeks."

"My father doesn't know I'm here." Helen turned to Edgar. "This is my friend, Edgar Scott."

"I'll ask Gladys to bring some cookies," Rosalee offered. "Usually I only have them on the weekends. My fitness instructor doesn't approve of store-bought cookies. They have too much sugar," she confided.

"You don't need a fitness instructor—you have a wonderful figure." Edgar took off his hat. "If I may say so, I've never seen better legs."

Helen gave Edgar a sharp look, but he ignored her.

"Do you think so?" Rosalee turned to Edgar. "The producer of *The Cocoanuts* said I had better legs than Clara Bow. She's a big movie star in Hollywood now. I could never move to California. I love New York."

From the wistful tone in Rosalee's voice, Helen guessed that wasn't true. Rosalee had probably auditioned for a Hollywood producer and was turned down.

"If Robert didn't send you, why are you here?" Rosalee wondered.

"Edgar is a writer," Helen explained. "He wanted to meet you."

"It must be so hard to write a book." Rosalee waved at a small pile on the side table. "I just checked out five books from Nassau Library. It's important to improve my mind." She gave a small sigh. "Most books aren't interesting, except for romances. They keep those behind the counter. I was too embarrassed to ask the librarian."

"I'll send you some books," Edgar offered. "I have stacks in my study."

Rosalee spread her hands in her lap.

"That would be very nice," she said happily. "You'd be surprised how long the days are when I don't have to prepare for a musical. That's why I'm excited about my party."

"The party is why we're here," Helen said. "If you have a party, people may ask how you got this house."

"I'll tell them the truth. Robert gave it to me."

Helen explained how that would hurt her family. All of Philadelphia society would talk about it.

"But he did give it to me," Rosalee persisted. "You don't know what it's like out here. At night, it's so quiet, I stand on the balcony and talk to the owls. If I don't meet people soon, I'll die of loneliness."

"We have an idea," Helen said.

She explained that Edgar would write a piece about Rosalee for *Town Topics*. He'd say that Rosalee was an heiress from Cleveland, and her great-aunt left her a large inheritance. Rosalee decided to move east because she loved the theater, and she settled on Long Island.

"It's not true." Rosalee frowned. "Besides my love of the theater."

"They often tell small white lies in gossip magazines," Edgar piped in. "You'll be the new 'it girl' of Long Island. I'll say that you won every beauty pageant in Cleveland. You only turned down being Miss Ohio because you were offered a part on Broadway."

Rosalee patted her bobbed hair.

"*Town Topics* only writes about people in society," she said thoughtfully. Then her expression changed. "But if I don't have the party, how will I meet people?"

"The best way to meet other women is to start a charity," Helen offered. "You could create a scholarship for girls from poor families to study theater. My mother belongs to the Children's Aid Society, and she hosts monthly teas at Dumfries."

Rosalee could host a charity luncheon at Chateau-sur-Mer and invite the women in Oyster Bay. She'd be invited to their estates too.

"Florence Guggenheim lives on the other side of Crescent Beach Road, and I've never been inside her house." Rosalee's voice was eager. "If she joins my charity, I'll suggest we hold a fundraiser at Sands Point."

Rosalee rang a little bell. "I'll ask Gladys to bring tea with the cookies. Edgar can interview me for the article now."

While Edgar and Rosalee talked, Helen sipped her tea and tried to avoid glancing around the living room. She didn't want to imagine her father enjoying his after-dinner brandy in front of the fireplace or kissing Rosalee on the daybed that faced the window. A humidor rested on the side table, and Helen wondered if it belonged to him.

An hour later, Edgar put away his notebook. Rosalee led them to the front door.

"This is the most fun I've had in ages," Rosalee said. Her large brown eyes fluttered under dark lashes. "You know, I'm sorry about everything. I never meant to cause any harm. I didn't know my own father, and my mother died when I was twelve. All I really wanted was a family. Robert said I made him so happy."

Helen and Edgar hardly talked on the way back to Philadelphia. Helen had so much to think about. By the time they pulled up at Dumfries, it was early evening. The sun dropped behind the hills, and the air was crisp and cool. She could hear the crickets chirping on the lawn.

Edgar stopped a little way from the house.

"I can write the article now if you like," he offered. "Then you can read it before I send it to the editor."

Helen didn't want to ask Edgar inside. She was tired and her head throbbed.

She shook her head. "I trust you to write it. I have a headache; I'm going to bed early."

Edgar glanced at her curiously. He reached up and touched her cheek.

"You've been crying. Your face is wet."

She wiped it with her sleeve.

"Of course I'm not crying. It must be sea spray from driving near the ocean."

She was too embarrassed to tell the truth. She wanted to hate Rosalee, but instead she felt quite differently. Rosalee grew up with nothing—she only wanted the things that came easily to girls in Helen's position. A loving family, a beautiful home, the ability to follow her dreams.

"Thank you for driving." She turned the door handle and stepped out of the car, an unexpected pang lingering in her heart.

Chapter Six

The morning of her debutante ball, Helen rose early and went for a ride around Dumfries.

She told herself it was her usual ride. Down to the gatehouse to take Abe, the gatekeeper, some of Mary's strawberry gelatin. A loop around the farm to check on a cow named Agnes who had just given birth. Trotting past the lake and up to the ridge, which had the best view of neighboring estates.

Dolobran, the shingle-style mansion built on 150 acres for Clement Griscom, who owned the American Steamship Company. Chanticleer, the home of the Rosengartens, who owned a pharmaceutical company. Last summer, Helen had a tour of Chanticleer's gardens—rhododendrons and peonies and irises as rich and bold as precious jewels. The flowers were so beautiful, she came home and asked the gardener to plant them at Dumfries.

And her favorite, Idlewild Farm, built for the chocolatier William Nelson Wilbur. Idlewild sat on the crest of a hill. The Wilburs often held parties, and the music drifted between the two properties, like a symphony heard from the back of an opera house.

This morning, Helen's ride was more than a way to exercise her horse. She was imprinting every part of Dumfries in her mind. If Harold didn't propose soon, some of it might be gone by next summer.

She had hardly seen Harold lately. She had been busy with last-minute arrangements for the ball, then Harold went away on business. Even when he was traveling, he was still attentive. He sent flowers, and he often called in the evenings.

It was almost noon by the time Helen returned to the main house. Her mother was in the living room, arranging a vase of birds of paradise.

"Aren't these spectacular," Charlotte said, looking up when Helen entered. Charlotte wore a pleated skirt with a white blouse and belt. "The Pews sent them. You'll have to thank them tonight."

The house was filled with flowers. A glass trumpet vase of lavender roses stood in the entry. The table in the morning room held a pedestal vase of lilies of the valley, and cylinder vases were filled with pink asters. Helen counted ten flower arrangements in the living room. Edgar sent a dozen Scottish roses with a note saying the article would appear in next month's *Town Topics*.

Helen had quickly removed the note before her mother could read it.

"I didn't know so many people sent flowers before a debutante ball." Helen opened a card attached to a bouquet of delphiniums. "It's almost like a wedding."

Charlotte stepped back from the birds of paradise.

"Speaking of weddings, Margaret Coe called this morning. She was in New York yesterday and ran into Harold outside of Black, Starr & Frost."

Black, Starr & Frost was a jewelry store in New York's diamond district. It sold some of the most famous diamonds in the world. Helen read in the newspaper that the former Ziegfeld girl turned socialite, Peggy Hopkins Joyce, just acquired the Portuguese Diamond, the largest blue diamond ever sold, from the store.

"Margaret Coe loves to gossip," Helen said, returning the card to its envelope.

"Margaret asked Harold what he was doing there, and he didn't answer."

"It doesn't mean anything. He could have been buying a pair of cuff links."

"Most young men only buy diamonds on one occasion," Charlotte said. "When they propose."

Harold had taken Helen out half a dozen times. She could tell that he liked her. He often commented on how clever she was, and they danced so well together. But she didn't want to get her mother's hopes up.

"Harold and I only met a few weeks ago," Helen replied. "He hasn't even kissed me."

"It doesn't matter how long you've known each other. Robert and I met at the Philadelphia Assemblies ball and were engaged a month later," Charlotte recalled fondly. "I still remember our first dinner date." Her eyes were bright. "The orchestra started playing before we ordered. We danced for hours. By the time we returned to our table, the kitchen was closed. We ended up eating cold sandwiches in my parents' kitchen."

Charlotte stopped to pull a twig from the birds of paradise.

"The important thing is that Harold is warm and kind and that he'll give you the type of life that you want."

Helen didn't want to talk about marriage with her mother. But Charlotte had brought it up.

"What if I can provide those things for myself?"

"The farm might make you happy now, but imagine when you're older. Family is the best thing in life. There's nothing worse than being alone."

Helen could think of worse things. Her father taking up with a showgirl. Lying to his wife and daughters, putting the family's fortune and social standing in jeopardy. But it was fruitless to try to change her mother's mind.

"Here are my two beautiful women." Robert appeared in the doorway. He held up two wine bottles. "I brought up bottles of champagne in case there's something to celebrate."

Helen still hadn't forgiven her father. She avoided being with him at the farm, and she couldn't bring herself to join the conversation at dinner. The few times he asked to talk in private, she made up an excuse. Harold was about to pick her up, or she needed to make a phone call.

Her father went upstairs to shower and shave, and Charlotte went to the kitchen to supervise the cooks. There was a knock, and then footsteps in the hallway.

Helen looked up from a vase of rhododendrons. "Harold!"

"The front door was open, so I walked inside."

"My mother sent the maid on an errand." Helen motioned for him to sit down. "It's been like a military operation around here. I never knew that getting ready for a debutante ball is so complicated."

"It will be worth it." Harold sat opposite her. He took off his hat and placed it in his lap.

Helen looked at Harold archly. "You must be tired of debutante balls. I can't imagine doing it for more than one season. It was nice of you to agree to come."

Harold seemed nervous, and Helen wondered if he was going to propose now. It made sense; Helen would be busy tonight greeting her guests. But she was wearing her riding clothes. What would her mother say when she learned that Helen got engaged wearing breeches and riding boots?

"That's why I'm here," Harold said. "I can't make tonight's ball."

He looked guilty of something.

"You can't?" Helen inquired.

She waited for him to explain. There was a family emergency, or he was sick.

"The past few weeks have been some of the most enjoyable I've ever spent." He took her hand. "I've never known a girl like you. You're intelligent and a wonderful sportswoman," he began. "But the thing is I met someone else, someone who . . ." He stopped, and his cheeks reddened.

Helen released her hand. She sprung up and strode across the room.

"Let me finish the sentence for you. A girl who always wears beautiful dresses and bobs her hair. Someone who listens to what you say instead of giving her opinion. She knows everything about you because she's already had tea with your mother, and she's planning a surprise party for your next birthday." Something hard pressed against her chest. "A girl whose main goal in life is to make you happy."

She pulled a bud from a vase of roses and noticed her hands were shaking.

"Something like that," Harold admitted.

"Well, there's no point in hanging around here." Helen rearranged the roses. "I'm sure you have a million things to do, and so do I."

Harold walked to the hallway and turned around.

"I'm sorry, Helen. Today is a rotten time to tell you. But I'm going away, and I wanted to let you know before I leave."

"Don't worry about me. I'll be fine."

Her pride wouldn't let her show how she felt. Even if she hadn't been in love with Harold, it was hurtful to be passed up for another woman when she had spent so much time dressing correctly and trying to be charming and witty. Even worse, she was no closer to reaching her goal of saving Dumfries. Her debutante ball was the most important ball of the season, and she didn't have any suitors.

~

Later that evening, Helen stood on the terrace and gazed out at the lawn. Even with the weeks of planning, she hadn't imagined it would look so beautiful.

Round tables were covered with tablecloths in every shade of pink. The pink of a hair ribbon to the palest pink of lipstick. Strands of pearls were looped around cocktail glasses, and there were vases filled with ostrich feathers.

Bartenders served drinks Helen had never heard of. Princess Kaiulani, made with gin and almond liqueur and pineapple juice. El Presidente, made with Cuban rum and vermouth and orange curaçao and garnished with an orange peel. The El Presidente was the warmest hue of gold and tasted like a drugstore soda. Helen drank three until she realized she was tipsy.

A stage had been set up for the orchestra, and there was a sitting area where guests could take their plates of hors d'oeuvres. Helen wanted to thank her mother, but Charlotte was surrounded by women wearing sequined evening gowns and men in top hats.

Helen would thank her later, when everyone sat down to dinner.

Clarence stood across the lawn, and she gave him a little wave. He nodded, and she noticed a pretty young woman holding his arm. Clarence had stopped calling when she started seeing Harold. Now he was seeing someone else.

The full scope of her predicament washed over her. The season was almost over, and she was no closer to finding a husband.

Suddenly she was desperate to be by herself. She slipped into the house and down the hallway to her father's study. A bottle of brandy sat on the bookshelf. Beside it was a photograph in a frame. It was of her father in front of the barn. He wore a panama hat and patted a large brown cow.

She hadn't looked at the photographs in the study in ages. Pictures of Helen and Daisy playing tennis, Helen and Daisy sitting on their ponies. A photograph of Charlotte from twenty years ago, in a white-and-black bathing suit and black silk stockings.

There was a whole row of photographs of cows. Under each cow, the date and cow's name were written. Flopsy, who had a large brown spot on her back. Agnes, who had ears like small trumpets, and Essie, who was all white, except for a brown splotch on her neck.

Helen poured herself a glass of brandy. She picked up each photograph and put it back. Her father loved the cows as much as she did. How could he have done something that risked losing them?

Edgar stood in the doorway. He was elegantly dressed in a black top hat and tails. A yellow handkerchief adorned his breast pocket, and he carried a pearl-handled walking stick.

"Edgar, what are you doing in here?" She put down the picture of Essie.

"I just got here. I saw you come inside," he answered. "Shouldn't you be greeting your guests?"

"I've been standing on the terrace for the last hour." She held out her hand in a mock handshake. "'How nice to see you, Mrs. Pew. Isn't it a lovely night for a ball? I'm glad you could come, Mrs. Patterson. You must be so happy—Julia told me she's engaged.'

"If I greet any more guests, my face will freeze from smiling."

Edgar studied her quizzically. "Are you all right? You seem quite drunk."

She did feel woozy, like when she'd stepped off the Ferris wheel at the Devon Country Fair.

"How could I be drunk? Besides this brandy, I've only had a few drinks. Most of them tasted like marshmallows."

"How many drinks?" Edgar inquired.

"I can't remember. The first one was this afternoon, after Harold left."

"Harold was here earlier?" Edgar asked.

Helen sunk into her father's leather chair. She told Edgar about Harold's visit. He wasn't going to propose. He was in love with another girl.

Edgar took off his top hat. He looked handsome in the warm light of the study. His light brown hair was slicked back, and his cheeks were smooth with aftershave. He gave her a long, appraising look.

"If Harold saw you in that dress, he'd realize he was a fool."

Earlier in the evening, when Helen stood in front of her dressing room mirror, with her hair brushed a hundred times and her brown eyes larger under Daisy's mascara, she thought she looked lovely. The dress was floor-length ivory silk, with a scooped neckline and a wide sash. The back was cut so low, she felt practically naked. She wore a diamond pendant and matching earrings.

But Harold wasn't here to see it, and none of the other young men were interested in her.

She reached for the brandy glass, and the hem of her dress caught on her shoe. Edgar leaned down and untangled it.

"Perhaps go easy on the brandy," he said. "You are going to have to go back to the party."

"I'm not drunk." She tried to stand up, but her legs were wobbly. "I should go. Half a dozen men asked me to dance. I'll be engaged by the end of the evening."

Edgar sat in a leather chair opposite her.

"Good, then. I won't feel guilty."

"Guilty about what?" she inquired.

"I'm afraid it's my fault that Harold isn't going to propose. He is in love with Jane."

It took a moment for Edgar's words to register.

"But you're going to marry Jane!"

"We got into a silly fight last week. She doesn't like the way I chew my steak." He played with his walking stick. "She called this morning and said she found someone more compatible. She was going to her parents' house in Newport, and he was going to join her."

Helen frowned. "But they've known each other for ages."

"Jane probably never saw Harold that way before." He sighed. "I talked him up so much, I made him sound like an ideal husband."

Men would always see Helen the same way. Someone to have a spirited conversation with at a dinner party or as a hunting partner at a weekend house party. They wouldn't see her as someone to fall in love with.

Helen wondered if it was her fault. Would Harold have asked her to marry him if she talked about a new dress or the cities she'd like to visit in Europe? She wanted to get married someday. Nothing was more important than family. But was it wrong to want more? To dream of starting her own dairy company? For the cows and farm to mean so much to her?

She picked up the photograph of Flopsy.

"This is the first cow my father let me name." She showed it to Edgar. "I called her Flopsy, after Peter Rabbit's sister in the Beatrix Potter book."

Helen was about to tell Edgar the names of the other cows, but her eyes were watery. It was silly to cry. She hadn't even been in love with Harold. But she had enjoyed his attention. Resting her head on his shoulder when they danced. Sitting in his car in front of Dumfries and wondering if he was going to kiss her.

Edgar jumped up and strode to the door.

"I have an idea. First, I need some very strong coffee."

He returned with a pot of coffee and a small cup.

"Now drink this." Edgar handed her a cup of black coffee.

"I think we should get married," he said when she drank it. "It's the least I can do after ruining things with Harold."

Helen put down the coffee cup. Her eyes blazed, and she was completely sober.

"This has nothing to do with you," she said. "Maybe Harold could tell that I didn't want to get married. I've never been good at hiding my feelings, and why should I? That's the problem with men: they think a woman shouldn't have a mind of her own. I'm glad he didn't propose. Now I can concentrate on the farm."

Helen knew what she was saying wasn't true. She would have accepted Harold's proposal if he had asked her. But she couldn't help getting angry. And she couldn't marry Edgar simply because he felt responsible.

"You might not have the farm if you don't find a husband," Edgar said gently.

"Then I'll find someone who loves me for who I am." She waved her hand. "Anyway, you aren't a good candidate. You want to be a writer instead of work in the railroad company."

"I work for my father now. I'll write in the evenings." He shrugged. "Besides, I was going to marry Jane. I'm tired of being a bachelor. I never have a good reason to refuse a dinner party invitation."

He poured a shot of brandy for himself. "I told you on the night we met that you're the bravest girl in the world. In the past few weeks, you've proven that. If you let yourself relax, you'd be quite beautiful."

"What do you mean, let myself relax?"

He touched her neck. His palms were soft against her skin.

"The muscles in your neck are tense. You keep your shoulders hunched." His hands moved to her face. "You have lovely cheekbones and a pretty mouth."

Edgar leaned forward, and she thought he was going to kiss her. She was surprised by how much she wanted him to. But he stopped and got down on his knee.

"Helen Hope Montgomery, will you marry me?"

Edgar's family was well respected. His grandfather founded the Philadelphia Railroad Company, and his father had been the second secretary at the US Embassy in Paris before he left to join the railroad company. Edgar's mother was on the board of the Philadelphia Assemblies ball, and his great-grandmother had started Saint Joseph's Orphan Asylum.

Helen had to marry someone. At least Edgar wouldn't object to her working on the farm.

They had to announce their engagement tonight. If they waited, she'd lose her nerve.

"We can't get engaged without a ring!" she exclaimed.

In the back of her father's closet was a chest of Helen's and Daisy's old dress-up clothes. Inside was a velvet princess gown and a string of glass beads. A small box held one of their mother's brooches and an opal ring. Daisy had borrowed them from Charlotte's jewelry box and never returned them.

Helen handed Edgar the ring.

"You can use this."

"I'd like to pick out the engagement ring." Edgar turned it over. "But it will do for now."

Daisy often talked about getting engaged. She wanted Roland to propose next summer on a trip to Paris. They'd be sitting at a patisserie near the Eiffel Tower, and Roland would bring out a black velvet box. Inside would be a diamond baguette from Van Cleef & Arpels in Place Vendôme. Helen hadn't known what she wanted. But she never pictured standing in her father's study in front of the photos of her favorite cows. Or that the groom never mentioned the word "love."

None of that was important. All that mattered was that her father would win his old clients back. Dumfries and the farm would be safe.

Edgar slipped the ring on her finger. He kissed her softly on the mouth. She wanted him to kiss her longer, but the orchestra started playing on the lawn.

"We should greet your guests," Edgar said.

Then he put on his top hat and offered her his arm.

Chapter Seven

The wedding was scheduled for the second week in October. Edgar's parents offered their cabin, Camp Pinecrest in the Adirondacks, for the honeymoon, and Helen didn't want to be there when it snowed. There was no point in waiting until Christmas. The sooner they were married, the sooner life could return to normal.

Helen's parents held an engagement party at Dumfries, and the Scotts hosted a second party at Fieldstone Manor. Edgar joined the Union League and the Philadelphia Club, and the two families were seen together at the Devon Horse Show. Helen began receiving invitations to bridal showers for girls in her circle. Instead of mucking around in Nellie's stall in rubber boots, she spent her afternoons eating cucumber sandwiches and talking about whether one's trousseau should come from House of Worth in London or Chanel in Paris.

The ceremony was going to be held at Christ Church, the oldest Episcopal church in Philadelphia. Helen would have preferred to have the ceremony at home, but she didn't have the heart to object. The point of the wedding was to make a big society splash.

The reception would be in the Bellevue-Stratford's ballroom. Two hundred and fifty guests with a five-course sit-down dinner and a twelve-piece orchestra. They'd spend the night in the hotel's honeymoon suite before driving to the Adirondacks.

Helen tried not to think about the wedding night. Edgar was handsome and witty, but she couldn't imagine sharing a bed with him. He hadn't really even kissed her. Sometimes, when they were listening to the phonograph in the living room or driving in his car, she wondered if things would be different if it were a normal engagement.

Then she'd remind herself that they wouldn't be engaged. The reason they were getting married was because of her father's affair.

Edgar's parents were building them a house as a wedding present. Until it was ready, they were going to live in a cottage on the grounds of Fieldstone Manor. Helen wanted to live in a wing of Dumfries, but Edgar put his foot down. It was the cause of their first argument.

"I don't see why we can't live at Dumfries," Helen said when they toured the cottage one afternoon in early September.

The cottage consisted of a sitting room and a kitchen on the ground floor. Upstairs there was a bedroom and an office that Edgar could use for writing.

"I don't want to slink into our bedroom at night like some overeager suitor when your parents are home," Edgar insisted.

They were standing in the cottage's bedroom. It had a sloped ceiling, so Helen could barely stand up straight. The kitchen didn't have a mudroom, so she'd have to bring her riding breeches upstairs and hang them over the bathtub.

"Dumfries is huge. They'd never know when we went to bed," Helen persisted. "We can't have dinner parties here. The point of the marriage is to entertain."

"We'll host dinner parties at Dumfries or Fieldstone Manor." Edgar poked his head into the office. He smiled cheerfully. "I quite like it. I feel like a character in a Charles Dickens novel."

"You're being pigheaded." The color rose to her cheeks. "The kitchen isn't big enough to hire a cook, and there's nowhere to do the washing. I'll have to take it to Dumfries."

"I can wash my socks in the sink, and I thought all women secretly like to cook," Edgar said. "My mother is always puttering around the kitchen on the cook's day off."

Helen was embarrassed to admit that she had never learned to cook anything besides soft-boiled eggs. Mary, the cook, had been at Dumfries for as long as Helen could remember. And the downstairs maids did the laundry. It wasn't that Helen was spoiled. She loved physical labor. But she didn't see the point of fussing over the sauce for a roast when she wasn't particularly interested in food.

"I suppose it's all right for a few months." She sighed, testing out the mattress on the bed.

Edgar touched her hand. His green eyes twinkled.

"I promise I'll be a good husband. When you come home from a long day at the farm, I'll be waiting with a pitcher of martinis. I'll even rub your back."

A frisson of something ran through her, like a bee sting when it started to wear off. She tried to ignore it. There would be time to think about Edgar in that way on their wedding night. At the moment, she had to worry about her wedding dress and the flowers and the music.

"If you're home at night." Her chin jutted out, and she crossed her arms. "You'll get sick of my cooking and take all your meals at the club."

Now it was the end of September, and Helen had taken the train to New York. She spent the afternoon in Saks bridal salon. Edgar was going to pick her up after his meeting with a publisher.

He was waiting in the car when she stepped out of the department store.

"How was your meeting?" she asked, slipping into the passenger seat.

"I don't want to talk about it." Edgar grimaced. "Publishers don't care about literature. They'd paste baseball cards between two book covers and call it a novel if it made money."

Edgar had finished three chapters of his novel. He'd started to make the rounds of New York publishers but hadn't had any success.

"They all have a different reason for rejecting it." He veered into traffic on Fifth Avenue. "It's not witty enough, or the characters aren't sympathetic. What they mean is it stinks."

"They wouldn't have agreed to read it if it didn't show promise." Helen adjusted her cloche hat.

"They read it because I could drop a Harvard professor's name over the telephone. That will get me a round of cocktails with an editor at the University Club, but it won't get my novel published," Edgar barked.

His usually sunny disposition had been replaced by a dark cloud. Helen tried to think of a way to cheer him up.

"Why don't we stop by Jack's art gallery showing. You only met him a few times, but he liked you very much."

Edgar honked at a taxi that swerved in front of him.

"That's a good idea."

Jack's paintings were being displayed at a gallery in Greenwich Village. The gallery was already crowded when they arrived. The artist Georgia O'Keeffe was there with her husband, and there was a well-known photographer named Paul Strand. The other guests were more bohemian than the people at Jack's gallery openings in Philadelphia. The men wore velvet vests. Their longish hair flopped over their eyes, and they carried shabby-looking coats. The women wore fringed dresses and silk bandeaus. Their eyes were made up with kohl, and they waved around cigarette holders.

The art on the walls was even more avant-garde than the guests. Jack's paintings were his usual still lifes, but the other paintings—which Helen learned from the pamphlet were representative of something called cubism and surrealism—were too modern for her tastes. The colors didn't complement each other, and the figures were odd and unsettling. One painting was supposed to be a cow, but the cow's body was a rectangle, and instead of ears it had horns shaped like cones.

"I've seen enough, we should go," Helen said to Edgar after they had been there for an hour.

"Jack suggested we go back to his place," Edgar answered. "He's invited everyone to come."

Helen didn't want to admit that she wasn't comfortable around this sort of people. Edgar already thought she was too narrow-minded. And Jack was her uncle.

"It will be fun." He took her arm. "Jack ordered from a Chinese restaurant in Greenwich Village. Egg rolls and pot stickers and shrimp rangoon."

The apartment was in a brownstone facing Gramercy Park. The flat was furnished in the art deco style. The walls were painted burgundy, and the floors were black and white marble squares. One wall of the living room was mirrored, and there was a mirrored coffee table. Velvet sofas were scattered around a rug, and there was a black armoire.

A hallway led to a bathroom, and Helen caught sight of a room that doubled as a bedroom and an artist's studio. Canvases rested against a bed, and there was an easel and an ottoman pushed next to the window.

The space was so different from Jack's place in Philadelphia. He had inherited that apartment from his parents. It was three floors of grand rooms with sweeping views of Fairmount Park and the Schuylkill River.

Edgar joined Helen in the kitchen. "You have to try the shrimp toast."

"No, thank you. I'm not hungry."

"You said you were hungry at the gallery, and you haven't eaten a bite." Edgar eyed her suspiciously. "You're worried because it's Chinese food. I bet you've never tried a pot sticker."

He handed her a flaky dumpling. She took a bite and put it on a plate. It was too spicy, and the shredded pork got stuck between her teeth.

"I've got nothing against Chinese food," Helen said haughtily.

"Then you don't approve of the guests," Edgar guessed. "Why else would you be hiding in the kitchen while everyone is enjoying themselves in the living room."

Helen leaned against the cabinet. Edgar seemed to be reading her thoughts. She may as well tell the truth.

"I haven't met Jack's New York friends before," she admitted. "The men here are outrageously dressed, and the women have skimpy dresses and wear too much makeup."

"Most of the guests are artists and writers. They can't afford expensive clothes," Edgar said. "The artists are better off than the writers. Small galleries are always willing to promote new artists, and it only takes one collector to make a sale. The writers are in a worse predicament. Their fates are in the hands of the publisher. Look at what happened to Theodore Dreiser."

Theodore Dreiser's first book, *Sister Carrie*, was banned in England for obscenity, and he was dropped by his British publisher. His latest book, *An American Tragedy*, had just been released in America and was already banned in Boston. The reason given was lewd and sexual content.

"Then it's right to be banned," Helen said. "Books should maintain certain moral standards."

"I disagree," Edgar argued. "Perhaps if people were allowed to read about the subjects in Dreiser's book—penury and lust and murder—they'd have more empathy for people who grow up in poor circumstances."

Helen's cheeks reddened. "I think you're wrong. Books should elevate you."

"We can't all keep a first-edition King James Bible on the bookshelf," Edgar snapped. "I'm just saying that the publisher should let the public decide what to read. If they publish my book and it doesn't sell, it will be my fault. At least I'll have had a chance. The way things are now, I'm a bloody horse that isn't allowed at the starting gate."

Helen knew that Edgar was just disgruntled, but she was still angry. He shouldn't take it out on her.

"Publishers are like teachers. They have a responsibility," Helen said.

"If it was up to some teachers, we'd still think the world was flat." Edgar's eyes flashed. "And what about Oscar Wilde? He's one of the greatest Irish playwrights who ever lived. He was tried for sodomy and spent years in jail. When he finally got out, he was flat broke."

Helen had heard of Oscar Wilde. She came across his novel, *The Picture of Dorian Gray*, at a bookstore. Daisy read it and thought it was fascinating. Helen read the back cover and decided she didn't want to read a novel about a man who was so worried about losing his looks, he wishes that the portrait of himself as a young man ages while he maintains his youthful appearance.

"I'd like to go home." Helen crossed her arms. "I'll drive. You've obviously had too much to drink."

They drove back to Philadelphia in silence. Helen wanted to apologize. She couldn't help the way she was raised. She wanted to try new things and meet new people. Of course, she didn't believe books should be banned. But she did think people should be protected from terrible things—that's why she didn't watch those horror movies that had grown popular.

But if she said anything, Edgar might think she couldn't have her own opinion. She was so flustered about what to do, she ran into the back of an egg truck. Edgar gave the driver twenty dollars for the broken eggs, and they helped him clean up the mess. After that, she was too miserable to try to explain how she felt.

Helen pulled up in front of Dumfries.

"If you don't mind, I won't come inside," Edgar said stiffly.

"I already apologized about the egg truck." Helen turned to him. "I'm still learning to drive; I've only had a few lessons."

"Then you should have waited until I was sober and could drive instead of driving yourself," Edgar fumed. "We're lucky the truck driver reacted so quickly; we could all have been killed. As it was, he lost all those eggs."

"I wasn't driving fast enough for anyone to get hurt," Helen countered. "And you didn't have to pay him. I offered to give him the money."

"I was only being a gentleman, something you know nothing about."

The color rose to her cheeks, and she turned to Edgar angrily. "What do you mean by that?"

"Exactly what it sounds like," Edgar retorted. He fiddled with his boater hat. "You may need a husband, but you don't want one. You'd rather do everything yourself."

"Of course I want a husband. As long as he's decent and polite." Helen's voice rose. "That doesn't mean I need anyone to save me. If I was looking for a Sir Galahad, I would have put an ad for one in the newspaper."

She waited for him to give a snappy reply. But his face took on a brooding expression, and he refused to look at her.

"Why don't we talk about it later, when we both cool down," Edgar said finally.

"We don't need to talk about it. I can tell by your expression what you think of me." Helen opened the car door. "Go on and say it. I'm spoiled and close-minded and think I'm better than everyone. Well, I don't want to change, and I won't be with a husband who doesn't respect me. I'll tell my mother to cancel the wedding."

Helen stormed into the house and placed her purse on the entry table. Her father's study door was closed, and she could hear her mother in the morning room.

She marched into the living room and poured a drink from the brandy bottle on the sideboard.

How dare Edgar accuse her of not appreciating a gentleman. And there was nothing wrong with wanting to take care of herself. Marriage should be an equal partnership.

Charlotte entered the living room. She was dressed for dinner in a red crepe gown.

"Your father and I already ate, but there are meatballs in the kitchen. I was on the phone with the florist. I told her you wanted snapdragons in your bridal bouquet."

"I'm not hungry, and you can cancel the florist." Helen gulped the brandy. "There's not going to be a wedding."

Helen told her mother about the egg truck and the things she and Edgar said to each other.

"It's just a quarrel. Tempers are always high before a wedding," Charlotte replied. "A week before our wedding, your father and I argued about whether we should name our first son after my father or his grandfather. It was so silly—we never even had a boy."

"Edgar and I don't agree on anything." Helen poured another shot of brandy. "And when I said I was going to cancel the wedding, he didn't try to stop me."

"Well, you can't marry Edgar if he doesn't make you happy," Charlotte said pensively. "If you're serious, we'll have to think of another plan. We could rent out Dumfries and live with my aunt in Ohio. Daisy doesn't need to have a season; she's practically engaged."

Helen looked past her mother to the brandy bottle on the sideboard. For once she wasn't thinking about saving the farm or sparing her mother from more embarrassment. She was upset for a different reason entirely.

She jumped up and strode to the front door. The driveway was empty—Edgar's car was gone.

"What's wrong? What happened?" Charlotte asked.

Helen pulled off her gloves. Her pulse raced, and she could barely breathe.

She turned to her mother. "I've made a terrible mistake."

Helen rushed up the staircase and threw herself on the bed. Instead of giving her a warm, fuzzy feeling, the brandy had made it perfectly clear. She was falling in love with Edgar.

She tried to think when it happened. Was it when he retrieved her cigarette case from Harold's car, or when he offered to go with her to see Rosalee? The way he looked so handsome when he proposed, and how she had wanted him to kiss her. He knew the names of her cows, and he was an excellent horseback rider. When they were together, she felt light and happy. As if life were a game they could win together.

She couldn't drive to Fieldstone Manor and beg him to take her back. And she refused to call him. If he loved her, he had to make the first move.

There was a knock. It was Daisy.

She wore a green sleeveless cocktail dress. A white cape was draped around her shoulders, and she wore long white gloves.

"Roland and I just came back from dinner. You and Edgar should have joined us."

"We ate in New York." Helen took off her cloche hat and shook out her hair.

"Well, you missed a lot of fun. We went to the new jazz club on South Broad Street." Daisy peeled off her gloves. "You're lucky that you're getting married soon. I still have a curfew."

Helen didn't want to discuss Edgar. Daisy would say that the fight was Helen's fault. If Helen had been more understanding about Edgar's mood, they wouldn't have gotten into an argument.

"I almost forgot." Daisy walked to the dressing table and picked up a magazine. "This came for you."

It was a copy of the *New Yorker*.

Her father read the *New Yorker* for its humorous articles and for the Talk of the Town column, which gave a wry commentary on the social scene in New York. But why had she received it, and why was one of the pages folded over?

She turned to the folded page.

The headline and byline read: My Philadelphia Princess by Edgar Scott.

> I met Helen Hope Montgomery at my sister's debutante ball. She wasn't floating across the dance floor in a ball gown like the other girls. In fact, she was standing at the stables. But I could tell right away she was a Philadelphia princess. It was the way she carried herself. That long, elegant neck and the way her light brown hair bounces at her shoulders.

Helen read on about how on her mother's side, she could trace her roots back to the Founding Fathers. One of her ancestors had been at the signing of the Declaration of Independence.

She came to the final paragraph.

> The reason Helen is a princess in my eyes has nothing to do with her bloodline. It's the way she treats others: buying a puppy for the stable boy, giving presents to the maid and the cook. Putting herself in uncomfortable situations to protect the people she loves. Like any princess she holds herself to certain standards. And she inspires those around her to do the same. I, for one, am a better man because of her.

Helen closed the magazine. She looked up at Daisy.

"Is Father's car here? I have to go and see Edgar."

"Edgar's out by the swimming pool. I saw him when I arrived."

Helen tore down the staircase and into the garden. Edgar was lying on a chaise longue. He wore the V-neck sweater and slacks he had worn in New York.

"It took you a long time," he said, looking up. "I thought I'd be out here all night."

She felt nervous. He must have written the article ages ago. What if he felt differently about her now?

"I thought you left." She stepped closer. "What are you doing by the swimming pool?"

"I couldn't leave in the middle of an argument."

Helen sat on the chaise longue opposite him.

"I read the piece in the *New Yorker*."

Edgar fiddled with his wristwatch.

"I was hoping you received it. I left it with the maid. It's my first magazine piece, besides the one in *Town Topics*."

"It was very good." Helen turned to face him. "I wondered if you still felt the same about me."

"Why shouldn't I? One small fight doesn't change anything." He shrugged. "But I realized there are two things wrong with our engagement."

Helen gazed down at her hands. She wasn't going to defend herself; it was too late for that. If Edgar didn't want to get married, she couldn't force him.

Edgar moved over to her longue. "We're getting married in two weeks, and I haven't told you that I'm falling in love with you."

Helen looked up at him.

"Are you falling in love with me?" she inquired.

"It seems that way." Edgar took her hand. "Why else would I be sitting out here in my clothes. I could be at home, enjoying a scotch and a nice, warm bath."

Helen's breath caught. The sky was dark, and fireflies glinted on the lawn.

"You said there were two things wrong with our engagement. What's the other one?" she asked.

Edgar moved closer on the longue. She smelled soap mixed with men's cologne.

"I haven't properly kissed you," Edgar whispered.

He drew her toward him and placed his arms around her. His mouth was on hers, and she kissed him back.

Chapter Eight

Two days before the wedding, Helen sat at the oak desk in the morning room. She had been to see Thomas Danforth at the creamery and was writing out notes in an old composition book.

The dairy industry was growing. Milk had recently been discovered to contain something called vitamins, a chemical compound that was essential to the health of children. It was going to be offered in school lunches and at children's hospitals.

Many farmers were producing sour cream—cream skimmed off from the top of milk and left to sour. Sour cream was excellent in baking recipes. Now that most homes had iceboxes, ice cream was a popular dessert. And canned evaporated milk was still a favorite, even though fresh milk lasted longer in refrigerators.

There was something about evaporated milk—its sweet, honeyed taste and rich flavor—that reminded Helen of the glasses of milk Mary served to her and Daisy as children.

Helen needed money. Dumfries had only four cows that produced milk. She needed to buy more cows to make enough butter and cheese to send to the creamery. There was now an electric butterfat tester that measured the amount of fat in each cow's milk. But her father needed every penny, and she refused to ask Edgar. When they returned from the honeymoon, she'd go to the bank and ask for a loan.

After she finished making notes, she bicycled to the barn. She spent the next few hours mixing the feed and replacing the hay in the stalls.

"We're going to make a great team, Nellie," Helen said. "One day your picture will be on milk bottles all over the East Coast."

She rubbed Nellie's udder with balm. The balm stopped the cow's udder from getting cracked by too much milking. Helen and her father had developed the recipe together. She recalled Mary's horrified expression when she found them stirring beeswax and butter and lanolin in one of her steel pots in the kitchen.

There was the sound of crunching hay. Her father stood at the barn door. He was dressed in a blazer and navy slacks. There were new lines on his forehead, but he was still handsome.

"I thought I heard someone." He joined her in the stall. "You always talked to the cows when you were a little girl. You'd tell them about a new doll or a story you wrote at school."

"Well, cows listen to you." Helen screwed the top on the jar of balm.

She still didn't know what to say to her father when they were alone.

"In two days, you're getting married and leaving home. You won't be my little girl anymore."

"I thought you noticed that I was grown up. That's why you took up with someone not much older than me," she snapped. "There must have been a better way to stop from feeling old. You could have gone on safari or learned to fly an airplane."

"I deserve that. I understand why you're so angry," Robert acknowledged. "I'm lucky that your mother has forgiven me. I bought you a wedding present," he said, changing the subject. "It's outside."

A young calf snuffled against the wall. A bell tinkled around its neck.

"Her name is Clara." Robert petted the calf's stomach. "She's from a cattle breeder in Illinois. She's a pure Ayrshire cow."

Helen put her hand under the calf's nose. She couldn't think of a better gift. She started to say something, but her eyes filled with tears.

"It's not the usual wedding present for a bride," Robert said to ease the tension. "But I thought you'd appreciate her."

"She's lovely." Helen nodded. "Her legs are quite spindly. Is she old enough to be separated from her mother?"

Robert stroked Clara's back. He let out a chuckle.

"Even when you were a child, you cared so much about the cows' feelings." He smiled at Helen. "Agnes was afraid of thunderstorms, so you'd throw a blanket over the window in her stall so she wouldn't see the lightning. And Essie had an aversion to spiders. You'd always sweep the ground for spiders before her evening feed."

Helen knew what her father was doing. He was hoping she'd remember the wonderful times they shared together at the farm. But it wasn't going to change the way she felt about what he'd done.

Sometimes, when she couldn't sleep at night, thinking about the wedding, she wished that she could feel differently toward him. Even Charlotte seemed happier lately. Robert was more attentive than he had been in years. A few times, Helen heard them dancing to the phonograph after she had gone up to bed. And once from her window, she saw them riding together. Helen felt like the beanstalk in the fairy tale "Jack and the Beanstalk" that she and Daisy loved as children. She was too rigid, but she didn't know what to do about it.

"I've been thinking. Perhaps next year, we can modernize the equipment," her father went on, as if he sensed her dilemma. "Concentrate on making butter rather than cheese. You can only sell cheese locally, but the creameries ship butter all over the country."

Helen raised her head sharply.

"What do you know about creameries? You only want the farm as a hobby."

"I heard you and Edgar talking about it after dinner. I know how important it is to you."

Helen placed her hands on her hips. She turned and faced her father. He was trying to buy her off, the way he had tried to convince Rosalee to give up Chateau-sur-Mer and buy a smaller house.

"You're right. We should produce more butter, and Clara is a thoughtful gift. But if you think taking an interest in the farm as a business and giving me a calf with a tinkly bell is going to make up for your affair, you're wrong." Her voice rose. "You and Mother made vows to each other. I'm going to make the same vows in two days, and I intend to keep them. You should have done the same."

"I tried to explain . . ." Robert began.

The color drained from his cheeks. He stuffed his hands in his pockets.

"I'm your daughter, I don't want an explanation," Helen stormed. "All I wanted was a father who set a good example. A man who loved his family too much to cheat on his wife and ruin everything." She hopped on her bicycle. "I have to go."

When she reached Dumfries, Helen flung the bicycle down and ran up the steps into the living room. Her mother was on the telephone. Helen was struck at how lovely she looked. She wore pale pink lipstick, and a pink scarf was knotted around her neck. Her voile tea dress stopped below the knee and accentuated her slim calves. Helen was reminded of the photographs of her mother as a ballet student. There were a grace and beauty about her that Helen wished for herself.

"I was on the phone with the caterer." Charlotte replaced the receiver. "I had to adjust the guest count. The Drexels aren't coming to the wedding."

"What do you mean they aren't coming?" Helen asked.

Marjorie and Joseph Drexel were part of the Drexel banking family. Marjorie was one of her mother's oldest friends—they had been classmates together at Bryn Mawr. Joseph Drexel ran the Radnor Hunt. Joseph and her father were often hunting partners.

Charlotte poured a cup of tea from the tea set on the sideboard. She settled on the sofa.

"The reason doesn't matter."

"Of course it matters." Helen sat opposite her. "Marjorie told me that they pushed back their holiday to Palm Beach so they wouldn't miss the wedding."

Charlotte stirred honey into her tea.

"If you must know, they were having dinner last week at the Paramount Grill in New York. A young woman came up to the table and greeted Joseph. Marjorie said she looked like a showgirl. Sleek, bobbed hair, and lots of makeup, but with some expensive jewelry. Joseph pretended not to know her, but she insisted they met before."

Her mother explained that one evening last spring, Robert and Rosalee were having dinner at the Commodore in New York. Joseph happened to be dining at the same restaurant. He came to their table to say hello, and Rosalee invited him to join them for a drink.

"Marjorie made up some excuse that they can't make the wedding because there's a leak at their house in Palm Beach," Charlotte finished the story. "They have to leave tonight. I could tell she was making an excuse. She was furious at Joseph for lying that he didn't know Rosalee."

Helen stared at the teacup. She hated seeing her mother in more pain.

"It's not your father's fault. Joseph should have mentioned it to her," Charlotte said, noticing Helen's expression.

"Of course it's his fault!" Helen exclaimed. "And what if Marjorie tells the Coes and the Phippses? By the time that Edgar and I cut the wedding cake, it will be all over Philadelphia."

Charlotte shook her head. "Marjorie and I always kept secrets for each other at college. She promised not to say anything."

Her mother deserved better. She could get a divorce. If her father refused to leave Dumfries, she could live with her and Edgar after their house was finished. In a year or two she could start dating again.

"Divorce is as big a scandal as adultery." Charlotte sipped her tea. "Robert might have done something that—"

"Please don't say that he needed to feel young again," Helen cut in. "You're still beautiful. In that dress you don't look a day over thirty."

Charlotte put down her teacup. She stood up and walked to the hallway.

"I appreciate what you're trying to do, but in a way, I'm happier than I've been in ages. It's easy for a married couple to become distant from each other when they have so many responsibilities. Since the affair, your father and I have been doing more things together. After your wedding, we're going to drive to Maine to see the leaves change. We haven't done that since you and Daisy were children. Now, I have to finish rearranging the tables. The Drexels did leave a hole in the seating arrangement."

After her mother left, Helen went into the morning room. She took out her composition book and continued making notes on the farm expenses. Footsteps sounded in the hall, then Jack stood in the doorway.

"I expected the house to be filled with people rushing around before the wedding, but there's no one here." Jack sat at the desk opposite her.

"Mother just left, and Daisy is getting her hair done," Helen said.

Daisy had been to the hair salon in Philadelphia three times, trying out different styles. Helen was going to wear a Juliet cap with a long veil. Her hair would be tucked into a bun and secured with bobby pins.

"I came to offer my services. If you need me to drive you somewhere or just want someone to talk to," Jack said. "But you appear so calm and collected. I'm probably bothering you."

Helen hadn't seen Jack since the gallery opening in New York. Here, sitting across from him, his hair golden and his eyes their deep aquamarine, she was reminded of how much she loved and trusted him.

"You could never bother me." She set down her pencil. "There is something, but I doubt you can help."

"Ask me anything," Jack offered.

Helen was still worried about the wedding night. She knew how sex between a man and a woman worked, but she didn't know what was expected of her. Should she change in the bathroom while Edgar waited in the bedroom, or should she ask him to help take off her wedding dress? Would Edgar want to shower or shave before they made love, and were they supposed to drink more champagne?

Her mother never mentioned the subject. Perhaps she assumed Helen discussed it at one of the bridal teas. Every time Helen tried to bring it up, she imagined Rosalee floating down the staircase at

Chateau-sur-Mer in her hostess gown. She couldn't ask Charlotte about sex when her father had been in another woman's bed.

Jack was too discreet to talk about his love life, but Helen saw how women adored him. He must have had dozens of liaisons over the years. Perhaps he could give her advice.

She haltingly explained. Jack waited until she finished, then he spread his hands in his lap.

"I can see why you don't want to ask your mother," he agreed. "There is someone you can talk to. Her name is April Coates. She's a recent widow and a good friend of mine."

"Are you sure she won't mind?" Helen questioned.

It would be good to get away from Dumfries, even if only for the afternoon. She needed to think about something other than Clara, her father's gift, and the fact that the Drexels weren't coming to the wedding.

"She'll be happy to have company." Jack stood up. "We'll go now. We'll stop and pick up some chocolates as a gift."

April lived at Whitewood Hall, a neo-Georgian-style manor built by Horace Traumbauer, whose firm designed the Philadelphia Museum of Art. Jack said it was as big as the White House in Washington, eighty-five rooms and thirty bathrooms and its own refrigeration plant. The main house was three stories with white columns and a bell tower. To the right of the house was a swimming pool, and there was a sports pavilion.

A maid in a black uniform led them into the living room. Helen expected April to be about her mother's age. Instead, they were greeted by a woman of about thirty. She was wearing riding breeches and drinking a cup of tea.

"Jack!" she exclaimed when they entered.

She rushed over and kissed Jack on the cheek. Helen noticed how pretty she was. Auburn hair tumbled down her back, and she had hazel eyes and a wide mouth.

"It's wonderful to see you. It's quiet as a tomb around here," April said wickedly. "I shouldn't say things like that. Alistair's only been dead for eight months. But I've cried so much, I created puddles wherever I went. Nothing will bring him back."

"Widowhood suits you—you're lovelier than ever," Jack replied. He turned to Helen. "This is my niece Helen. She's getting married in two days."

April gave Helen a small hug.

"Then it's a doubly nice surprise." April beamed. "I've been at Whitewood Hall for three months. The only people I've met are Alistair's acquaintances from childhood. They pretend to be my friends, but they're only seeing how long I last before I give up running the estate and sell it."

Whitewood Hall had belonged to Alistair's parents. When they died, Alistair had inherited it, but he preferred living at their townhouse in Philadelphia. Alistair was killed in a trolley accident in February.

"I've always loved the countryside, and I don't mind living in a big house alone," April said when the maid brought them cups of tea. "Alistair spoke so fondly of his childhood here, I'm determined to keep the estate."

"If anyone can do it, you can," Jack said approvingly. He reached into his pocket. "I almost forgot, we brought you a box of chocolates."

April opened the chocolates and handed them to Helen.

"Jack knows I have a terrible sweet tooth. I'm lucky that I'm so active, or I'd sit around and eat sweets and ruin my teeth." She smiled coyly. "The only time I did that was when I was an artist's model. That was different. I was paid to lie around and do nothing."

Helen had never known an artist's model. She imagined them to be scandalous, like the women at Jack's apartment in New York. April was the opposite. There was something open and fresh about her.

"You were an artist's model?" Helen said.

"That's how I met Jack. I modeled for his art class. I fell madly in love with him, of course." Her hazel eyes twinkled. "It never came to anything. He treated me like a sister."

"I would have had too much competition," Jack said gallantly. "Every man in the class was in love with you."

"I didn't model for long. My parents found out and dragged me back to New York." April sighed. "Thank God I met Alistair. I might never have escaped."

They chatted for a while, and then Jack said he had to run an errand. Helen and April could talk privately—he'd pick her up in an hour.

April poured two more cups of tea, and Helen told her about her fears.

"It's not the sort of thing I've ever discussed with a stranger," Helen finished. "But I didn't know who to ask."

"I had the same worries when I got married. The only instruction my mother gave me was to do whatever Alistair asked and pretend to enjoy it," April said. "I was barely twenty. I wasn't going to spend my life doing something I didn't like. No one else would tell me anything, so I read novels about the great French courtesans: *The Lady of the Camellias* by Alexandre Dumas *fils*, and *Chéri* by the female French author Colette."

For some reason, Helen wasn't embarrassed to talk about sex with April. April was straightforward and matter-of-fact. It was as if they were talking about what kind of eggs Edgar might like, or whether to garnish a sidecar with a twist of orange or lemon.

"From the first night of our honeymoon, I let Alistair know that I wanted to be equal partners. We discovered sex together; it was one of the best parts of our marriage."

Helen wondered how many women Edgar had been with. She would never ask him; it was none of her business. She assumed he had enough experience to guide them.

"You've been very helpful." Helen put down her teacup.

"Society doesn't think a woman should enjoy sex, just like it doesn't believe a woman can run a large estate," she mused. "I intend to surprise everyone. Why don't I show you the stables? I could use a friend. When you return from your honeymoon, we can go riding together."

Helen followed April down the hallway. A large painting hung on the wall. It was a portrait of April. She was sitting on a chair by the window, holding a book.

"That was the last painting Jack did of me. I gave it to Alistair as a wedding present."

"I didn't know Jack painted portraits."

"He was the best portrait artist in his class," April said. "After graduation, he went off to Europe. When he came back, he wouldn't paint portraits anymore. He never told me why."

The portrait had a warmth and poignancy that wasn't present in Jack's still lifes.

"What do you think happened?" Helen asked curiously.

"What makes anyone do anything?" April shrugged. "My guess is that someone broke his heart."

Helen was silent on the drive back to Dumfries. She wondered whom Jack had been in love with. He never said anything about his relationships. Her earliest memories of Jack were at her parents' garden parties, looking dashing in a top hat and tails, with a different dazzling woman on his arm.

How could Jack have let a love affair interfere with his passion for painting? She thought about April and Alistair. They had been happily married. But would it have lasted, or would they have ended up like Helen's parents?

Helen might be falling in love with Edgar, but she wasn't going to depend on him for her happiness. After the honeymoon, she was going to get the loan from the bank. Dumfries was going to produce the best dairy products in the Lehigh Valley.

"Drop me off at the barn," she said when Jack's Roadster pulled into Dumfries's driveway.

She leaned forward and kissed her uncle on the cheek.

"What was that for?" he asked.

"For showing me that if I want something badly enough, it's up to me to go out and get it."

"How did I do that?"

"It doesn't matter. Right now, I've got to do something even more important than prepare for the wedding. I've got to introduce Clara, the new calf, to Agnes and Nellie."

Chapter Nine

The morning of the wedding, Helen woke up early.

She expected to feel grown-up and mature. She and Edgar were getting married. When their house was finished, she'd be in charge of her own household. Neither of them wanted to start a family right away. Edgar was intent on finishing his novel, and Helen wanted to start her dairy company. But Edgar was excited about having children. He was going to teach them to climb trees and swim in the lake.

They'd host dinner parties and weekend hunts. If Edgar got his book published, they'd drive to New York to see his editor. Afterward they'd take in a Broadway play or go dancing at the Waldorf-Astoria hotel. Helen would join charity committees like her mother and perhaps start a horse club for women.

Instead of feeling confident and excited, she was trembling so badly she could barely brush her teeth. She did the one thing that always soothed her nerves when she was a girl: she crept into Daisy's room and curled up in the armchair by the window.

Daisy woke drowsily, and they talked about their joint birthday parties when they were children. One year there was a magician. He pulled two rabbits out of a hat, and Helen and Daisy were allowed to keep them. Another year, their mother hired a man on stilts and a juggler. There was always a large birthday cake and treats for the other children.

They recalled their first trip to Rome with their parents. Daisy was fourteen and fell madly in love with a boy named Franco. She and Franco carved their initials on an arch in the Piazza del Popolo. When it was time to leave, Daisy wept and swore she'd never feel the same about a boy again.

After Helen and Daisy finished talking, they went downstairs for breakfast. Helen was surprised to discover that she was hungry. She ate two portions of Mary's eggs Benedict and asked for extra toast and jam. Her mother kept jumping up to receive deliveries, and her father made a quick appearance before he left to pick up a new top hat.

Helen's heart had never felt so full. She had a family that she adored, and she was marrying a man who was good-looking and considerate and said he was falling in love with her.

There was the moment at the church when Helen was tempted to flee out the back door. How could she walk down the aisle on her father's arm when some of the guests might know about his affair? But then she saw Daisy and the other bridesmaids in their pink organza gowns and watched the flower girls sprinkle rose petals on the floor and knew she couldn't disappoint everyone.

Edgar had been waiting at the altar in white tie and tails. Helen couldn't believe how handsome he looked. His shirt was perfectly starched, and he wore a black topcoat and white gloves. He had a white pocket square in his vest and topaz cuff links.

When he saw her, his nervous expression turned to one of wonderment, and she knew she looked lovely. Her wedding dress was from Saks couture bridal salon. Floor-length silk trimmed with lace, in the most delicate shade of ecru. The dress had a long lace train sewn with appliqued flowers. A pearl choker was fastened around her neck, and she carried a bouquet of snapdragons tied with an ecru satin ribbon.

After the ceremony, she and Edgar climbed into the back seat of a Rolls-Royce Phantom for the short drive to the reception. Edgar sat beside her, smelling of cologne, and held her gloved hand in his.

The reception was a heady blur of champagne and dancing and speeches. The ballroom at the Bellevue-Stratford was even more beautiful than the lawn on the night of her debutante ball. The room had white pilasters and low-hanging chandeliers. Tables were covered with black tablecloths, and the chairs were upholstered in pristine white satin. There was a chocolate-and-vanilla wedding cake and champagne bottles wrapped in white beads.

Helen danced with her father and Edgar and Jack. By the time the cake had been cut and the final toast had been given, she was giddy with exhaustion and happiness. It wasn't until her mother hugged her and made her promise to call when they reached the Adirondacks that her anxiety returned.

The wedding wasn't some wonderful party that she and Daisy would talk about in Daisy's bedroom. It was the beginning of a new life. She and Edgar hardly knew each other. What if he regretted marrying her? Or if Helen missed living at Dumfries? Being able to bicycle to the farm, riding her horse whenever she liked. She searched for Jack. He would understand how she felt. But he had already left.

Finally, the reception was over and Edgar led her to the hotel elevator. The honeymoon suite was on the sixteenth floor. From the window, Helen could see Independence Hall and the Centennial Bell. John Jacob Astor IV spent his wedding night in the same suite, and Theodore Roosevelt had stayed there with his wife, Edith.

The suite had been recently decorated in the French art deco style. There was an oval-shaped living room and a half-circular bedroom and a Turkish bath. The walls were papered in beige silk, and the floors were polished ebony. A grand piano stood near the window, and there was a white desk.

"Well, Mrs. Scott," Edgar said when they were both sitting on the velvet love seat. He took his pocket watch out of his vest. "We've been married for six hours. Does it feel different?"

"Different?" Helen repeated.

"The usual things the bride and groom feel after the wedding. The groom worries that his carefree bachelor days are over. Instead of getting up in the morning and reading the newspaper with his breakfast, he'll be expected to make conversation. He'll spend all day in an office, when he longs to go rowing on the river or watch a pretty girl walk in the park. When he arrives home, he has to remember to ask his wife about her day. And if he falls asleep straight after dinner, he'll never hear the end of it.

"The bride is afraid that he won't be as generous as her father with her allowance. Instead of spending the afternoon shopping for a new hat with friends, she has to go home and supervise the cook even though it's only her and her husband at dinner. And she can't read at bedtime, because her husband is waiting to make love."

The hair on the back of Helen's neck bristled.

"You make marriage sound as appealing as drinking molasses to cure a sore throat."

"I'm only repeating what I hear at dinner parties." Edgar chuckled. "I'm sure it will be different for us."

Helen was too nervous about the wedding night to respond. She stood up and walked to the hallway.

"If you'll excuse me, I'm going to take a bath."

The bathroom had a black marble counter and diamond-shaped mirrored tiles. Fluffy white towels were piled on the side of the bathtub, and matching his-and-her robes hung from pegs on the wall.

Helen unfastened the pearl choker and laid it on the counter. Next, she undid the pearl buttons on her wedding dress. When she wore only a slip and underwear, she gazed at her reflection. She never worried about her looks. But tonight, she couldn't help critiquing her small breasts and narrow hips.

Jane had full breasts, and a curved waist. Is that why Harold had fallen in love with her? And what about Daisy? No man could help falling in love with her sweet smile, those cornflower blue eyes. Charlotte had been much more beautiful on her wedding day than Helen. She had seen photographs of her parents in an album.

What if Edgar didn't find her sexually attractive? He said those terrible things about marriage. Perhaps he was regretting it already.

The door opened; Edgar stood beside her. He had removed his top hat and gloves.

"I didn't hear the bathwater. I wondered what you were doing."

She turned from the mirror. "I was resting for a minute."

"You weren't about to take a bath; you're still wearing a slip." Edgar frowned. "You're upset about something."

Helen took a deep breath. "If you must know, it's because you made all those comments about marriage. Well, for your information my parents share the morning newspaper. And they both read before bed; there are piles of books on their bedside tables. Before my father's affair, they were madly in love. If you think that marriage is some torture chamber designed to rob you of the next fifty years, then you can go back to the church and get it annulled."

Edgar took out his cigarette lighter and lit a cigarette.

"You can't smoke in here; the whole place will smell like smoke," Helen said in horror.

"Of course I can. I'm paying for the suite." He lit another cigarette and handed it to her. "So can you. We're adults—we can do whatever we like. If we want, we can skip the Adirondacks for our honeymoon and take a cruise to Alaska to see the polar bears instead. If we get tired of living in the countryside, we can buy an apartment in New York. And if we don't want our cook to make pot roast for dinner, we can give her the night off and eat baked beans on bread."

Helen accepted the cigarette.

She turned to Edgar. "What are you saying?"

"I didn't point out the good things about marriage. No one can tell us what to do. We're bound to make mistakes, but they'll be our own. And no matter what, we'll know that we have each other to count on."

Edgar took her cigarette and dropped it into the sink. He moved the hair from her shoulders.

When he kissed her, it wasn't the gentle kisses she'd known when they were engaged. This kiss was long and probing. He pulled her against him, cupping her chin with his hand. She gasped, and something unfurled inside her, a balloon that had come loose from its string and floated to the sky.

Edgar took her hand and they walked to the bedroom. She sat on the bed and watched him undress. His black suspenders, the shirt with its stiff collar, finally his slacks. There was a smattering of hair on his chest, his shoulders were broad, his legs were long and sinewy.

He lifted her slip over her head and drew her down onto the bed.

"We can wait if you like," he whispered. "We can take all the time you want."

Helen didn't know if it was the boldness of his kisses or the closeness of his naked body, but she felt confident and desirable.

"No." She shook her head. "I don't want to stop."

"Are you sure?" He placed his hand on her breast.

She arched her back, her body reaching instinctively for his. One hand moved under her, drawing her closer. His mouth covered hers. It felt like it was exploring and protecting her at the same time.

Something hard pressed against her thigh. She was afraid to look down—she'd never seen a penis before.

"Perfectly sure," she whispered.

He kept kissing her, cradling her in his embrace. His fingers caressed her breasts, sending a tingling down her stomach. Then his body was on top of hers, and her legs dropped open.

She stayed with him. Her hands grabbed his shoulders and she felt a buildup, and then an exquisite sensation she had never known. He murmured her name, then his throat made a guttural sound and he collapsed onto her chest.

Afterward, they sat against the headboard. Helen took a proper look around the bedroom. A Chinese divan was upholstered in rose-colored silk. The walnut floor was covered by a round pink rug.

"Now what do you think of marriage, Mrs. Scott?" Edgar asked.

Helen had never imagined she could be so intimate with a man. But she had to be cautious. She couldn't give her heart completely. Look at what happened to her mother.

"It's very good," she said.

Edgar's tone was light and bantering. "Good? That's all you can say?"

"Well, I have nothing to compare it to," she said archly.

"Take it from me, it was exceptional."

~

Edgar's parents' cabin in the Adirondacks was on Upper Saranac Lake, next door to the compounds owned by the Vanderbilts and the Huntingtons.

The area had been nothing but forests and lakes until forty years earlier, when the railroads made it possible to travel there from New York and Philadelphia. All the great families—C. W. Post, who founded the Post cereal company, J. P. Morgan, and the Rockefellers—had built summer homes. During the season, the lake was filled with sailboats and wooden fishing boats.

The first week of the honeymoon, Helen and Edgar fell into a companionable routine. They ate breakfast in the timber kitchen, and then Edgar disappeared with his notebook. Helen spent her days reading in a hammock in the garden or drifting along the lake in a raft. One afternoon they went fishing together. Helen caught a trout, and Edgar cooked it on the stove.

Toward the end of the week, Helen invited Harry Flagler and his wife, Anne, to dinner. Harry had been one of her father's clients, but he left the firm because of Robert's affair with Rosalee. It was the perfect opportunity to show him that Helen had married into a good family.

Except Harry and Anne were sitting in the living room and Edgar wasn't there. He knew the Flaglers were coming. She couldn't imagine what was keeping him.

Helen kept running from the living room to the front porch to see if he was walking up the path. To make things worse, the electricity had stopped working and the living room was freezing. Helen bundled herself in a fur coat she found in the closet, and Anne was wearing a scarf and gloves.

"Are you sure you don't want a coat?" Helen asked.

Anne was a thin woman in her forties. She had angular cheekbones and a pointed nose.

"I think I'll take you up on that." Anne rubbed her hands together. "I'm used to October nights in Florida."

Harry's father, Henry Flagler, had started the Florida East Coast Railway. Harry owned hotels in Saint Augustine and Palm Beach, and he was building a new hotel in Key West.

Helen went to the closet and dug out a full-length racoon coat.

"I don't know what's keeping Edgar. He said he'd be back by six p.m." Helen glanced nervously at her watch.

Harry had hardly spoken since they arrived. It was up to Helen and Anne to keep the conversation going. Helen tried to think of something to say, but they had already talked about the wedding and Harry's hotels.

"I can help you prepare dinner," Anne suggested. "You know what men are like—they think with their stomachs. Harry is as noncommunicative as a bear when he's hungry."

Helen didn't want to admit that she didn't know how to use the coal stove. Instead, she took a sip of her old-fashioned. At least the ice in the icebox hadn't melted, and she had been able to mix a pitcher of drinks.

"Young people these days don't care about being punctual," Harry grunted. "Just last week, I had to let a junior associate go. The young man thought a Princeton degree in economics allowed him to take three-hour lunches."

Helen heard the sound of someone singing, and then Edgar appeared on the front porch. He wore a flannel shirt and wool slacks. A cadet cap was perched on his head.

"It looks like the stands of a Harvard football game in here," Edgar said. "Why are you wearing my mother's racoon coats?"

Helen jumped up and took Edgar's hand. She led him into the living room.

"This is Harry and Anne Flagler. They're friends of my parents. I told you yesterday that they were coming for dinner."

Edgar seemed genuinely surprised.

"It must have slipped my mind." He shook Harry's hand. "When I'm writing, I don't think about anything else."

"You're a writer?" Anne inquired.

"Edgar writes in the evenings," Helen said quickly. "He works for his father in the railroad company."

Edgar walked to the pitcher on the coffee table and poured a drink.

"For now," he said cheerfully. "I've never thought about it until this week. But now I see the railroads have a lot to answer for. The Adirondacks was unspoiled wilderness until the railroads came in. Now the whole lake is overrun by summer people. Next, they'll build hotels, and all the natural beauty will disappear."

Harry frowned. "I disagree. The railroads employ more workers than any other industry, and hotels aren't far behind. The US economy would collapse without them."

"Edgar is joking, of course." Helen looked at Edgar pointedly. "Harry's family owns the Florida East Coast Railway and all the hotels from Saint Augustine to Miami."

Helen excused herself and dragged Edgar into the kitchen. Edgar threw two large trout into a frying pan. He turned to Helen.

"You're angry about something. You can at least tell me what I've done."

Helen set the gelatin salad on the counter. She told him how Harry Flagler had been a client at her father's firm. This was her chance to win him back, and Edgar ruined it.

"First you were late. I had to entertain them by myself. Then you said those horrible things about railroads and hotels," she fumed.

"I apologized for being late; the dinner slipped my mind," Edgar conceded. "And Harry must have heard it before—the newspapers have been saying those kinds of things about railroads for years. Not everyone likes progress, and this week I can see their point. I've never spent so much time in nature before. I've written the best work of my career."

She wanted to say that Edgar's writing wouldn't save the firm or Dumfries's farm. But arguing with each other while Harry and Anne were waiting in the living room would only make things worse.

Edgar went to the refrigerator and took out cheese and a jar of olives. He arranged them on a platter and handed it to her.

"Take these to our guests. Let me do the rest. I promise I won't let you down."

Twenty minutes later, Edgar appeared in the living room. An apron was tied around his waist, and he carried a large serving bowl.

"Follow me, everyone. Dinner is on the table."

The trout was perfectly cooked in butter and accompanied by sautéed vegetables. There was the Jell-O salad and a Waldorf salad Helen prepared that morning. For dessert, Edgar brought out the chocolate cake Helen bought at the bakery and a bottle of his father's port.

"The port is delicious," Harry said approvingly. "It's hard to find a good port during Prohibition. The bootleggers only sell whiskey and bathtub gin."

"There are more bottles in the cellar. You can take one home," Edgar said generously. He turned to Helen. "I ran into Alain Locke fishing today. He's on sabbatical and he's staying at Camp Sagamore, the Vanderbilts' compound."

"You know Alain Locke?" Harry asked with interest.

Alain Locke was born and raised in Philadelphia and had attended Harvard. He was the first Negro to become a Rhodes Scholar at Oxford; now he was a professor at Howard University. The newspapers called him the "father of the Harlem Renaissance" for encouraging black authors and poets and artists. He edited an anthology of their work called *The New Negro*.

"He was a visiting professor when I was at Harvard," Edgar said.

"I graduated from Columbia, but I spent two years at Harvard." Harry leaned back in his chair. "Alain was a year behind me. Even then one could tell that he was a genius. I haven't seen him in twenty years."

"I asked him to dinner the next time he's in Philadelphia. You'll have to join us," Edgar suggested.

Harry finished his port. He beamed at Edgar. "I'd like that very much."

After Harry and Anne left, Helen and Edgar loaded the dishes in the sink. Helen was still upset. She wondered if Edgar meant the things he said about working at the railroad company. They'd never survive without his paycheck, and she still had to win back her father's clients.

Edgar scraped chocolate cake from the plate. "You're very quiet."

She told him what was bothering her.

Edgar wiped his hands on the apron.

"Writers aren't like most men. They can't help the way they are," he said grimly. "Do you think Dickens would have chosen to be a legal clerk or Anthony Trollope would have worked at a post office if they could have been content with proper careers? Jack London stole oysters from an oyster farm in San Francisco to support himself before he was published." He took Helen's hand. "But I made you a promise, and I intend to keep it."

They finished cleaning up and went to the bedroom. But for the first time since they'd arrived at the cabin, they didn't make love. Perhaps it was a coincidence. They were both tired from being in the sun and fishing.

Helen turned on her side and fell asleep.

Chapter Ten

The first two months of their marriage were a great success. Helen and Edgar hosted a dinner party in the main house at Fieldstone Manor. Percival Foerderer and his wife, Ethel, who owned the estate La Ronda in Bryn Mawr, came, and so did the Van Leers. During the cocktail hour, William Atbury, the president of the Philadelphia Club, stopped by with the former US president William Howard Taft. President Taft shook Edgar's hand and said Edgar fixed the best sidecars he'd drank since the war.

It was Edgar's idea to have a regular table at the Warwick Hotel and invite their friends. Helen enjoyed it more than she imagined. She and Daisy went shopping at Wanamaker's and bought her a fashionable wardrobe. Sleeveless cocktail dresses, beaded gowns with dropped waists, and a gold mesh evening bag. Helen even got her hair styled. It wasn't as short as a bob, but it was cut squarely above her shoulders.

When she caught her reflection in the mirror, she almost didn't recognize herself. The hairstyle softened her cheekbones, and her mouth seemed wider. Daisy showed her how to use face powder, and her skin was as lustrous as the pearls around her neck.

Helen and Edgar always arrived before the other guests and told each other funny stories about their day. Helen learned to dance the Charleston and the shimmy, and their table was always filled with laughter. Many nights after the others left, Helen and Edgar stayed, drinking coffee and listening to the orchestra. Helen often thought that was her favorite part of the evening.

She spent most of her days at the farm. She used her savings to buy an electric butterfat tester. And she spent hours researching the new glass butter churns that produced butter faster than their old-fashioned churn.

On the weekends, Helen and Edgar took long drives and went riding together. For their one-month anniversary, Edgar gave Helen a new foal. Edgar tied a blindfold around Helen's eyes and led her into the stable. When he removed the blindfold, the excitement in his voice almost giving it away, Helen gasped. The foal was eight months old, with large, doleful eyes and a wet nose. Helen named her Belle, after the horse in *Anne of Green Gables*.

Helen's present to Edgar was a new Royal typewriter. She had never seen him so touched. He peeled off the blue bow and typed a few sentences. Then he spun her around and declared he was going to write a bestseller.

This morning, Helen was sitting in the reception area of the bank, waiting to talk to the bank manager. She was going to ask for a loan to buy more cows.

"Mrs. Scott, Mr. Fairbanks will see you now," the secretary announced.

Helen gathered her purse and entered Mr. Fairbanks's office.

Helen hadn't seen him in months. He was a large man with dark hair and small blue eyes. He wore a suit with a vest, and he smelled of cigars.

"Please, sit down. Can I offer you something to drink?" he asked.

"No, thank you." Helen sat opposite him at the desk. She had dressed carefully in a jade-green dress with a flat collar and a bow tie. She wore white gloves and Mary Jane pumps.

"I remember the day you and your sister received your first bankbooks. Now you're a married woman," Mr. Fairbanks said jovially.

"What can I do for you? Are you depositing more money into your little nest egg?"

"Actually, I came to ask for a loan."

Helen told him about wanting to invest in the farm. Dumfries's Dairy Products was going to be her company, and she didn't want to ask her father or Edgar for money.

"The bank doesn't lend money to women," Mr. Fairbanks said when she finished.

"I understand, but maybe you can make an exception. You've known my family for years, and it would mean so much to me." She smoothed her gloves. "Haven't you always wanted something of your own? Perhaps, a car that you've seen in a showroom window or a boat to sail on the river. It's much more special when you pay for it yourself. No one can take it away."

"I'll tell you what. I'll check yours and Edgar's bank history. If they both check out, we can offer you a small loan," Mr. Fairbanks suggested. "I have a daughter your age. It's nice to see young women take the initiative."

Helen waited while Mr. Fairbanks went downstairs. He returned twenty minutes later.

"Your account is fine, but your husband's personal account is overdrawn."

It wasn't possible. Edgar deposited his paycheck into a joint account once a month. He gave her a household allowance and put money into a personal account for his own expenses.

"My husband's account has nothing to do with me," Helen said.

"Those are bank rules. I'm afraid there's nothing I can do." Mr. Fairbanks shuffled some papers. "I'm taking my Christmas holiday next week. Why don't you work things out at home. We can talk again in the new year."

It didn't make sense. Edgar was frugal when it came to money. They made a budget for gas for his car and for his shoeshines. He even suggested they set up a savings account for when they had children.

A few hours later, she sat in the cottage's living room, waiting for Edgar to come home. The situation reminded her of her father and Roland. What if Edgar was spending money on another woman, or betting on horses? By the time the front door opened, her nerves were frayed and her hands felt like ice.

"You didn't have to wait for me to have an evening cocktail," Edgar greeted her. He kissed her and set his hat on the peg in the entry.

He fixed two glasses of gin and seltzer water and handed one to her. Helen placed her glass on the coffee table.

"I'm not thirsty. There's something I want to talk about."

She told him about her meeting with the bank manager. Edgar jiggled the ice in his glass.

"The account is overdrawn by sixty-five dollars and thirty-three cents," he said. "That's hardly a cause for alarm."

"It stopped me from getting a loan." Helen looked at Edgar levelly. "What did you spend it on?"

"Not showgirls, if that's what you think," he said, as if he could read her mind. "It's not important. You could use your money to fly an airplane or take flamenco lessons, and I wouldn't say a word."

Since they'd returned from the honeymoon, Edgar had been so loving. In the mornings, he made the coffee before she came downstairs. He often called during his lunch hour just to tell her that she made him happy. But now, his brow was furrowed, and there were lines around his mouth.

"You must have spent it on something," she insisted.

Edgar went to the sideboard and refilled his drink.

"If you must know, I hired a writing instructor."

Edgar had written another four chapters of his novel. Every night after dinner he went into his office and she heard him typing. But the book wasn't finished, and he hadn't sent it to more publishers.

"You paid someone to help with your writing?" Helen said incredulously.

"You make it sound like I was running a bootlegging ring," he retorted. "I didn't hire him to write the words, just to help me see the novel as a whole. When I find a publisher, I'll replace the money."

The book was only halfway done. It could take Edgar months to finish it and get a publisher. In the meantime, the bank wouldn't give her a loan.

"What if you don't need him? Just because a few editors rejected it doesn't mean others will do the same. You could offer it to publishers now."

Edgar set down his glass and went upstairs to his office. He returned with a stack of typewritten pages, neatly separated and secured with paper clips.

"I haven't sent out the novel, but I've submitted short stories to different publications." He unfastened the paper clip.

"From the desk of Ellery Sedgwick," he read out loud. "Dear Mr. Scott, thank you for submitting your short story. While your theme is thought-provoking, your characters aren't sympathetic enough to engage the reader. I'm afraid we'll have to pass. Sincerely, Ellery Sedgwick, editor in chief, *The Atlantic*."

There were similar notes from the editor at the *Saturday Evening Post* and *Vanity Fair*. The publisher of *Collier's* praised Edgar's writing style but said the plot was trite.

"My writing is missing something. I've gone over the pages a dozen times, but it's like a jigsaw puzzle. I can fit together the pieces, but I can't see the finished whole."

Helen had never seen Edgar appear so defeated. She had to do something. He was charismatic and full of ideas; he could do many different jobs.

"If you don't like the railroad company after a year, you could choose a different career," she suggested. "You're so creative, you could go into advertising."

In the last ten years, advertisements in newspapers and magazines had become popular. It was the cigarette industry that brought them to the forefront. Full-page color ads for R. J. Reynolds Tobacco Company and Lucky Strikes were in every issue of Helen's father's *New Yorker*.

"You want me to go into advertising?" Edgar repeated in surprise.

"It might not be as prestigious as the railroad business or banking, but it's becoming well respected. You'd be good at it," Helen said. "Roland's brother works for J. Walter Thompson. One of his clients is General Motors. He gets to test-drive new cars before anyone else."

"I only care about writing novels," Edgar fumed. "I may never be a great writer like Tolstoy or Chekhov, but I want to create something lasting. A book that some kid picks up and it inspires him to be a better person. A novel that will be read by someone in a nursing home who thinks his life is over." He picked up his glass. "You wouldn't understand."

"What do you mean I wouldn't understand?"

"All you talk about is how much you want to start your own dairy company. I support you, of course. I want you to succeed," Edgar replied. "And I'm all for equality for women. My mother fought for the suffragette movement. I believe women should get the same salaries as men for doing the same work."

"It is harder for women, especially in society." Helen couldn't keep the frustration out of her voice. "My mother refuses to divorce my father because it's frowned on for a woman to live alone. Daisy wants to be a decorator when she finishes college, but she's smarter than that. If anyone encouraged her, she could be a lawyer or a doctor. And the only way I could save Dumfries was by marrying someone respectable."

Edgar stood up and paced around the room.

"You don't see anything past those damn pearls around your neck." He clenched his jaw. "You're too self-centered to even notice how I feel. Do you know what's harder than being deprived of what you want because of society or the amount in your bank account? It's not being able to do the one thing you live for, the one thing you need to stay alive, because you're not good enough and never will be."

"Perhaps you just have to learn to be patient." Helen crossed her arms. "And how dare you talk to me like that. It's not my fault that you don't have a publisher."

The minute the words left her mouth, she regretted them.

Edgar's green eyes were bright. He grabbed his hat and opened the door.

"I'll see you later. I'm going to finish my cocktail someplace where I'm not a constant reminder that your husband is a complete failure."

Helen couldn't remember being so angry. Edgar shouldn't have walked out; she had only been trying to help. He wasn't a starry-eyed college student anymore; he was a married man. He needed a profession. Yet she felt slightly guilty. If someone told her that she'd never have her dairy product company, she didn't know what she'd do.

It was too late to go to Dumfries, and she didn't have a car. Besides, she wasn't going to be one of those brides who ran home at the first sign of trouble in the marriage. She tried calling Jack—he would give her advice. But the concierge at his apartment building said he was in New York. She telephoned his flat there, but he didn't answer.

Helen ate a piece of chicken at the kitchen table and left the rest in the refrigerator.

Before she went to bed, she took Edgar's robe and slippers and laid them on the small sofa in his office. He had to come home sometime. It would be better if they talked in the morning.

The next day, Edgar was contrite at breakfast. He apologized for walking out and promised it wouldn't happen again. But when he kissed her goodbye, there was a tension between them. And when he called at lunch, neither of them could think of anything to say.

Helen had to talk to someone. She decided to go and see April. April had been married; she would know what to do.

When Helen arrived at Whitewood Hall, April was sitting in the living room. A tea tray rested on the side table.

"Helen, how nice to see you," April greeted her. "Let me get another teacup."

Helen had seen April a few times since she returned from the honeymoon. April was bright and lively, and Helen found they had a lot in common. April spent her mornings riding around the estate, inspecting the outbuildings and drawing up plans to update the stables and greenhouses.

The living room looked different from her last visit. There was a blue velvet settee and chrome chairs. A Lalique chandelier in the shape of a pineapple hung from the ceiling, and in the corner was a mirrored cocktail cabinet and an Oriental screen.

"This room looks beautiful," Helen said. She admired the ebony secretary next to the window and the oval mirror above the fireplace.

"Do you like it?" April beamed. "I got rid of Alistair's parents' Victorian furniture and hired an interior decorator. I can give you his name, for when your house is finished."

"I don't know if Edgar and I will be moving into our new house," Helen said glumly. "We got into a terrible argument."

She explained how the bank wouldn't give her a loan because Edgar's account was overdrawn. When she suggested he choose another career, he stormed out.

"All marriages have ups and downs." April sipped her tea. "Marriage is like driving in a sporty new car. There's nothing more fun than cruising along in a Roadster, but the minute you hit a pothole, you wished you had walked instead."

"We've only been married for two months, and we've been so happy." Helen stirred sugar into her cup. "Edgar shouldn't have overdrawn his account, and if he did, he should have told me."

"Perhaps he was embarrassed," April suggested. "Men want to take care of their wives."

"I don't need anyone to take care of me. But if Edgar was short of funds, he should have trusted me enough to tell me," Helen said staunchly. "Marriage should be a partnership."

"Even partnerships are never equal. I learned that from my father. He's in the diplomatic services. I was a much better horsewoman than

Alistair, so I always let him ride ahead. Then I'd pretend that I had to catch up with him."

Helen disagreed—marriage should be based on trust and honesty. But she missed Edgar. She missed the warmth between them. And she didn't know how to get it back.

Her mind went to the previous night, when Edgar left. Waking up in the morning, without his muscular body beside her. In the last two months they had grown so close. She loved cooking with him on the evenings they ate at home. He was a surprisingly good cook—he learned during a summer he lived in Italy. He prepared the main dish—a delicious pork roast, or bowls of spaghetti—and Helen made the salad and cut up fruit for dessert.

And she liked living in the cottage at Fieldstone Manor. His parents had an indoor swimming pool, and she and Edgar swam laps together. Afterward, they bundled up in Edgar's old college overcoats before driving the short distance to the cottage.

"I have an idea," April interrupted her thoughts. "Do you have an extra copy of Edgar's novel?"

Helen nodded. "He keeps two copies in his desk drawer."

"Then we'll stop by the cottage on the way to New York." April set down her teacup. "First, we're going to see Alistair's family's stockbroker. He works for J. P. Morgan Bank, and he's very clever. If you give him a small amount of money, soon you'll have enough to start the dairy company."

Helen was nervous about withdrawing money from her bank account, but if she wanted to buy more cows, she had to do something. And she didn't know much about the stock market. But the radio announcers were always talking about something called the bull market. Stocks had been rising steadily for eight years. Wall Street was doing so well, new millionaires were made every day.

"That is a good idea," Helen agreed. "Why do I need Edgar's novel?"

April's hazel eyes danced with excitement. "Because after that, we're going to see my godfather, Max Perkins. He's one of my father's oldest friends, and he happens to be the editor of F. Scott Fitzgerald and Ernest Hemingway."

Edgar often talked about Max Perkins—he was every author's dream editor. After graduating from Harvard, Max became a reporter at the *New York Times* and then an editor at Scribner. He began his career by editing established authors like Edith Wharton and Henry James before discovering Fitzgerald's first novel, *This Side of Paradise*.

"Do you really think he'd read Edgar's novel?" Helen asked in awe.

"He'd do anything for me. He and my father were at Saint Paul's School together. My father was a year older than Max, and he protected Max from being bullied by the older boys. Max loves finding new talent. One of his favorite dinner party stories is how nobody would publish Fitzgerald; now he's the most successful author in America."

Edgar hadn't sent his novel to other publishers because he thought it wasn't good enough. But Helen had liked the chapters she read. Perhaps he just lost his confidence. All he needed was for someone in the publishing business to praise his work.

It was against her principles to submit the novel without asking Edgar first. But they were hardly speaking. It was a golden opportunity; she couldn't pass it up. She pictured Edgar's expression when he learned that Scribner was going to publish his novel. He'd hold book signings and readings. Perhaps one day he'd teach a writing course at Harvard.

Helen nodded. "All right, let's do it."

"I'll go upstairs and change and call Frank, my chauffeur," April said happily. "I'm an excellent driver, but if we get good news, we might want to open a bottle of champagne and celebrate. Then I'll be too tipsy to drive home."

~

Scribner occupied its own building on Fifth Avenue between Forty-Eighth and Forty-Ninth Streets. The bottom floor was taken up by a bookstore, and the higher levels contained offices.

Helen and April sat in the reception area and waited for Max to appear.

"April!" Max stood in the doorway. He was about fifty, with dark brown hair and a long nose. He wore a navy suit with a spotted handkerchief in the breast pocket. "What are you doing in New York?"

April jumped up from her seat. She had changed into a yellow crepe skirt and matching jacket. She wore a yellow cloche hat and carried a leather handbag.

"Coming to see you. You're so important now, you must be terribly busy." She kissed him on the cheek.

"Never too busy for you." Max's eyes traveled to Helen. "Who's this?"

"Helen Montgomery Scott." April smiled mischievously. "Helen is a blue blood from Philadelphia, but you'd never know by being with her. She's the most fun person I've met since I lived on the Main Line."

Max and Helen shook hands, and Max led them into his office. It was completely different from her father's offices or the offices at the bank. There was a black-and-gold settee and a coffee table scattered with ashtrays and bowls of hard candy. One wall was taken up by a bookshelf, and the walls were covered with framed book covers.

"What a beautiful office." Helen admired the marble bust on the sideboard.

Max followed her gaze. "That's a bust of Benjamin Franklin. He was the first person to promote the printing press in America."

"Max's office always has the best sweets." April unwrapped a Tootsie Roll. "I used to visit him after school just to eat his peppermint Life Savers."

"Most of my visitors are nervous authors," Max explained to Helen. "If I don't stock candy and cigarettes, they'll ask for hard liquor instead. Recently, I made the mistake of offering Scott Fitzgerald a drink while I was editing his novel *The Great Gatsby*. He got so agitated waiting for my notes, he finished off a bottle of whiskey."

The secretary brought tea and little cakes, and they talked about April's parents and Max's daughters. Eventually, Helen told him about Edgar's book.

"Edgar has had pieces published in *Town Topics* and the *New Yorker*. What I've read of the novel is very good."

"You're brave being married to a writer," Max said with a smile. "Most of the authors I know are so miserable, they'd give their last dollar to do something else. One of my writers donated his typewriter to charity and got rid of every notepad and pencil in his house. It didn't do any good. One night, he and his wife went out to dinner. By the end of the meal, he had asked the waiter for his pen and started scribbling ideas on a napkin."

Helen recalled the pain in Edgar's expression before he walked out the door.

"Max is being too serious. Everyone knows that successful authors are treated like film stars," April chided. "Scott and his wife, Zelda, spend all their time in the South of France. And Hemingway's novel *The Sun Also Rises* was so successful, he's already divorced his first wife and found a rich, young new one."

"Leave the manuscript with me; I'll read it over the weekend." Max handed Helen a card. "Call me on Monday, and I'll give you an answer."

Helen planned on telling Edgar what she had done over dinner. But when she arrived home, she wondered if they were having company. The dining table was set with the fine china that Helen had brought over from Dumfries. Edgar had even taken out the silver candelabras they received as a wedding gift.

Edgar entered the living room, and Helen was reminded of how handsome he was. This evening, he wore an open-necked white shirt and tan slacks. His shirt sleeves were rolled up and showed the light brown hair on his forearms.

"There's my darling wife," he greeted her. "I was afraid you'd packed a suitcase and gone back to Dumfries. I wouldn't blame you—I acted like a heel."

Edgar's mood was completely different than it had been that morning. There was a spring to his step, and he had been humming a show tune.

"Are we having people to dinner?" she wondered.

"Just the two of us." He set a soup tureen on the table. "We're celebrating. I took the afternoon off and went to the Philadelphia library."

Helen and Daisy had spent many summer afternoons at the library's previous location on Locust Street. It wasn't grand like the new building on Logan Square that resembled a Greek temple and had been funded by Andrew Carnegie. But Helen had loved the wooden shelves on the third floor that contained books on farming. And Daisy adored the selection of fashion magazines and the illustrated books about interior design.

Edgar brought out a glazed ham and duchess potatoes. There was mandarin orange gelatin and warmed bread rolls.

"I sat in front of a display of signed first editions and realized I was behaving like a spoiled child." Edgar poured two glasses of wine. "The shelves are lined with volumes by authors who spent their lives writing a few great books. I couldn't expect my work to sit next to *Don Quixote* by Cervantes or *The Count of Monte Christo* by Dumas when I'd only been trying for a short while. I have to do what all authors do—throw out what I've written and start again."

Helen almost dropped her soup spoon.

"What do you mean start again?" she asked nervously. "You've been working on your novel for months."

"That's the problem." Edgar's voice was eager. "I'm like the parrot at the pet shop that only repeats what it hears. I can't write something meaningful while I'm still thinking about what I was taught at Harvard or a story I read in the *Saturday Evening Post*. I have to write something new, something that hasn't been done. For instance, a novel about an explorer who travels to the jungles in Peru."

"You've never been to Peru." Helen's throat constricted. "You're the one who told me that F. Scott Fitzgerald's first book was about a wealthy society boy, and it became a bestseller."

She had to make him be sensible. It would take him ages to finish a new novel. And why would writing something new be different? If it was rejected, he would get disillusioned all over again.

"That's my point. I can't write the same thing as Fitzgerald and expect people to buy it," Edgar said. "I might never have been to Peru, but I can research it at the library." He picked up his wineglass. "You were the one who said I needed to be patient. You were right. I don't know how to thank you. Thank God I didn't show my book to other publishers. If they hated it, they'd never read anything else I write."

Helen thought about Edgar's manuscript sitting on Max Perkins's desk. She couldn't tell him that she had given it to Max now. He'd be furious.

"You don't need to thank me," she said bleakly.

Edgar's eyes were warm in the candlelight. He reached across the table and touched her hand.

"I always knew the best part about marriage would be finding someone who understood me. I'm in love with you, Helen. Let's never fight again."

Chapter Eleven

Helen phoned Scribner on Monday, but Max was home with the flu. His secretary told Helen to call back at the end of the week.

She hardly saw Edgar all week. Every evening he arrived home with a stack of research books in his arms. At dinner they talked about when their house would be finished and whether they should go skiing after Christmas. But Helen knew he wasn't listening. The minute the dishes had been washed and put away, he kissed her and climbed the stairs to his office.

Every time the phone rang, she hoped it was Max saying he loved Edgar's novel. She was tempted to tell Edgar what she'd done. But each time she went to knock on his door, she couldn't do it. Edgar was happy—he was consumed with new ideas.

Max would call eventually. If it was good news, Edgar would think she was a star. If Max didn't like it, she would have to tell Edgar the truth. She couldn't live with herself if she wasn't honest in the marriage.

Now it was Friday, and Helen was driving to Dumfries to help her mother wrap Christmas presents. Every year Dumfries held a Christmas party for the employees. Helen's father dressed up as Santa Claus, and there was a puppet show for the children. Helen had worried that this year there wasn't enough money to hold the party, but Charlotte assured her that she wouldn't cancel it.

Charlotte was in the morning room when she arrived. Wrapping paper was scattered over the desk, and there was a pile of bows and ribbons.

"Daisy is in her room; she'll be down soon," Charlotte greeted her. "Your father just tried on his Santa Claus suit." She smiled. "He's quite pleased with himself. He's worn the same costume for twenty years and it still fits." She picked up a green bow. "He went to his barber. We've been invited to the Drexels' holiday ball at Maybrook. The leak at their house in Palm Beach is fixed, and they're back in Philadelphia," she said archly. "And your father's membership at the Old Philadelphia Club has been reinstated. William Atbury called personally and complimented him on his son-in-law."

Helen was glad for her mother, but she still hadn't forgiven her father. And she tried not to think about Rosalee. But she couldn't put her out of her mind entirely. She still scoured *Town Topics* for photographs of parties in the Hamptons, and whenever she and Edgar attended a Broadway play, she made sure Rosalee's name wasn't in the playbill.

Charlotte kept talking. "Robert and I decided not to exchange Christmas presents this year. Instead, we're going to the South of France next summer. You and Edgar should join us."

Helen shook her head. "I don't think so. Edgar started a new novel, and I'll be busy with the farm."

Charlotte tied the bow around a jar of homemade jam.

"It would be good for you. You didn't take a long honeymoon, and the Riviera is beautiful in August."

Helen put down a sheet of wrapping paper.

"Just because the Old Philadelphia Club reinstated Father's membership and the Drexels are speaking to him doesn't mean I've forgiven him." Her voice was sharp. "He hasn't done anything that says he's sorry."

Helen knew that wasn't quite true. Her father had given her Clara as a wedding gift. And whenever she came to Dumfries, he tried to talk to her about the farm. But it wasn't enough. It still didn't erase what he'd done.

"Sometimes it's not about what a person has or hasn't done." Charlotte examined the bow. "Forgiveness is something you find in yourself. It's in the Bible."

"So is not cheating on your wife," Helen snapped.

She bit her lip. There was no point in arguing with her mother. But it wasn't right. The only reason her father was being accepted in Philadelphia society was because of Helen's marriage.

"If it wasn't for Edgar's parents' social standing, you'd be spending the holidays sitting in the living room, listening to Paul Whiteman's orchestra play Christmas music on the radio."

"You really should try to be nicer to your father. I know you don't like to hear it, but he's working hard to be a better husband. We signed up for a ballroom dancing class so we can learn the newest dances. He only did it to please me." Charlotte sighed. She looked at Helen pensively. "You are happy, aren't you? You and Edgar seem like a perfect couple."

Helen decided not to tell her mother about their fight. She and Edgar had made up. And she had vowed to herself that she wouldn't let it happen again.

"Of course we're happy," Helen answered. "I couldn't live with someone if we didn't get along."

"I'm glad. Marriage isn't easy. And I'm not talking about your father's affair." Charlotte selected a piece of ribbon. "You spend the first year discovering each other's faults. Your father grinds his teeth, and I'm terrible at playing bridge. Then there are the baby years. I was miserable when I was pregnant. I got hungry for the strangest things—Lorna Doone cookies with hot milk, baked potatoes with mustard instead of butter. I'd send Robert down to the kitchen, and by the time he returned, I craved something else. After you and Daisy were born, it was worse. Even though we had a baby nurse and then a nanny, I was still exhausted. Now there's always something at Dumfries that needs repairing or a dinner party that we have to attend when one of us doesn't want to go."

"Why are you telling me this?" Helen asked.

She would never leave Edgar simply because they were fighting, but she refused to be unhappy. And she couldn't keep her opinions to herself just to make Edgar feel better.

Charlotte finished wrapping a fruitcake. "All newly married couples could do with some advice. Talk to Edgar about coming with us to the South of France. We'd have so much fun, strolling along the promenade in Nice and swimming in the Mediterranean."

"I will, but I don't think we'll come," Helen said before she could stop herself. "If I were you, I'd be careful. Father loves following native customs. The French are notorious for having mistresses as well as wives. They see it as a badge of honor."

An hour later, Daisy hadn't come downstairs. Helen went up to her bedroom.

Daisy's room still had her childhood bed and white headboard. But the floral wallpaper had been replaced by a silver-and-green satin wallpaper. There was an ottoman with a green throw rug. The dressing table had a large mirror, and a vase of winter irises stood on the bedside table.

Helen entered the room. "What are you doing? We were expecting you downstairs."

Daisy quickly picked up a hairbrush. She slipped a piece of paper into a drawer.

"I'm sorry, I've been busy," she replied.

Helen could always tell when Daisy was hiding something. When they were children, Daisy was hopeless as a partner in hide-and-go-seek. She started fidgeting while the other children were trying to find them. And she could never wait until Helen's birthday to tell her what she was getting as a present. She blurted it out the minute she and Charlotte returned from shopping.

Daisy was hiding something now. Helen could tell by the way she avoided Helen's gaze and the heightened color in her cheeks.

"Busy doing what?" Helen asked.

Daisy glanced up from the dressing table. Her blue eyes were rimmed with tears.

"I can't tell you."

"You have to tell me." Helen sat on the day bed. "You've been crying."

Daisy fiddled with the hairbrush.

"Roland got expelled from Harvard."

Helen put her hand over her mouth in surprise. Roland's father must be furious. His father and grandfather had gone to Harvard. There was even a building named after their family.

"Roland studies hard, but he still gets terrible grades." Daisy sighed. "His father threatened to disown him if he failed, so he paid someone to write a paper. The dean found out and asked him to leave."

"What will he do?" Helen asked.

Daisy opened the drawer. She handed Helen the sheet of paper.

"He wrote a letter saying that he was going away. His father threw him out of the house and cut him off. He said he loves me, but he doesn't want to ruin my life."

"He's right." Helen read the letter. "Next year, you'll have your season. You'll meet someone new."

Daisy snatched back the paper. Her eyes were round with shock.

"I'm in love with Roland!" she exclaimed. "The minute I received the letter, I went to see him. We're going to elope and move to Italy. His aunt left him a villa in Portofino. We're going to fix it up and turn it into a hotel."

Portofino was a small fishing village near Genoa. It had become fashionable recently as a holiday resort. Helen had seen photos in a magazine of lush gardens and craggy cliffs leading down to the sea. It would be a wonderful place to visit, but Daisy and Roland couldn't live there. Neither of them spoke Italian, and they didn't have any experience running a hotel.

"You can't elope. You just started at Bryn Mawr," Helen said.

"I don't care about college. I'm not telling anyone but you, so you have to keep it a secret," Daisy warned. "We're going to leave next week. We'll say we're visiting one of Roland's relatives for Christmas. By next summer, the hotel will be ready for visitors."

Daisy's whole life was on the Main Line. She loved it as much as Helen. And she had her future planned out. She wanted a large house, and children, and her own interior design company. She couldn't change her whole life for a man.

"Roland was caught cheating. He deserves to be thrown out of Harvard!" Helen exclaimed.

"He only paid a student to write a paper; he didn't cheat on an exam," Daisy countered. "Anyway, it doesn't matter. We love each other. Everyone can't be like you—then no one would stay married."

"What's that supposed to mean?" Helen demanded.

"I hear you talking to Mother. You still think she should have kicked Father out."

Helen did think her mother would be happier with someone who respected her. But Charlotte was determined to see Robert in a new light, and Helen had given up trying to change her mother's mind. This was different. Daisy was barely eighteen. She had her whole life ahead of her.

Helen tried again. "You can't give up everything you dreamed of for a man."

"I'm not giving up my dreams for Roland; I'm doing it for myself," Daisy said firmly. "I don't want to live without him. You're married now; you should understand."

Helen wondered what she would do in Daisy's position. She didn't believe in divorce, but she couldn't stay with Edgar if he lied or cheated. And being in love wasn't the only thing that mattered. No matter what, she had the cows and the farm.

"Women are supposed to have come so far, but you and Mother act as if it's the nineteenth century." Helen's eyes flashed. "Eloping to Italy sounds romantic, but just wait. If you don't have enough money, you won't be able to heat the villa in winter, and you'll die of cold before you fix it up. If you do manage to turn it into a hotel, you won't be able to afford a maid or a cook, and you'll have to do everything yourself. Do you really want to spend your days scrubbing floors when you could be riding and attending house parties? You belong on the Main Line—anything else is the plot of one of Mother's romance novels."

Daisy looked at Helen narrowly. Her mouth was harder; her cheekbones seemed more pronounced. She was a woman rather than an eighteen-year-old girl.

"I couldn't be happy without Roland, and I won't give up on him because he made one mistake," she declared. "If you won't support me, I have nothing more to say."

"What do you mean?" Helen asked.

"Exactly what it sounds like." Daisy's voice was adamant. "Roland and I are a team. He has to come first. If you really loved Edgar, you would understand."

∼

Later that evening, Helen sat at their table at the Warwick Hotel, waiting for Edgar. She was still upset about Daisy. But she couldn't worry about it now. She and Edgar were having dinner with Leonard and Gloria Biddle. Leonard's father was the secretary of the Union League. If Edgar and Helen made a good impression, her father might be allowed back into the club. But Edgar was late, and the Biddles would arrive any minute.

"Are you sure Mr. Scott hasn't called?" Helen asked the waiter. She lit another cigarette. It was her third of the evening, but as soon as she finished one, she wanted another.

Instead of answering, the waiter disappeared to the front of the restaurant. He returned with a telephone with a long cord.

"Maybe this will make you feel better. You can keep it at the table." The waiter set the phone down beside her.

Helen was about to say that wasn't necessary when a young couple approached the table. The man had short, dark hair, and the woman had an auburn bob. They were both dressed in evening clothes, and the woman wore a bandeau adorned with an ostrich feather.

"I'm Gloria and this is Leonard," the woman said as they sat down. "I'm so glad my mother suggested we get together. Leonard and I have been married for six months. It's so nice to meet other newlyweds."

Leonard's great-grandfather had been the founder of the Second Bank of the United States. Leonard and Gloria had recently moved to a large estate in Radnor. Helen knew she should say something: she'd introduce Gloria to the women at Merion Cricket Club or invite her to join her mother's charity. But she was too distracted. Edgar was never late to dinner at the Warwick.

She was about to ask if they wanted to order when Edgar appeared. He wore a topcoat and tails. His cheeks were freshly shaven, and he carried his walking stick.

"Sorry I'm late." He slid into the booth. "I usually keep my evening clothes at the office, but I had to go home to change."

Helen breathed a sigh of relief. Nothing was wrong—he was late because he had to go back to the cottage. She introduced them, and Edgar set his walking stick beside him. He glanced at the telephone.

"That's an interesting piece of furniture at the dining table," Edgar commented.

"I thought you might call. I didn't know where you were," Helen explained.

Edgar turned to Leonard and Gloria. Something about his manner made Helen nervous. His eyes were unnaturally bright, and his breath smelled strongly of peppermint, as if he'd eaten a whole roll of Life Savers.

She wondered if he had been drinking. Edgar never drank before the cocktail hour. It was one of the things that he was adamant about.

"Wives always talk about marriage being based on trust. But then they do things that show they don't trust you, even when you haven't done anything wrong," Edgar commented.

Edgar poured a gin rickey from the pitcher on the table. He turned to Leonard.

"The thing is, not all wives can be trusted. Take you and Gloria, for instance. How do you know that she's not making eyes at some good-looking young man—the teller at the bank or the milkman—while you're slaving away at the office?"

Leonard's forehead puckered, and Gloria's cheeks turned red.

"I would never cheat on Leonard!" she said hotly.

"Of course you wouldn't," Helen cut in. "Edgar didn't mean it." She glared at him, but he was calmly sipping his cocktail. "Edgar is writing a novel. He's always talking about men and women's relationships."

Leonard's brow smoothed over. Gloria gave a little sigh. She picked up her glass and squeezed her husband's hand.

"I suppose that's all right. A friend of Leonard's is writing a novel. He's always bringing up delicate subjects." Gloria looked at Edgar with interest. "Are your books in the bookstores?"

"Well, I was hoping they would be someday." Edgar set down his glass. "But my wife didn't believe in me enough to let me accomplish it by myself. I got a call from an editor while I was home. Max Perkins—you may have heard of him." Edgar took a long sip of his cocktail. "He told me that I don't have the talent for writing fiction. If he were me, he'd give it up and stick to my job at the railroad company."

Helen's stomach dropped. She felt sick. Max must have called after she left for the restaurant.

"I'm sure he's wrong," Helen interjected. "All editors have different opinions."

Edgar ignored her. He turned to Leonard. "So tell me. What would you do if your wife went behind your back and did the one thing you asked her not to?"

"If you two would like to talk in private, we're happy to get another booth," Leonard suggested.

"I wouldn't dream of spoiling everyone's evening." Edgar stood up.

He collected his walking stick and made a small bow. Helen was about to stop him, but the walking stick knocked over his glass, and the gin rickey spilled on the table.

Edgar glanced at the liquid seeping over the tablecloth. "If you'll excuse me, I have to go. Helen can ask the waiter to clean the tablecloth. Her favorite activity is clearing up other people's messes." He paused and glared at Helen. "It makes her feel superior."

Leonard and Gloria were silent. Helen wondered what they were thinking. She couldn't run after Edgar and leave them sitting there. She had to stay and apologize.

"I'm sorry for Edgar's behavior," Helen said after he left. "I didn't know writers were so high-strung until I married one." She gave a nervous chuckle. "Edgar will take a brisk walk around the block, and he'll be fine."

Leonard ordered French onion soup for everyone and swordfish with asparagus as entrées. Gloria kept up a monologue about their plans to build a summer house in Newport. Helen nodded at the appropriate times, but her head swam and she could barely eat a bite.

"It's been a lovely evening," she said when the dessert plates had been cleared. Edgar hadn't returned. She wondered if he'd gone home. "Next time, we'll have to invite you to Fieldstone Manor."

"You can't take a taxi to Villanova," Leonard objected. "Gloria and I will drive you. It's on our way."

Leonard was right. It was beginning to snow, and the taxi driver would grumble that he had to drive all the way out to the Main Line.

She climbed into the back seat of Leonard's Model T Ford. Outside the window, the tree branches were white with snowflakes. She wished she were driving with Edgar. His hand would be on her knee, and he'd slow down to point out a deer or to let a squirrel cross in front of them.

Her mind turned to their first argument on the way back from Jack's gallery showing in New York. She'd been so afraid that Edgar wanted to call off the wedding. She found him outside by the swimming pool, and they shared their first proper kiss.

It was the night she realized she was falling in love with him.

How did she feel about Edgar now? They were married, and in many ways her feelings were stronger. She loved his sunny outlook. He never let ordinary things get him down—the previous weekend they'd driven to New York to see *Show Boat*, the new Broadway musical that everyone was talking about. At the last minute it was canceled because Helen Morgan, the lead actress, came down with laryngitis. All the other shows were sold out, and they couldn't get a table at a restaurant in the theater district without a reservation.

So Edgar had driven to Katz's Delicatessen on Houston Street on the Lower East Side, and they ate roast beef sandwiches instead. The owner of Katz's convinced them to see a play at the Yiddish theater on Second Avenue. The play ended up being wonderful—neither of them had ever laughed so hard.

Later, Edgar had shown her a review of the play in the *New York Times*, which said that theatergoers received a Broadway experience at Second Avenue prices. They both felt so cocky, as if they had discovered some wonderful secret.

But tonight, Edgar shouldn't have walked out on the Biddles. It reminded her of her birthday lunch at the Plaza with Jack when she noticed her father and Rosalee in a booth. That day she had been so mortified, all she wanted was to run out of the restaurant and burst into tears.

"Are you sure you'll be all right?" Gloria asked when Leonard pulled up in front of the cottage. "Leonard can see you inside."

Edgar's car was in the driveway; a light was on in the living room. Edgar had probably calmed down. He'd be drinking black coffee to sober up, and he'd kiss her and apologize.

Helen thanked them. "Don't worry about me, I'll be fine."

Edgar was sitting in an armchair next to the fireplace. He still wore his evening clothes. A bottle of brandy was on the side table.

"I see you made it home," he said icily.

"The Biddles drove me." She pulled off her gloves. Edgar made no move to get up. She felt her anger rising. "How dare you leave me there. I had to stay for dinner. We are the ones who invited them."

Edgar's eyes glinted under the light.

"If you hadn't given my manuscript to Max Perkins, none of this would have happened."

Helen explained that Max was April's godfather. She couldn't pass up the opportunity.

"I see it all perfectly now." Edgar refilled his brandy glass. "You knew Max would hate it. It would be the end of my writing career. We'd laugh about it at weekend house parties. 'All young men have fantasies about becoming artists and writers. Thank God, Edgar came to his senses before we ended up living in a garret.'"

"I gave him your manuscript because I believed in you," Helen shot back. "I still do. You had those pieces published in *Town Topics* and the *New Yorker*."

"I studied journalism at Harvard. I can string together a few decent paragraphs. But that's entirely different from writing a whole novel."

Helen moved to the fireplace. She had never seen Edgar behave this way. Like a small boy on the verge of throwing a tantrum.

"There's nothing stopping you from writing a new book," she reminded him. "That's why you're doing all that research."

Edgar took a swallow of his drink.

"Publishing is a small world." He stared at the gold liquid. "If Max Perkins says I'm finished, then I don't stand a chance."

The rage boiled up inside her. None of this was Helen's fault. She poured herself a shot of brandy.

"You can't quit. Just because the bank won't give me a loan doesn't mean I'm giving up on starting my dairy company. If you want something badly enough, you'll find a way to get it."

Edgar stood up. He paced back and forth on the rug.

"I'm sick of your high-minded advice. That may have worked for your great-grandfather who came over from Scotland, but it doesn't work for me," Edgar seethed. "You can't compare writing a novel to tugging the udder of a cow. If you could, every damn farmer in the country would hang up his rubber gloves and make his living as an author instead."

Edgar twisted his cuff links. The cravat on his shirt was crooked, and the handkerchief from his vest pocket was missing. They were both upset. It would be better if they discussed it later.

She set down her brandy. "I'm going to bed. I invited the Biddles to dinner at Fieldstone Manor. It would help if you wrote a letter of apology first. They're quite important—Leonard's family owns the largest bank in Philadelphia."

She had never seen his eyes quite that color. A green as luminous and charged as the satin wallpaper in Daisy's bedroom.

"You skewered my writing career as if it was a raw piece of meat thrown to the lions, and all you care about is staying in the Biddles' good graces." He glared at her. "Well, I'm tired of hearing about the Pews and Biddles. If you really cared about people, it would be different." He paused for a moment. "Maybe instead of trying to improve your father's social standing, you should ask him why he cheated in the first place. I have a feeling it had nothing to do with his wife or Rosalee and everything to do with having to always live up to his daughter's standards."

Helen was completely quiet. Her emotions from the events of the day—Daisy announcing that she and Roland were eloping to Italy, her mother pressing her and Edgar to go on vacation, the mortification of Edgar walking out during dinner—overwhelmed her. She grabbed the Lalique vase that had been a wedding present. Without another thought, she hurled it toward Edgar. It smashed into pieces at his feet.

Edgar jumped back in shock. His eyes flew to hers, and he grabbed the poker from the fireplace. Then he flung it on the floor and strode out the door.

Helen's body went rigid. She could hear the snow falling on the roof. Edgar would be freezing without his overcoat. Then she crouched down on the rug and started to clean up the broken smithereens that were her marriage.

Chapter Twelve

Helen spent the following morning at the barn at Dumfries. Edgar hadn't come home, and she didn't want to be alone in the cottage. A few hours with the cows would make her feel better.

All night she had tossed and turned, waiting to hear the front door open. She picked up the phone half a dozen times to call the main house at Fieldstone Manor. What would she say if Edgar was there? They couldn't go on this way. Next time, the vase might hit him, or Edgar might throw the poker at her instead of tossing it on the floor.

Helen didn't understand how their marriage had come to this in a few short months. Edgar knew from the start that she had to help her father rise from the scandal. And blaming her for her father's affair was ridiculous. For a moment, she yearned for her childhood. Summer vacations to the coast of Maine. Eating apples in the back seat of the car with Daisy, while her parents chatted happily in the front.

She stared blankly at the snow-covered valley outside the barn window. The cows snuffled in their stalls, and the new foal raised its head. For the first time that she could remember, the nearness of the animals didn't soothe her. She felt cold and alone.

She grabbed a brush and let herself into Essie's stall.

"You're lucky you don't live with any bulls. All they're good for is breeding more cows." She brushed Essie's back fiercely. "Everyone talks about doing things for those who are less fortunate, but charity begins at home. If we don't strive to do the right thing with the people we love, how can we achieve the really big things: create opportunities for the poor, give women the same rights and privileges as men."

That's what Edgar and Daisy and her parents didn't understand. One needed to maintain high standards. It was the only way to make people act decently. Since Helen's marriage, she was trying to be less rigid. It was the only way to be happy when one lived with another person. But that didn't excuse bad behavior.

"If we allow our politicians to lie and cheat, others will do the same," she said to Essie.

"Personally, I don't know any cows that are politicians," a male voice said.

Helen turned around. For a moment, she thought it was Edgar. But it was Jack.

"Who told you I was here?" she wondered.

"No one. It was a lucky guess." Jack's aquamarine eyes twinkled. "Where else would a beautiful young society woman be on a snowy morning the week before Christmas?"

Jack was jauntily dressed in a beaver fur coat and brown trousers. A wool scarf was knotted around his neck, and he wore suede driving gloves.

"The cows still need to be brushed and fed," she defended herself. "Anyway, it's warm and peaceful in the barn. Much nicer than the cottage at Fieldstone Manor."

Helen knew that wasn't true. She loved the little cottage. It wasn't Dumfries, with its light-filled reception rooms and wide terraces. But she loved reading in the small living room and preparing meals with Edgar in the kitchen. She would miss it. But she couldn't keep living there with Edgar if they fought all the time.

"That's why you're wearing three sweaters and still shivering," Jack pointed out.

Helen could never hide her feelings from Jack. He knew her too well.

"My shivering has nothing to do with the temperature of the barn," she admitted with a sigh. "It's because of Edgar. We got into a terrible fight. This time I think our marriage is over."

"Edgar showed up at my door last night." Jack perched on a stool beside her. "He's staying at my apartment."

Helen was shocked. How dare Edgar go to see Jack. Jack was *her* uncle.

"I didn't expect you to take sides," she said briskly.

"It was snowing, and he didn't have an overcoat. I had to let him in."

Helen pictured Edgar appearing in the middle of the night, still wearing his topcoat and tails.

"Well, you can tell him that if he wants a divorce, he'll have to wait until after Christmas. It would create too much of a scandal at the holiday balls."

"He didn't say anything about a divorce. He gave me this." Edgar reached into his pocket and took out an envelope. "He said you'd understand."

Helen unfolded the letter.

Dear Helen,

I am a writer; I should be able to express myself. But I suppose I'm too close to what happened to put it down on paper.

What I do know is that life is full of opportunities. Some I've worked towards my whole life, but when I was given them, they weren't what I expected. Others came out of the blue, and they brought me more happiness than I thought possible. But a gentleman has to know when he is beaten. It's not about quitting or giving up. It's about being a good loser. One day, I hope you'll see that.

Edgar

Helen didn't want to be the winner in their marriage. She only wanted to feel loved and be happy.

She recalled her first night at boarding school. Foxcroft had a tradition that a current student sat with a new girl at dinner for the first week of classes. Every night, Helen waited at a table in the dining room, but the girl never showed up.

It was only later that Helen found out the girl came down with the measles and never returned to school. By then it was too late. All the other girls had found friends to eat with, and Helen was alone.

She had the same feeling now. For the first time, she wanted to be part of something besides her family and the farm. She wanted to be Edgar's wife and eventually a mother. But she couldn't change who she was. Perhaps they would never get along.

Jack let out a cough. She had almost forgotten that he was there.

"I'll go up to the house and write him a letter," she said stiffly. "You can tell him I'll file for divorce after New Year's."

"I have a better idea," Jack suggested. "You and Edgar should go away for a few months."

"Why would we do that?" Helen asked.

Jack unwrapped his scarf. He studied her closely.

"Because you're in love with Edgar. It's written all over your face." His tone was gentle. "Edgar looks exactly the same."

"My mother invited us to the South of France this summer. Edgar and I could do that."

Jack shook his head. "You need to be somewhere alone. I have a little house in Sussex next door to a group of artists and writers who call themselves the Bloomsbury Group. Virginia Woolf and her husband, Leonard, own a publishing company. Perhaps they'd publish Edgar's novel after it's finished."

Jack had never mentioned a house in England. He loved restaurants and the theater; she couldn't imagine him living in the English countryside.

"What would I do there?" Helen wondered.

"There are lots of farms. And Edgar could work on his novel."

They'd miss the rounds of cocktail parties and dinners, but it would be better for her father's reputation than if she got a divorce. And Edgar's father would let him take a few months off from the railroad company if Edgar said it was important.

"It is a good idea," Helen said hopefully. "What if Edgar says no?"

"I'll drive you to my apartment. We'll stop at the travel agency." The smile came back to his expression. "You can give Edgar the ocean liner tickets as a gift. Only a scrooge would turn down a Christmas present."

~

Edgar was in the living room of Jack's apartment. He wore a pair of silk pajamas that must have been Jack's. He was hunched over a brandy snifter.

"I haven't started drinking before noon," he said when he saw her. "I caught a cold. I'm inhaling the brandy."

Jack had wonderful taste in decor. The room was furnished in the neoclassical French style. Every piece was a different shade of white. Off-white velvet armchairs were arranged around a glass coffee table. A cream-colored sofa with gold tassels stood near the fireplace, and an ivory divan was placed under a mirror.

Helen sat on the sofa.

"Don't worry, I put away the fireplace poker on the chance that you might come," he said archly, following her gaze. "I should have written that I'd give you a divorce. It would have saved you the trip into Philadelphia." Edgar inhaled the brandy. "I'll take the blame, of course. I'll invent a mistress."

Helen wanted to say so many things. That she didn't want to imagine Edgar having a mistress. That she didn't know why she got so angry—she couldn't help it. She didn't want a divorce, but something had to change.

Before she could say anything, Edgar picked up a small box from the side table.

"This is for you."

Inside was a diamond-and-emerald ring. Edgar had never given her a proper engagement ring. She still wore the opal ring she'd found on the night they were engaged. She didn't understand why he was giving one to her now.

"I had my grandmother's diamond ring reset," he said. "I was going to give it to you for Christmas. I want you to have it. You can sell it and use the money to buy more cows."

The diamond was an oval cut, circled by emeralds and set on a platinum band. It was perfect—she couldn't love a ring more. If only he were giving it to her for a different reason: because he loved her and wanted to stay married.

Tears came to her eyes. She brushed them away before Edgar noticed them.

She handed him the envelope from the travel agent.

"I have something for you too."

Edgar took out the ocean liner tickets.

"Jack has a house in Sussex," she explained. "He thought we could stay there for a while. You could finish your novel, and I could work on the dairy products."

Edgar looked as surprised as if she had asked him to fly to the moon.

She was tempted to say it had been a bad idea. A divorce was a much better solution. In a few months, they'd be free and they wouldn't have to see each other again.

But something stopped her. She had never backed down from a challenge. When her horse missed a jump, she simply coaxed him over the next hurdle. Instead of asking her parents to pick her up from boarding school because she was lonely, she became secretary of the Pony Club and joined the yearbook. She wasn't going to quit now.

"How would it look if we got divorced after we've only been married a few months?" she asked. "It's better this way."

She told him about the Bloomsbury Group, and Leonard and Virginia Woolf's publishing company.

Edgar's cheeks were smooth under the light of the chandelier. She remembered the night they met at Ivy's debutante ball. He had looked so handsome in a rumpled work shirt and boots. And he had been easy to talk to. She wanted that camaraderie back now.

"That's the only reason you want to go away." He turned the tickets over. "So people won't talk about our divorce."

"Well, you seem to think divorce is the best solution." She took a deep breath. "But I disagree."

"On what grounds?" Edgar said with interest. His eyes seemed brighter. He almost looked like he was enjoying himself.

She was about to remark that this wasn't a courtroom and she didn't have to defend herself. But this wasn't the time. She had to be completely honest.

"On the grounds that I'm in love with you."

Edgar pushed away the brandy snifter.

"Well, that does change things. Do you always throw vases at the people you love?"

"Only when they behave atrociously," she said before she could stop herself. "But I've decided I want to try again."

"You were right about my writing," Edgar said. "Even if my novels don't get published, I can't give it up. And I still think you're terribly brave."

Helen's cheeks flushed with pleasure. But Edgar hadn't said that he still loved her.

"You said that my being in love with you changes things," she prompted.

"I did, didn't I?" He moved beside her on the sofa. "That's because it's easier staying married to someone who loves me than to a wife who wants to poke my eyes out."

"So, you do want to stay married?"

Edgar picked up her hair. He brushed it to the side and kissed her. "More than anything," he whispered.

~

Later, they joined Jack at Wanamaker's to do some Christmas shopping. Every year the Grand Court was transformed into a magical Christmas setting. One year it replicated a scene from King Arthur's Round Table. She and Daisy had been so enraptured by the knights in shiny armor and the princesses wearing long velvet dresses. They slipped away from their parents and climbed into the display. Helen recalled her father's amused expression when the man in charge demanded he take Helen and Daisy away.

She thought about that now. One day, Edgar would be a wonderful father. He loved children. He bought a bag of holiday mints and offered them to every child he met. And he was incredibly patient. When she couldn't decide which bracelet to buy her mother, he happily waited while Helen tried on each one.

In the evening, they prepared to drive to Dumfries for dinner. Helen dressed formally in a floor-length red chiffon gown with bell sleeves. She borrowed Daisy's curling tongs to do her hair and applied her new red lipstick.

"Mrs. Scott is looking exceptionally beautiful this evening," Edgar commented as they stepped into his car.

"It's almost Christmas, and Mother and Daisy always dress so elegantly."

She had decided she would try one more time to convince Daisy not to elope. Except, when they arrived, only her parents were having cocktails in the living room. Daisy wasn't there, and Roland's yellow Packard wasn't parked in its usual spot in the driveway.

"Daisy and Roland went to visit his aunt in Detroit," Charlotte said.

Daisy had said that they were leaving the following week, but they were already gone. Helen excused herself and went upstairs to Daisy's room. A Raggedy Ann doll was propped against the headboard. Helen and Daisy both had received Raggedy Anns on the first Christmas that the dolls were available in stores. Helen lost her doll ages ago, but Daisy's Raggedy Ann still sat on her sister's bed.

Helen picked up the doll. Daisy was one of the people she loved most in the world. She hated the rift that had grown between them. She could write and beg her to change her mind, but she knew Daisy would tear up the letter.

She went downstairs to join Edgar and her parents for dinner.

Chapter Thirteen

Sussex, England, March 1928

Daisy's telegram had arrived three weeks after Christmas, when Helen was packing her steamer trunk.

Helen's mother read out loud, "Roland and I are married and living in Italy. Letter to follow. Very much in love and very happy—Daisy."

Helen expected her parents to be devastated, but Charlotte didn't seem terribly upset.

"I'll miss planning their wedding. Daisy has been waiting to be a bride since she was a little girl," Charlotte said wistfully. "But what else could she do? She's in love with Roland. She couldn't stay behind."

Helen wanted to tell her mother that she was wrong. Her parents could sail to Italy and bring Daisy home. Daisy should finish college and build something of her own. Without that, she'd be dependent on Roland for everything. And there was Daisy's dream of being an interior designer. Female designers like Elsie de Wolfe and Syrie Maugham were becoming quite famous.

The previous year, Charlotte took Helen and Daisy to the Colony Club in New York. Elsie de Wolfe had transformed the dark Victorian interiors into a space that resembled an outdoor pavilion. The ceiling was painted an avocado green, and the wallpaper had a trompe l'oeil design that made one believe one was sitting in a tropical garden. The club was such a success that everyone in New York and Philadelphia was clamoring for Elsie's services.

Syrie Maugham had her own interior design shops in New York and London. She was well known for her all-white rooms. *Vogue* did a piece on some of her outrageous antics—once, she dipped silk drapes into white cement to get the perfect shade of white; another time she installed a white birdcage in a drawing room and filled it with white doves.

Daisy could be as successful, but now it was too late. She'd spend her youth catering to British tourists who only cared that they could eat their favorite English marmalade while they were on holiday.

Helen and Edgar had sailed at the end of January on Cunard's RMS *Aquitania*. The ship's public rooms were decorated by the same team that designed the Ritz in London. There was a sauna and an indoor orangery. Helen's favorite was the smoking room. She and Edgar often sat together in leather wingback chairs, drinking port and smoking cigars.

It took a while to get used to the cigar's taste. But she loved the pomp of lighting it and then waving it around while she and Edgar discussed books and farming.

The best part of the trip was the times they spent away from other passengers. She loved their morning walks around the deck and dancing in the ballroom late at night. Helen, wearing one of her mother's fabulous Chanel gowns, rested her head on Edgar's shoulder. The orchestra played Lee David and Billy Rose's hit song "Tonight You Belong to Me," and she was almost glad they'd had a terrible fight. She'd never been happier in her life.

Jack's house in Sussex was a three-story manor house set in a park. There was a garage filled with bicycles and an Aston Martin. Helen convinced a neighboring farmer to let her work for no pay. In exchange, he was teaching her how his farm made butter and cheese. She kept a notebook of the different techniques and planned to use them at Dumfries.

The first month, they explored the countryside in the little car. Helen refused to drive in it by herself. The roads were crowded with sheep and cows, and the steering wheel was on the wrong side. The last thing she needed was to run into another egg truck, like she had driving back from Jack's apartment in New York.

This evening, Helen and Edgar were invited to dinner at Charleston Farmhouse. Charleston was owned by Vanessa Bell and her husband, the art critic Clive Bell. Vanessa's sister, Virginia Woolf, and her husband, Leonard, and other members of the Bloomsbury Group would be there.

The house wasn't a farmhouse at all. It was a Georgian-style mansion with a summer house and a walled garden. A black car was parked in the driveway, and there was a wheelbarrow filled with cut flowers. A young girl opened the front door, and they were shown into a library. A man in his late twenties lay on the divan next to the window. He had a long beard and wore a shabby-looking coat. His eyes were closed, and he was snoring.

A woman appeared in the doorway. "You're here," she said. She was in her early thirties, with brown eyes and a wide mouth. Her hair was covered by a floppy hat, and she wore a Spanish-style flamenco skirt and lace-up velvet boots.

"I'm Vanessa Bell. Please excuse me, I don't usually dress like this. My nieces are here; they convinced me to play charades after dinner." She smiled and held out her hand. "I should have warned you over the phone. But we have heaps of costumes—you can both borrow whatever you like."

"We'd love to play charades," Edgar answered for both of them. "We met one of your nieces. She answered the door."

"That's Clarissa. She's twelve. Sophie is here too. They're my husband's nieces." Vanessa's eyes traveled to the man asleep on the divan. "That's Lytton. He just finished writing a biography of Queen Victoria."

"Does he always sleep in public?" Edgar asked curiously.

"Only when he's been writing." Vanessa's eyes danced merrily. "He says it's because he has to do so much thinking, his mind gets tired. I believe it's the amount of wine he drinks at lunch."

Helen shook Vanessa's hand.

"It's wonderful to meet you. Jack didn't say much, except that you lived next door."

Vanessa took off her hat. She was quite pretty. Her dark brown hair was pinned into a bun, and she had a small nose and high cheekbones.

"That's because we haven't seen Jack in years. We miss him." Her expression was thoughtful. "I miss him the most. Jack and I were very close."

The figure on the divan opened his eyes. Vanessa took Helen's arm.

"Let's leave the men to fix cocktails. I'll give you a tour of the house."

The rooms were filled with oversize wooden furniture. Every surface was painted a different color. The dining table was royal blue, and the chairs in the drawing room were painted orange. There was a sunroom with a purple coffee table and a study with apple trees painted on the ceiling.

"Duncan and I bought the house ten years ago, at the end of the war." Vanessa led her into a parlor. "It was completely run-down. We fixed it up and painted it ourselves."

Helen noticed a framed Renoir on the wall, next to a painting that resembled something she and Daisy could have done as children.

"Bunny made most of the furniture," Vanessa said. "Bunny is David Garnett, the artist. He'll be at dinner. Everyone calls him Bunny."

Helen frowned. "You and Duncan bought the house? I thought your husband's name is Clive."

"Clive is my husband, but he doesn't own this house," Vanessa corrected. "Duncan and I live here together."

Outside the window, a girl of about six climbed into the wheelbarrow. She had wheat-colored hair and round hazel eyes. The wheelbarrow was being pushed by the most handsome man Helen had ever seen.

His hair was the same color as the girl's, and his eyes were dark brown and covered by thick lashes. He wore a wool sweater and slacks with leather boots.

"That's Duncan." Vanessa pointed outside. "And that's Angelica, our daughter."

Vanessa noticed the puzzled expression on Helen's face.

"I have two sons with Clive. Julian and Quentin live with Clive and Mary in London," she continued. "Clive comes to visit often, and he brings Mary. We all get along very well."

Mary was Mary Hutchinson, a respected art dealer. Vanessa explained that Angelica believed Clive was her father and that Duncan was her doting godfather.

"Angelica became attached to Clive when she was a baby, and she's crazy about her older half brothers."

"What does Duncan say?" Helen wondered. She had never heard of such an outrageous arrangement. But Jack had warned her that the Bloomsbury Group prided themselves on being unconventional.

"Duncan never wanted to be a father. I had to beg him to have Angelica." She let out a small sigh. "He was so beautiful. I wanted a daughter who looked just like him."

It was the oddest way to describe a man, but Duncan was beautiful. His mouth had a wonderful shape, and he had wide, strong hands. Pushing the wheelbarrow, his strong body had a grace that Helen hadn't seen in a man.

"Of course, he's crazy about Angelica now." Vanessa turned from the window. "Let me show you the rest of the house."

Vanessa showed her the writing room that Virginia used when she visited and the children's playroom that overflowed with dolls and toys.

When they returned to the library, Edgar was sitting next to a young woman about Helen's age. She had auburn ringlets and almond-shaped green eyes. She was very pretty and wore a green velvet evening gown and a silver bandeau.

"And this is my niece Sophie Bell," Vanessa introduced them. "Sophie is a budding writer."

There was something about the young woman, the way she was sitting so close to Edgar, that made Helen uncomfortable. She told herself she was being silly. Edgar met dozens of beautiful women at parties and never gave Helen a reason to feel jealous.

Dinner was held in the dining room. Vanessa sat at the head of the table, and Duncan sat at the other end. Helen was seated between Bunny and Lytton. Edgar was across from her, next to Sophie. Virginia had come down with a migraine, and she and Leonard didn't come.

"How did you meet Jack?" Helen asked, eating a pork chop. There was steak and kidney pie and Yorkshire pudding.

"An art gallery in London was showing Jack's work. Clive thought he was very talented. He brought him to Charleston Farmhouse to paint my portrait," Vanessa replied. "Jack stayed with us for a while, then we convinced him to buy the house next door."

Helen wondered if Vanessa was the woman that broke Jack's heart. Perhaps Jack had fallen in love with her, but she was already involved with Clive and Duncan.

After dinner, they returned to the library. Duncan and Bunny paired up for charades, and Vanessa insisted that Helen be her partner. That left Edgar and Sophie to make a team. Edgar and Sophie took ages to pick their subject. They finally chose a phrase from the hit song "When My Baby Smiles at Me." Helen was surprised—Edgar still wasn't fond of jazz. She didn't like the way they huddled together or how Sophie flashed Edgar a triumphant smile when Duncan guessed the answer.

Later in the evening, Edgar stayed in the library to talk about writing, and Vanessa showed Helen some of Jack's paintings.

"That's my favorite." Vanessa pointed to a portrait of herself and Duncan. They were sitting on a bench in the garden. Vanessa was wearing a yellow sun hat, and Duncan was dressed in a blue shirt.

"Duncan and Bunny had just finished making all the furniture. I was pregnant with Angelica, and I was so happy. My first two pregnancies were miserable, but with Angelica I had never felt better."

Helen didn't approve of Vanessa living with a man who wasn't her husband, but she couldn't help but admire her. Charleston Farmhouse had been purchased with Vanessa's own money, and she still earned a living with her art. She didn't seem dependent on any man, and she was a good mother. After charades, she had gone upstairs and put Angelica to bed herself.

"You and Duncan look so in love," Helen commented.

Vanessa's face took on a distant expression.

"We were. I still believed love could conquer everything and life would stay the same forever. It took me years to realize I was wrong."

"What do you mean?" Helen wondered.

"I'd never had the deep feelings for a man that I had for Duncan," Vanessa mused. "It was the headiest drug—waking up beside this wonderful man and believing he was mine. I could watch him shave in the morning for ages, and every conversation was infused by an electric current."

"What happened?"

"Duncan was involved with someone else before we got together, but I thought it was over. He said he loved me, and we were having a baby."

"Who was he involved with?"

Vanessa gazed at the painting.

"I thought you could tell at the dinner table." She pulled her eyes away. "With Bunny, of course. They've been crazy about each other ever since I can remember. It taught me a lesson. We never really belong to others. The only person we can count on is ourselves."

~

The month of March flew by. Helen spent her days on the farm, while Edgar worked on his novel. Most evenings they were invited to

Charleston Farmhouse. Different cars were always parked in the drive-way, and new people sat at the dining table and played games afterward in the library.

Life at Charleston Farmhouse was so different from that at Dumfries, but Helen enjoyed Vanessa's company. Vanessa had her own set of standards. She surrounded herself with interesting people, and they were all passionate about what they did. She didn't put up with anyone who lied—during an after-dinner game of checkers, a guest cheated and was never invited back again.

Helen met Vanessa's sister, Virginia, at the "Friday Club" held at Virginia and Leonard's house in Gordon Square. The novelist E. M. Forster and the artist Roger Fry were there, and everyone talked about art and literature. Edgar was radiant—he didn't stop talking about that night for days.

An editor at Chatto & Windus was considering Edgar's novel. Leonard was helping Edgar edit it. Sometimes, Leonard joined them for dinner. Edgar made big pots of spaghetti, and they talked about authors Helen had never heard of. James Joyce, who was Irish and wrote novels full of dense language, and a French author named Marcel Proust, whose book had just been translated into English.

Today, Helen sat at the kitchen table, watching a soft rain fall on the driveway.

Edgar appeared at the kitchen door. He wore a long overcoat and carried a rectangular box.

"You're home early. I thought you'd be at the farm," he said, kissing her.

"It was too cold in the barn." Helen sipped her tea.

She wasn't used to the weather being so cold and rainy in late March. This time of year on the Main Line meant horseback riding and cocktails served in Dumfries's grand reception rooms. It meant rooms filled with vases of her mother's greenhouse flowers. But she didn't mind. Edgar's writing was going so well, and she was enjoying working on the farm.

"Leonard says it rains in England from now until September." Edgar took off his overcoat. "You won't be cold tonight. I bought you a present."

Inside the box was a silver fox cape. Helen ran her hands through the fur. It was lovely, but it wasn't the kind of thing one wore to dinner at Charleston Farmhouse.

"It's stunning, but what's the occasion?" she asked.

"I was hoping you'd like it. I never bought fur for a woman before." Edgar beamed. "Tonight is an important evening. We're dining with Malcolm at the Savoy Hotel."

Malcolm Osgood was the editor at Chatto & Windus who was interested in Edgar's novel.

"He called this morning," Edgar continued. "He loves the pages I sent him. He wants to talk about publishing the book."

Helen frowned. "That's wonderful news, but it's not finished."

Only the previous evening, Edgar said the latest chapters needed work.

"Finishing it can wait." Edgar waved his hand. "What's important is that a publisher is enthusiastic about my book. I read that Max Perkins signed a new writer named Thomas Wolfe. Everyone is excited about his book, and it doesn't come out until next year. What if the same thing happens to me?"

Edgar hadn't appeared so animated since Max's rejection. She didn't have the heart to say that he and Leonard worked so well together, he should wait until the novel was done.

"You'll be my good luck charm at dinner." Edgar kissed her. He draped the cape around her neck. "You'll have to get used to wearing furs and dining at places like the Savoy. Soon, you'll be the wife of a successful author."

～

The Savoy Hotel was in the heart of London, near Covent Garden. It was built in the 1890s to mirror the luxury hotels in America. The lobby's potted palm trees and deep velvet armchairs reminded Helen of the Plaza in New York. The restaurant had a stage for an orchestra and a dance floor. Fred Astaire often stopped by after a performance of the musical *Funny Face* to drink White Russian cocktails and dance with his dancing partner, Adele.

Helen and Edgar sat in a booth across from Malcolm. At the other tables, men were dressed in topcoats and tails, and the women wore beaded evening gowns and fringed hems. Everyone was laughing and drinking cocktails. Helen ordered a drink called a hanky panky. It was invented twenty years earlier by Ada Coleman, the first of only two female bartenders the Savoy ever employed.

"I read your recent pages, and I'm impressed," Malcolm said to Edgar.

Malcolm was in his early fifties. He had dark hair and a thin mustache.

"We don't read much American fiction over here, besides Hemingway and Fitzgerald. Your language isn't as flowery as Fitzgerald, and it's not as blunt as Hemingway. And you describe a young man falling in love in a way I haven't read before."

Edgar beamed with pride. He squeezed Helen's hand.

"My inspiration is sitting beside me. I couldn't have written it if I wasn't married to my beautiful wife."

Helen sipped her hanky panky. It was delicious—gin and vermouth with a splash of Fernet-Branca and a twist of orange. It tasted tart but sweet and had even more of a punch than the Mary Pickfords served at the Warwick Hotel.

"Leonard Woolf has his own publishing house, but it doesn't have the reputation of Chatto & Windus," Malcolm continued. "We'd want to buy the rights here and in America, and we're willing to give a good advance."

"How much of an advance?" Edgar wondered.

"Five thousand pounds."

Five thousand pounds was almost ten thousand dollars! Edgar wouldn't have to go back to the railroad company; he could keep writing. He could pay off the shortfall in his bank account, and the bank would give Helen a loan.

"I don't usually take on a writer with an unfinished manuscript," Malcolm said. "As long as you turn it in by the beginning of June, we can put it in the winter catalog."

June was less than two months away. What if Edgar didn't finish it in time?

"It's a wonderful offer. Edgar and I should talk about it," Helen said.

"I don't need to talk about it." Edgar held out his hand to Malcolm. "I accept."

Helen was speechless. She stood up and gathered her mesh evening bag.

"If you'll excuse me, I need to use the powder room."

Helen sat on an ottoman in front of the powder room mirror and tried to control her emotions. This was everything Edgar had worked toward, and she wanted him to accept. But the nagging uncertainty wouldn't go away. What if his writing stalled and he had already spent the advance? It would be safer to finish the novel first.

When she returned to the table, Malcolm had left. His place was taken by a young woman wearing a red evening gown. Her back was facing Helen, but she could see the diamond tiara in her hair and the low-cut back of her dress.

"Helen, look who's at the Savoy," Edgar said.

It was Sophie. This evening she looked particularly beautiful. Her eyes were rimmed with kohl, and her mouth was coated with orange-red lipstick and shaped in a Cupid's bow.

"Edgar said you were in the powder room." Sophie smiled at Helen mischievously. "The powder room at the Savoy is a girl's best friend. I've often used it as an excuse to avoid a man."

Sophie hadn't been to Charleston Farmhouse in weeks, and Helen had let herself relax. Now she was reminded of how lovely Sophie was. It was impossible for any man to ignore her charm. She had a sophistication mixed with a fresh-faced youthfulness that was captivating.

"Edgar didn't say anything. I would have come back sooner if I'd known you were joining us," Helen said smoothly.

"We just bumped into each other. I'm waiting for my date." Sophie waved at a young man standing by the door. "He's here now. You have to meet him."

A man in his early twenties joined them. He had floppy blond hair and round glasses. His tie was knotted in a Windsor knot, and he wore some kind of luxury watch.

Sophie introduced them. "This is Lord Aubrey, also known as Tommy."

Tommy shook their hands and slid into the booth beside Sophie.

"Tommy is down from Cambridge for the weekend."

"It's been an unsuccessful visit so far." Tommy took out his cigarette case. "I asked Sophie to marry me, and she refused."

"We're too young to get married," Sophie explained. "Tommy keeps prattling on that all the previous generations of his family were married by our age."

"Last time I came to London, Sophie thought it was a good idea," Tommy said petulantly.

"I do want to marry you." Sophie turned to Tommy. "I want to have some fun first."

Helen briefly wondered if Edgar was part of the reason Sophie rejected Tommy's proposal, but she quickly shook it off. Tommy was quite handsome, and he seemed to be in love with her.

Edgar changed the subject. "I ordered a bottle of champagne. Sophie and Tommy can help us celebrate."

The waiter poured four glasses of champagne, and Edgar told them about his book deal.

"You must be so proud." Sophie turned to Helen. "Edgar will be a celebrity. You'll be invited to all the best parties."

"Edgar isn't doing it for the fame. He loves to write."

"A little fame will be nice." Edgar sipped his champagne. "Writing can be isolating. You're stuck at a typewriter all day, and you never know what people think of your work."

Helen was surprised. Edgar had never talked like that about writing before.

"I have an idea." Sophie's eyes lit up. "We're all going to Deauville for the month of April. You and Helen should join us."

Deauville was a holiday resort a few hours from Paris. It was famous for its casino and for the horse races. Helen's father and Roland used to talk about it.

Vanessa and Duncan were taking over a suite of rooms at the Barrière Le Royal Hotel.

"We can't afford it," Helen said quickly. "And Edgar has to finish his book."

"Vanessa pays for rooms for everyone. Clive is friends with the owner of the hotel," Sophie said. "Leonard will be there. He and Edgar can work together."

"It's a good idea," Edgar agreed. "There's been so much rain. Deauville will be much nicer."

Deauville was on the sea; it would be beautiful in April. And there were many dairy farms nearby. Normandy cows produced some of the creamiest milk and cheese. Helen and her father sampled some a few summers ago when they were in Paris.

Helen couldn't think of another excuse to say no.

She nodded. "All right, we'll go."

Edgar poured another round of champagne. She and Edgar had been so happy in Sussex, and she didn't want to be around Sophie for a whole month. She drank the champagne in one gulp.

Chapter Fourteen

Deauville, France, April 1928

The following week, Helen and Edgar took the ferry to Calais and the train from Calais to Deauville. Vanessa and Duncan joined them, and Bunny and Lytton, and Sophie and Tommy. Leonard and Virginia came a few days later. Angelica was staying with Clive and Mary in London.

From the moment they arrived and Helen saw the ceramic rooftops and explored the cobblestone streets, thick with thatched-roof cottages and grand Belle Époque–style mansions, she was entranced. Deauville was a perfect blend of medieval charm and modern elegance.

Every afternoon the Promenade des Planches was filled with women carrying parasols and men wearing boater hats. Coco Chanel had a boutique on rue Gontaut-Biron and held fashion shoots on the boardwalk. Photographers snapped photos of film stars, and members of the Polo Club took breaks between matches to inhale the sea air.

The Barrière Le Royal Hotel and its neighboring casino were as grand as the luxury hotels in Philadelphia and New York. The hotel was built in the Belle Époque style, directly opposite the sand. The whole lobby was decorated in red. Red velvet sofas, crystal vases filled with red roses, and valets in red uniforms and red-and-gold peaked caps. Even the gift shop held a selection of red dresses and scarves. Edgar insisted on buying Helen a red silk scarf so she would never forget their time in Deauville.

Her fears about Edgar finishing his novel, and Sophie trying to get Edgar's attention, subsided.

Edgar worked all day on the book, only stopping to join Helen for lunch. Sophie and Tommy sat in a beach cabana and played boules with the others on the hotel lawn. At night the whole group gathered for drinks at Bar du Soleil and then went on to the casino. Helen wasn't fond of gambling, but she adored the casino. The men and women were glamorously dressed, and the women smoked Gauloises cigarettes and moved around the tables without needing a male escort.

During the day, her favorite thing to do was to take a taxi and visit the neighboring farms. Every few miles, she got out to pat the noses of the large, placid cows standing at the side of the road. They reminded her of Nellie and Essie.

This afternoon Edgar had a surprise for her. She sat at a café and picked at her plate of shrimp, waiting for him.

"There's my beautiful wife," Edgar said as he joined her.

He had a light tan and looked handsome in a blue blazer. Helen's complexion didn't do well in the sun. She left the hotel once without a hat and ended up with freckles on her nose.

"You're lucky—you don't burn." She sighed.

"I like you with freckles. You've never looked prettier," Edgar said, kissing her.

"Mother never leaves the house without a hat." Helen put down her shrimp fork. "She always says that beauty fades, but a woman can always keep her creamy skin."

Helen often thought about her mother and Daisy. She wrote Charlotte long letters, and a few times she booked a transatlantic call through the hotel operator. Hearing her mother's voice and imagining her standing in Dumfries's living room eased the pain of missing the farm. But she didn't reach out to Daisy. She wondered if they'd ever speak to each other again.

"You haven't told me where we're going," Helen said.

She had planned on spending the afternoon at a farm that specialized in Neufchâtel cheeses. She had tried a slice of Neufchâtel at a patisserie. The crumbly yellow rind was tart and salty, and the rich center was like eating Mary's whipped cream straight from the bowl.

"You'll find out." Edgar took out his wallet and put some francs on the table.

He took her arm, and they turned onto a side street. Edgar stopped in front of a jewelry store. BOUCHERON was written in cursive above the window. Inside, the space consisted of a small showroom with a sitting area. A gold display case was filled with clear white diamonds.

"What are we doing here?" Helen asked.

Boucheron was one of the most famous French jewelers. They couldn't possibly afford any of the pieces. And Helen didn't need jewelry. She had her pearls, her gold watch, and the diamond-and-emerald wedding ring.

"Leonard arranged a dinner party tonight at the casino," Edgar said. "Scott Fitzgerald and Zelda will be there. I want you to have something special."

Helen couldn't help thinking how her father had spent all their money on Rosalee and Chateau-sur-Mer. She never wanted to worry about money again.

"I don't want any jewelry. There are better things to spend the advance on," she said irritably.

"Please, just this once," Edgar begged. "It could be one of the most important nights of our lives."

Edgar had been working so hard. And Scott Fitzgerald was one of his literary idols.

"All right," she relented. "But it can't be anything too expensive."

The salesgirl showed her small diamond earrings and a gold-and-amethyst bracelet.

"You don't want the earrings," a male voice said.

Helen looked up. The man was standing near her at the counter. He was about forty with very dark hair and a thin mustache. He was good-looking for his age; he reminded her of an older Rudolph Valentino.

She glanced around for Edgar, but he had gone outside to smoke a cigarette.

"I beg your pardon," she said stiffly.

"The diamond earrings are the kind of thing a man gives his mistress," he continued. "They're so discreet, one would never suspect that the woman he's with is not his wife. A husband wants to show his wife off." He pointed to the bracelet. "The bracelet is a better choice."

"How do you know I'm not a man's mistress?" she said archly.

The man made a small bow.

"I saw you come in together. You're too refined to be a mistress. And if you were a mistress, it wouldn't be to an ordinary man like your husband."

Helen was about to demand an apology, but Edgar walked back in the store. She tried on a pair of sapphire earrings before choosing the gold-and-amethyst bracelet. She told herself it had nothing to do with what the man said. The bracelet was pretty, and Edgar liked it.

～

A few hours later, Vanessa greeted them at the entrance of the casino. Vanessa wore an emerald-hued, drop-waisted dress and silver lamé sandals. A rhinestone clip was fastened in her hair.

Helen and Vanessa had grown quite close. Often in the evenings, they sat and talked on the hotel terrace. Vanessa told her about growing up in Victorian society, where she and Virginia were expected to marry men with titles and not have careers. She was given art lessons so she'd have a hobby, and it became her grand passion.

"You look positively French." Vanessa noticed Helen's bracelet. "Is that new?"

Helen grimaced. She wished Edgar had saved his money.

"Edgar insisted I have it. He's so excited about meeting Scott and Zelda." She gave a little smile. "You'd think he was meeting the president."

Dinner was held in the Empire Lounge, behind the game room. Sophie and Tommy were there, and Leonard and Virginia. Duncan looked more handsome than ever. His hair was golden from the sun, and his forearms were covered with light blond hair. He was seated between Bunny and Vanessa. Helen still wasn't comfortable with Vanessa's revelation about their odd arrangement. But Vanessa and Duncan and Bunny seemed happy, so she told herself it was none of her business.

Leonard ordered kir royales—champagne with crème de cassis—for the table, and they ate beef with truffles and baked potatoes. They talked about everyone's recent projects. Vanessa and Duncan had new art exhibits in London. Sophie's short story was accepted by a literary journal, and Bunny was making furniture for a townhouse in Mayfair.

"And you, Mrs. Scott," Scott Fitzgerald addressed Helen. "What do you do?"

"I raise cows." She smiled coyly. "Not everyone can be a great writer or artist, but we all have to eat."

Everyone laughed. Scott told a story about a scathing *New York Times* review of *The Beautiful and the Damned*, and Zelda described her renewed passion for learning ballet.

After dinner, Scott and Zelda left for another party, and the group moved on to the gaming tables. Helen and Edgar stayed behind to finish their coffee.

Sophie appeared at the table. "Do you mind if I borrow Edgar?" she asked. She leaned over Edgar's shoulder. "Tommy had to go back to the hotel, and he left me a pile of chips. I'm a terrible gambler; I don't want to lose them."

Sophie looked striking in a floor-length gold evening gown. A feather headband was arranged over her auburn curls, and she carried an ostrich feather.

Edgar and Sophie joined the others at the roulette wheel, and Helen walked out to the casino's terrace. The sky was a velvet black, and stars shimmered on the sea. Yachts bobbed in the harbor, and men and women swathed in furs strolled along the promenade.

Helen took out her cigarette case. She had almost quit smoking before she arrived in Deauville. But everyone in France seemed to smoke. She told herself that it was the sweetness of the kir royale, mixed with the bitter French coffee, that left an unpleasant taste in her mouth and made her want the cigarette. But it was the image of Sophie leaning so close to Edgar. She refused to be jealous. There was nothing wrong with either of them having friends of the opposite sex, and Edgar had never given her any reason to doubt him.

"You don't have to come out here to have a cigarette," a male voice said. "In France, it's acceptable for women to smoke in the casino."

It was the man she had met at the jewelry store.

He joined her at the railing. "Or are you out here so you don't have to watch that woman fawn all over your husband?"

Helen's eyes flashed. She inhaled her cigarette.

"I don't know who you are or why you think you can comment on my marriage," she said stormily. "But I'd like you to stop."

"You're right, I haven't introduced myself." He held out his hand. "I'm Louis Renault."

He announced it as if she was supposed to know who he was. Perhaps he was a famous French film star, but she had never heard of him.

"Well, Mr. Renault." She waved her hand. "It's a large terrace. You can stand somewhere else."

"I'd rather stand here. There's a better view of the ocean. See down there." He pointed at the bay. "That's my yacht, *La Voiturette*, named after the first model of my cars. I'm a car manufacturer; I own the biggest factory in France."

"I don't know anything about French cars. My father and husband drive Fords."

"Henry Ford makes a fine car, but it's not as good as a Renault." His dark eyes twinkled under the outdoor lights. "Perhaps you'll allow me to take you for a drive."

Helen was shocked. No man had ever been so forward with her before.

"As you noted in the jewelry store, I'm a married woman. I would never go for a drive with another man."

"Never is a long time. You'd be missing out on many experiences." His voice was smooth. "For instance, I'd show you the mushroom farms near Deauville. If you haven't eaten a French mushroom, you've never lived."

Helen stubbed out her cigarette. She raised her chin and crossed her arms over her chest.

"There's a casino full of women who I'm sure would love to pick mushrooms with you. I suggest you ask one of them. If you'll excuse me, I'm going to join my husband."

Edgar wasn't at any of the gaming tables. She wondered if he had gone back to the hotel. She went to the coat check and asked the girl for her fur cape.

"What a beautiful cape." The girl handed it to her.

Helen draped it over her shoulders. If Edgar had left recently, she could hurry and they could walk together.

"If you don't mind me asking, what kind of fur is it?" the girl continued. "My fiancé wants to give me a gift." She giggled self-consciously. "I told him that girls like me don't wear fur, but he insists."

Helen turned her attention to the girl. "It's a silver fox."

"How odd, I've never seen a silver fox before," the girl commented. "But tonight, I hung up another just like it."

When Helen arrived at the room, Edgar was sitting at his writing desk. He was still wearing his topcoat and tails, and he was hunched over his typewriter.

He looked up. "There you are. I couldn't find you at the casino. I thought you left."

There was no reason to mention Louis Renault. She would never talk to him again.

"I needed some air. I was on the terrace." She set down her evening bag.

"Everyone is still at the casino, but I wanted to do some writing." Edgar beamed. "Scott said he'd read my novel when it's published. He gave me his address in Saint Louis."

Helen went to the closet to hang up her cape. The lining was a different color; she hadn't noticed it when the girl handed it to her. It couldn't be her cape. She'd have to go back and exchange it.

She crossed the lawn to the casino. More people were starting to leave. The driveway was filled with European sports cars, and there was the sound of drunken laughter.

"Excuse me," Helen said to the girl at the coat check. "You gave me the wrong cape."

"I'm very sorry, I told you that two capes were exactly the same. The other woman just picked up the other one."

"Do you know where she is?" Helen wondered.

The girl pointed to the casino entrance.

A young woman was wearing a gold evening gown. The silver fox cape was draped over her shoulders.

It was Sophie.

Edgar had given Helen the cape the night of their dinner at the Savoy with Malcolm. Had he bought one for Sophie too? The idea seemed ridiculous, yet it was too much of a coincidence. She couldn't think of another reason why Sophie would have the same cape.

Helen waited until Tommy and Sophie left. Then she stepped through the revolving doors. The night air felt damp and chilly against her skin. She hugged the cape around her shoulders and walked quickly back to the hotel.

Chapter Fifteen

The weather in April was so mild, Vanessa decided to extend their stay until the end of May. Tommy returned to university at Cambridge and came back to Deauville occasionally. Leonard and Virginia went to Paris to stay with Sylvia Beach, the American writer who owned an English-language bookstore on the rue de l'Odéon.

Helen wanted to go back to Sussex, but Edgar was close to finishing the book. He insisted they stay in Deauville, and reluctantly she agreed.

She never asked him about Sophie's fox cape. Whenever she got up the courage—when they were sitting at an outdoor café in the Place de Morny and enjoying café au laits sweet with sugar and cinnamon, the mornings they visited the stables at the racetrack, when they rented a sailboat to explore the little inlets—she didn't know what to say.

Helen worried about other things too. Edgar's mood had changed. At first, it was little things. He didn't join Helen in the hotel dining room for breakfast. The first month they were there, the French continental breakfast—tartine with blackberry jam and fruit juice—was his favorite meal of the day. Now, when he did appear—unshaven and with circles under his eyes—he spent the meal reading the American newspaper and didn't eat a bite.

Eventually, Helen realized what was wrong. The book was due in less than a month. Since Leonard left for Paris, Edgar hadn't written a word.

The worst part was that when Helen asked, he lied and said the words were flowing and he couldn't get them down fast enough. It was only when she reached into his closet for a pillowcase that she discovered the truth. The typewriter was stashed under a set of towels. Edgar hadn't touched it in days.

It was early evening and Helen was getting dressed. Jack had sent a cable that he was in Paris. He was taking the train to Deauville and would join them for dinner.

Edgar entered the room in a pair of tan trousers and a V-neck vest. He held his boater hat in his hand. Suddenly she longed to be back on the Main Line. They'd be dressing for dinner at Dumfries with her parents. Instead of her spending the meal worrying about the book and Sophie, they'd talk about the Devon Horse Show. After dinner, they'd go for a swim. The stars would be out, and they'd lie on chaise longues and revel in the soft country air.

"Where have you been?" Helen asked. "Jack will be here soon."

"I spent the afternoon at the library." Edgar set his hat on the coffee table. "I left my typewriter there. I have my own little cubicle."

Helen picked up her hairbrush. She was tempted to confront Edgar, but something stopped her. What if this had to do with Sophie? He was in love with Sophie and couldn't concentrate on writing until they were together.

Whenever Helen allowed herself such thoughts, she became furious with herself and with Edgar. How dare he lie to her about the typewriter. Helen didn't need a man, and she refused to turn into her mother or Daisy. But she still loved Edgar, and she wouldn't let Sophie win. Sophie might be beautiful and alluring, but Edgar was her husband.

Before she said anything to Edgar, she would share her concerns with Jack.

"Jack is meeting us in the lobby. We're going to Chez Gabriel for dinner, then we'll join the others at the casino."

"I can't come. I already have plans," Edgar replied.

"You said you would," she reminded him. "I told you about it yesterday."

"Something came up." Edgar poured a glass of water from the pitcher on the side table. "There's a French publisher who Malcolm wants me to meet. He's only in Deauville for one night."

"He can join us. I'll change the reservation."

"Not this time. Jack will want to talk about other things." Edgar moved to the dressing table. "Tell Jack I'll see him at breakfast." He reached down and kissed her. "I'll take the day off from writing. We'll pack a picnic and explore the countryside. You can introduce Jack to some of those Normandy cows."

"A whole day? Are you sure?" Her voice was slow and measured. She wondered if he would finally admit that he hadn't been writing after all.

Edgar opened his mouth as if he were about to say something. Instead, he set down the glass and picked up his hat.

"That reminds me, I have to send Leonard my new chapters."

~

Chez Gabriel was tucked into a corner of rue Désiré le Hoc. Blue leather booths lined the walls, and baroque chandeliers hung from the ceiling. Children crowded around the lobster tank that took up the middle of the room.

Helen couldn't remember being happier to see anyone. Jack looked so wonderfully American. His blond hair was cut short and parted to the side. He wore a white blazer and a watch with a leather band. The women at the adjoining tables couldn't take their eyes off him.

"Gabriel will lose customers," Helen said happily. "None of the women are interested in their food. They think you're an American film star."

"The only woman in Deauville that I'm interested in is you." Jack sipped his martini.

Helen had ordered for both of them. Artichokes as their appe-
tizers and lobster with vegetables for the main course. Dessert would
be cheese and fruit and glasses of Calvados—cider brandy made with
apples from a nearby orchard.

"I don't want to talk about myself. Tell me everything about
Dumfries and the Main Line." Helen leaned forward eagerly, as if Jack's
words could transport her to her childhood bedroom. She could almost
see the view of the paddocks and the swimming hole where she and
Daisy spent so much of their summers.

Jack told her that many of her father's clients had returned to the
firm. Her mother was planning a weekend house party for the Fourth of
July. Jack had seen the new musical *A Connecticut Yankee* on Broadway,
and the stock market was doing better than ever.

"Your parents miss you, but they're glad you're happy." Jack studied
her carefully. "Are you happy?" he pressed her. "You haven't said a word
about the dairy farms or Edgar's writing."

Helen told him about the identical fox capes and the typewriter
hidden under the towels. Edgar hadn't been himself; he disappeared for
hours and said he was writing at the library.

"Perhaps he was at the library," Jack offered. "And the capes might
be a coincidence."

"Both capes had the same pearl buttons, and they came from the
same fur shop in Mayfair." Helen shook her head. "The typewriter is in
the room. He couldn't have been working at the library."

"There still might be an explanation," Jack persisted.

"The way my father had an explanation for having lunch with
Rosalee at the Plaza." Helen sliced an asparagus. She was so angry, she
was afraid the knife would cut straight through the plate.

"Edgar is in love with you," Jack said gently. "He wouldn't throw
away your marriage."

"You're the one who said that men don't think clearly around
women like Rosalee." Her voice was sharp. "Sophie is striking and beautiful. It's impossible for men not to fall in love with her."

The lobster was soft and pink on her plate. Jack had ordered lobster at her birthday lunch at the Plaza. She remembered wishing she had ordered the same thing, because the lamb chop required chewing and lobster melted in your mouth. But now she couldn't swallow a bite.

She still believed her mother should have made her father leave after his affair with Rosalee. And Daisy shouldn't have followed Roland to Italy when he cheated on his exams. Even if Edgar admitted the truth, it might not be enough.

Perhaps she wasn't meant to be married. The cows made her happy, and the farm. She loved horses and riding. She even found new things to love in Deauville. Beautiful clothes, music, and dancing. The buzz of the casino, the scent of Gauloises cigarettes and men's cologne. She couldn't be with someone who lied, and she couldn't forgive Edgar if he had an affair.

"Let's talk about something else," she urged. "Tell me about Daisy."

Before coming to Paris, Jack had spent a few weeks in Portofino. Daisy and Roland's villa was tucked high in the hills above the bay. There were olive trees and a winding path down to the sea. The village was filled with trattorias that served spaghetti with seafood. The local people were the friendliest he'd ever met.

"Did she say anything about me?" Helen asked.

She missed Daisy. If they were speaking to each other, Daisy and Roland could have come to Deauville. Edgar would have taken Roland to watch the polo matches, and Helen and Daisy would have visited Coco Chanel's boutique.

Jack nodded. "She asked about you and Edgar." He looked at Helen. "Daisy is your family. You need each other."

"Daisy has a new family. All she wants is Roland." Helen recalled their conversation in Daisy's bedroom. She wanted to change the subject. "I promised Vanessa we'd meet them at the casino. She wanted to join us for dinner, but I wanted you all to myself."

Helen wondered again if Jack had been in love with Vanessa and she was the reason that he stopped painting portraits. But it was none of her business, and she didn't know how to ask.

Jack was about to pay the check when a man wearing a dark suit approached their table. Helen recognized him. It was Louis Renault. She hadn't seen him since the night at the casino.

"Helen, what a nice surprise." Louis made a small bow. "I thought you left Deauville. I haven't seen you at the hotel."

She introduced the two men.

"Your niece had never heard of Renault cars," Louis said to Jack with a smile. "I felt quite insulted. I hope you have, or I'm going to have to fire my American advertising company."

They talked about the Renault showroom in New York and how Louis visited Henry Ford the last time he was in America.

"I admire American businessmen," Louis said smoothly. "They're not afraid of going after what they want." He turned to Helen. "Perhaps tomorrow, you and your uncle would like to come for a drive. I can convince you both to buy Renaults."

Helen shook her head. "I'm sorry, we have plans tomorrow."

Louis reached into his pocket and took out a business card. He handed it to Helen. "Take this. We'll try another time."

～

After dinner, Jack went to his room to change into black tie and tails for the casino. Helen went to put on an evening gown. She had just stepped out of the elevator when she saw Sophie walking down the hallway. Sophie's back was to Helen, but it was definitely her. She wore the diamond tiara she'd worn on the night at the Savoy, and a rose-colored gown. The man with her was dressed in black tie and tails. He carried a top hat. It was Edgar.

They stopped at Sophie's room, and Edgar fumbled with the key. Sophie leaned forward and kissed him. It was a short kiss. Then they disappeared into her room.

Helen walked quickly to the other end of the hall. Her breath came in short gasps. Her hands shook so badly, it took three tries to unlock the door. She entered the room and poured a glass of brandy from the decanter on the sideboard.

Edgar was supposed to be having dinner with a French publisher.

She picked up the housephone and asked the operator to dial Jack's room number. She hated lying to Jack, but she wasn't ready to tell him what she had just seen, and she wanted to be alone.

"I'm not coming to the casino; I've come down with a terrible headache," she said when he answered the phone.

"Would you like me to bring a cup of warm milk and honey from the hotel kitchen?" Jack offered. "It always worked when you were a child."

"I just need a good night's sleep." Helen thanked him. "Give Vanessa and everyone my love."

She hung up and sipped the brandy.

They had spent many nights making love in this room. Edgar would pour two brandies and they'd talk about their day: how well a new chapter was coming, how Helen learned to blend herbs into cheese. Then they'd move to the bed and undress each other. That was almost Helen's favorite part of lovemaking. Edgar's hands on her zipper, her own fingers unknotting his tie. They'd only lie down when they were completely naked. Edgar didn't like her to wear a negligee; he said her body was more beautiful than any piece of silk.

How could Edgar cheat with Sophie when Helen's father's affair had hurt her so badly? And the hotel staff knew that Edgar was married. If anyone saw him go into Sophie's room, it would create a scandal.

She opened her evening bag. Inside was Louis Renault's card. Her heart pounded. She picked up the phone and called the hotel operator.

"Louis Renault's room, please."

The phone kept ringing. She was about to hang up when a male voice answered.

"This is Louis."

"This is Helen Montgomery Scott." She gripped the phone. "I've changed my mind. I'd love to take a drive tomorrow."

Louis paused as if he was going to ask a question.

"Excellent. Let's say eleven a.m." His tone had a smile to it. "An older man like me needs his beauty sleep when he's going to spend the day with an attractive young woman."

~

The next morning, she told Edgar she had a headache and was going to spend the day in the hotel spa. He and Jack should go for a drive without her.

"Are you sure?" Edgar asked. He was sitting on the bed, buttoning his white shirt.

Helen searched for some trace of guilt. But he appeared exactly the same. She wondered if other women experienced the same feeling—a tug of war within herself of wanting to ask for the truth, mixed with the fear of being humiliated.

Had her mother guessed that her father was having an affair and chose to ignore it? Helen refused to behave in the same way. But she couldn't confront Edgar now. She already told Louis that she would go for a drive. Tonight, she would ask Edgar about Sophie.

"You and Jack haven't seen each other in months," Helen said to Edgar. "And the hotel already prepared a picnic. It shouldn't go to waste."

"All right." He grabbed his hat and kissed her. "It won't be as much fun without you."

After Edgar left, she spent twenty minutes choosing what to wear. She had never gone for a drive with a strange man before. She chose a blue pleated skirt and a polka-dot blouse. She paired them with a straw hat and short white gloves.

"Mrs. Scott?" The concierge approached her when she stepped out of the elevator. "I have a message from Mr. Renault. He's been delayed in his suite. He asked you to meet him there."

"In his suite?" Helen repeated.

"Suite 320 on the third floor."

Helen didn't want to go up to Louis's suite. But if she sat in the lobby, Vanessa or Sophie or someone might see her. And she didn't want to ask Louis to come to her room.

"Thank you." She nodded. "Tell him I'll be right there."

"Please make yourself comfortable," Louis greeted her. "I apologize for keeping you waiting. I have to finish a phone call."

Louis's suite faced the ocean and took up half the floor. She realized he must be very wealthy. The living room was done in gold and marble. A gold coffee table had pedestals shaped as gargoyles. There were gold Baccarat candelabras. Helen caught a glimpse of a dining room with gold chairs. At the end of the hall was a closed door that Helen presumed was the bedroom.

Louis disappeared through the door. A few photos stood on the coffee table. One was of Louis with a pretty young woman. She had dark hair and was dressed to go skiing. Another was of the same woman with a little boy.

"Ah, you found the photos of my wife." Louis entered the room. "Christiane is very beautiful, isn't she? She's not much older than you." He picked up the first photo. "This was taken last winter in Chamonix. It was our first time skiing. She was a much better skier than me."

"And this one?" Helen pointed to the other photo.

"That's our son, Jean-Louis." Louis beamed proudly. "He's almost two. He's the thing I love most in the world besides my cars."

Louis put down the photo. He turned to Helen.

"You might want to take off your gloves. No one wears gloves in Deauville. It's a holiday resort."

Helen pulled at them. "Well, I do."

"I already know that you're married." He arched his eyebrows. "Or aren't you wearing your wedding ring?"

"I don't know what you're talking about." Helen's voice was sharp. Suddenly she wished she hadn't come. She was tempted to make an excuse and go back to her room.

"The night we met, you wouldn't even stand next to me on the terrace at the casino," Louis reflected. "Now you're in my suite. Something must have changed."

"Nothing has changed in my marriage. The only reason I'm in your suite is that you weren't ready. I'll go wait in the lobby."

Louis put his hand on her arm.

"Please don't leave," he apologized. "You don't know what it's like, traveling for business, not being home with my wife and son. It's not often that I meet a woman I feel I can talk to."

Helen let out her breath. Louis was married, with a baby. Perhaps this was perfectly innocent. He was simply lonely and wanted company.

She asked why his family wasn't with him.

"Jean-Louis is too young to travel, and Christiane refuses to leave him at home with the nanny," he said indulgently. "Wait until you have children. You think it's your own life, then a child comes along and wraps you around his little finger. Come"—he patted the side of the sofa—"let me pour you a drink, then we'll go for a drive."

Helen sat down and took off her hat. Louis poured two glasses from the pitcher of orange juice on the sideboard.

"This isn't orange juice," she said after he handed her the glass. It tasted sharper than orange juice, and it was fizzy.

"It's a French cocktail called a mimosa. Orange juice with a splash of champagne."

"Should you be drinking if we're going for a drive?" Helen wondered.

"Don't worry about me." Louis sat on the sofa beside her. "French children are brought up on champagne. I had my first glass when I was ten. Tell me about yourself."

Helen told him about Dumfries and her goal to start a dairy company. She had been working at a farm in Sussex; now she was learning about Normandy cows.

"Women are becoming so successful," he said approvingly. "I was one of Coco Chanel's first supporters. When we met, she had a woman's hat store on rue de Chabon in Paris. Now she has her own fashion house with perfumes, and boutiques in Paris and New York."

The mimosa made her feel more relaxed. She told him about Thomas Danforth's creamery and her dream to sell her dairy products in supermarkets all over the East Coast.

"In business, one can never dream too big." He nodded. "I started as a mechanical engineer. Several car companies wanted to buy the gearbox I invented, but I turned them down. Why should I sell them my product so they could get rich? I pawned everything I owned to buy the parts to build my first car."

Louis took her glass and refilled it. Helen had one sip and put it down. She was feeling light-headed.

"It's getting late. We should go." She stood up and walked to the door.

Louis smiled at her. There was something different about his smile. As if he were addressing a child.

"We both know we're not going for a drive," he replied.

"I don't know what you mean."

"Of course you do. You never wanted to go for a drive." Louis walked over to her. He took her hand and led her back to the sofa. "Even beautiful American women don't go to men's hotel suites except for one reason. You're aware that I find you attractive, and you want to see what it's like to be kissed by a man who isn't your husband."

Before she could stop him, he leaned forward and kissed her. It was a long, deep kiss. His mouth remained on hers for a moment, then she pushed him away. He moved closer to kiss her again. There was the sound of shouting, and the door flung open.

Edgar entered the living room. He held a small gun.

"Get away from my wife." He moved closer to the sofa.

Helen wrenched herself from Louis's embrace. Her eyes were wide, her heart pounded.

"Edgar, what are you doing here?" she gasped.

"I came back to the hotel. The concierge said that Louis asked you to come to his suite." Edgar waved the gun at Louis.

Louis's voice was calm. "Helen and I are good friends. We're about to go for a drive."

"Helen isn't going anywhere but back to her room." Edgar kept the gun pointed at Louis. He nodded at Helen. "Get your hat and your purse."

Helen's eyes flashed, and there was a tightening in her chest. How dare Edgar tell her to leave when he had kissed Sophie. She wasn't going to be treated like a tennis ball in a match between two men. And she wasn't going to be humiliated in front of Louis.

"Louis is right—we were about to go for a drive," she said, smoothing her skirt.

Edgar was about to say something, but Louis turned to the side table. He opened the drawer and took out a pistol.

He pointed it at Edgar.

"You see, your wife wants to stay," Louis said to Edgar. "You're the one who should leave."

Then everything happened so quickly. Edgar fired the gun. The bullet grazed the sofa cushion next to Louis. Louis glanced at the cushion in disbelief and turned back to Edgar. Louis's hands shook, and he pulled the trigger.

The bullet pinged off Edgar's gold watchband. Edgar's expression changed to one of terrified surprise and confusion. At the same moment, the door opened wider and Jack appeared in the living room. He was dressed all in white and carried his panama hat.

Helen and Jack ran to Edgar's side at the same time. Helen's gaze flew between the two men she loved most in the world, and she let out a gasp. Her knees buckled, and then everything went black.

Chapter Sixteen

The Deauville chief of police was a good friend of Louis's. The alter-cation between Louis and Edgar was hushed up in exchange for a brand-new Renault for the chief and a fleet of Renaults for the police department.

Louis offered to pay for Edgar and Helen's and Jack's accommo-dations at the hotel. Helen politely declined. Vanessa was still paying for their room, and Jack had plenty of money. Helen didn't want to be indebted to Louis for anything.

It was a miracle that Edgar wasn't injured. It had been a small pistol, and the bullets didn't have a far range. Helen wondered whether Louis had a habit of making passes at other men's wives and kept a pistol in order to frighten any husband who caught him.

She had been so relieved when the doctor examined Edgar and said he hadn't received a scratch. Edgar made a joke that marriage was good for something. The gold watch was a wedding present; a leather band wouldn't have offered the same protection. Helen didn't find it funny and left the room without saying a word.

The person she was most angry at was herself. What had she been thinking going up to Louis's suite? She hadn't planned on having an affair. Yet she had let the attention of an attractive man sway her because she was angry at Edgar.

She wanted to discuss it more with Jack, but he had gone to Paris for several days. His visit had been arranged earlier, so it was something he couldn't get out of. Helen missed him more than she could put into words. He had always been there for her during a crisis; without his calm advice, she didn't know what to do next.

After a couple of days, Helen moved into a room of her own. She was still furious at Edgar for kissing Sophie. She needed time to think about their marriage. She couldn't sleep and found it difficult to swallow. Every day at lunch and dinner, Vanessa ordered room service and forced Helen to eat the consommé the hotel chef prepared especially for her and to take the sleeping powder the hotel doctor gave her to sleep. None of it helped. Helen wanted to feel hungry. The emptiness in her stomach masked the deeper ache in her heart. When she slept, she had nightmares. It was better to stay awake.

What if the bullet had injured or killed Edgar? Or if Jack had walked in moments earlier and the bullet had struck him instead? She was so ashamed and mortified, it was hard to look in the mirror.

She called her mother and told her what happened. Charlotte was sympathetic, but Helen could tell she was perplexed. Helen had never been involved in any kind of scandal. She even accepted a call from her father. But her own actions didn't mean that she could forgive him. In a way, it made it worse. She couldn't help recalling seeing her father having lunch with Rosalee at the Plaza, and then picturing Edgar kissing Sophie outside Sophie's hotel room. She hung up, longing for when they had been close. That time seemed as distant as the places in the books she and Daisy read as children.

Daisy sent a telegram saying that Charlotte told her about Edgar and Louis, and she was glad no one had been injured. Helen reread the slip of paper a dozen times, searching for something more. The word "love" in the signature, or a line saying how much Daisy missed her. There was nothing except a polite sentence saying she wished she and Roland could come to Deauville for a few days, but they couldn't leave Portofino. They didn't have much money, and there was no one to run the hotel.

Edgar was suffering as much as Helen. For the first couple of days, after she moved into her own room, she didn't hear from him. Then he started sending flowers and notes. Arrangements of lilies of the valley from the hotel florist. Primroses and bluebells from the fields around Deauville. Three dozen roses from the most expensive florist in Paris. The notes all said he had to talk to her.

"Nothing Edgar could say can make a difference," Helen said to Vanessa.

It had been five days since the incident. Helen didn't know what she was going to do. She wasn't ready to go back to Philadelphia, and she didn't want to return to Sussex. The only thing she was certain of was that she couldn't stay married to Edgar.

"As soon as I feel strong enough, I'm going to call a divorce attorney," Helen said briskly. The thought of doing something productive made her feel more alert than she had felt since the morning in Louis's suite. "Paris must be full of good lawyers. All those wronged wives deserve to get something out of their husbands."

"You have the rest of your life not to speak to Edgar," Vanessa ventured with a small smile. "You can spare him thirty minutes."

Helen thought of all the times they had spent together. The first time they met, when she thought he was a stable hand and he didn't correct her. Finding him at the head of the table the next morning, reading the newspaper. Driving to Oyster Bay to see Rosalee and pretending to be a reporter for *Town Topics*. The piece he wrote about her in the *New Yorker*.

"All right." Helen nodded. "But you should wait in the hallway. If we're alone, I might be tempted to throw a vase of flowers at his head."

Edgar looked thinner than when she'd last seen him. His clothes hung on him, and his chin was covered in stubble. His eyes were bloodshot, and his hand shook when he tried to light a cigarette.

"You look like one of those skeletons Mother used to decorate the house with on Halloween," Helen said, pacing around the living room.

She couldn't sit still for long. It was easier to stop thinking when she was moving.

"Having a pistol fired at you doesn't do much for one's appetite. You don't look any better." Edgar appraised her. "You must have lost five pounds, and you didn't have anything to lose."

"Yes, well, sitting in the hotel dining room and eating the chef's potatoes dauphinoise hasn't sounded appealing." She waved at a platter of fruit and French cheeses. "You're welcome to some fruit and cheese. The maids keep refreshing the sideboard."

Edgar picked up a piece of cheese. He leaned against the cushions and started talking.

"Jack and I came back to the hotel because he forgot his hat," he began. "I asked the concierge to leave you a message, and he said you were in Louis Renault's suite. I was worried. Men like Renault only invite women to their rooms for one reason."

"I was quite capable of taking care of myself," Helen retorted. "Did you ever think that I might want to be with Louis rather than a husband who lies about everything?"

Edgar ate another piece of cheese with a crust of bread, and the story poured out.

The first few weeks in Deauville, he had never been so happy. He could feel the novel taking shape, like a soufflé that went into the patisserie oven as a mix of eggs and flour and butter and came out as soft and billowy as the sail on a sailboat. After he finished working, he'd stroll past the bookshops on the promenade, picturing his novel wedged between Fitzgerald's *The Great Gatsby* and Hemingway's *The Sun Also Rises*. Once he even stopped at a fortune teller. The woman read his cards and said his books would be sold in twenty countries.

Then Leonard left for Paris, and Edgar stopped writing. At first he thought he had been working too hard and needed a few days off. He went to the racetrack at La Touques and bet on a few races. The first two times his horse won. He was relieved—his luck had changed. He could return to the book. But he sat at the typewriter for hours, and the words wouldn't come.

"I gave up and went back to the racetrack. I had used up the advance, so I asked the local bank for a line of credit. I lost four races in a row," Edgar continued. "If I didn't finish the book, I'd have to pay back the advance, and I didn't have it."

Helen was shocked. They had been so careful with money. Each night, they set aside ten francs for dinner and the casino. Neither of them spent any more.

"Where did the advance go?" she asked.

Edgar looked so weary. His mouth sagged at the corners.

"I paid off the fur and the bracelet." He waved his hand. "There were other things. I lent some money to Tommy a few times at the casino."

Helen wondered if he lent money to Sophie too. But her parents were wealthy. They owned a townhouse in Westminster facing Hyde Park.

"I saw you and Sophie go into her hotel room," Helen said.

"Tommy had written her a letter with an ultimatum," Edgar explained. "Either she accepts his marriage proposal, or he was going to start seeing other women. Sophie got very drunk at the casino, and I escorted her back to her room."

"You kissed her," Helen said.

"She kissed me," he corrected. "It was nothing. I did the only gentlemanly thing. I took her inside and stayed with her until she sobered up. It took three cups of coffee and a number of aspirin. Then I put her to bed. Nothing happened—you have to believe me."

When Edgar had found out that Helen was in Louis's hotel suite, he couldn't think clearly. He only meant to scare Louis with the gun. He didn't know that Louis had one too.

"This morning, I sent a cable to my father asking to borrow the money," Edgar finished. "We'll go back to Philadelphia; I'll finish the novel there. We can live at Dumfries until our house is finished so you're close to the cows and the farm."

Edgar had lied about his writing. He bet on the horses without telling her. Even if he was telling the truth about Sophie, what he did wasn't right. Sophie could have found someone else to take her back to the hotel.

Helen couldn't live with Edgar on the Main Line. Having cocktails with her parents, swimming in the pool on a starry night. Even if they were invited to parties, everyone would be talking about them behind their backs. Memories of their previous lives would be everywhere. If they dined at the Warwick Hotel, she'd be reminded of the many nights they danced on the dance floor and she'd felt light and happy. If they rode horses together, she'd think of the plans they had to build a stable once their new house was finished.

She and Edgar were like two pieces of sandpaper rubbing together. They sparred with each other all the time. This was the second time their marriage almost led to disaster. The first time was when she smashed the vase and he threw the fireplace poker. It was quite clear that they couldn't remain a couple any longer.

Helen would file for divorce; she'd stay in Europe for a while. Eventually, when any gossip had died down, she'd go back to Dumfries and find the money to start her company. She'd join her mother's charities and create a scholarship for underprivileged girls to attend Foxcroft.

"I'm going to contact a divorce attorney," Helen said to Edgar. "You don't have to worry about being at fault or inventing a mistress." She arched her eyebrows. "Given the circumstances, I'm quite sure any judge would grant us a divorce."

Edgar jumped up from the sofa. "I don't want a divorce."

"Well, I do. We never should have gotten married in the first place. Your writing will never make you happy, and I wasn't cut out to be a wife. We can't be in the same room without wanting to throw something at each other. I'm going to stay here until Jack returns from Paris. Then I don't know what I'm going to do." She took off her wedding ring and dropped it on the table. "I'm sure you can go back to Sussex. If it rains too much during the summer and the farmhouse gets damp, you can always stay with Sophie in London."

Edgar opened his mouth to say something, and then closed it. His expression reminded her of Christopher Robin in *Winnie-the-Pooh* when he had to leave his beloved stuffed animals—Pooh and Piglet and Eeyore—and return to boarding school. The book had come out two years ago and was the most popular children's book in England. Helen had heard Vanessa reading it to Angelica at bedtime and was so entranced by the characters and setting, she stayed for the whole story.

Edgar was experiencing his own terrible loss, but he was too proud to let it overcome him in front of Helen.

After Edgar left, Vanessa entered the guest room.

"That was more painful than my meeting with the headmistress at Foxcroft when I told her my parents were taking me home for good," Helen said bleakly. "The headmistress pretended to dissuade me, but I knew she was secretly happy. I never fit in. The other girls would be relieved that I was gone."

"What are you talking about?" Vanessa asked. "Edgar loves you. I could tell when he walked into the hall. He looked as defeated as the matador in one of Ernest Hemingway's short stories."

"He might be in love with me, but our marriage will never work." Helen shook her head.

She glanced at the plate of fruits and cheeses. She was filled with a new emptiness that no orange wedge of Camembert or ripe plum could fill.

"It's the best thing for both of us. Things could have ended up so much worse."

Vanessa refused to let Helen be so unhappy. The shooting wasn't Helen's fault. She didn't know that Edgar would come after her. Or that either man had a pistol.

"I'm going to throw a garden party," Vanessa announced. "We'll take over the lawn in front of the hotel. It's what we need to clear the air."

Helen glanced at Vanessa in disbelief. The last thing she felt like doing was putting on a pretty dress. And she didn't want to stroll around the hotel's gardens. What if Louis was still staying there or all the employees knew what happened? But Vanessa insisted. Helen couldn't stay cooped up in her room forever. And planning the party would give everyone something to do. The party would have a springtime theme. Vanessa and Bunny would provide clothes in spring colors for the guests to wear.

The next morning, Helen accompanied Vanessa and Bunny to the outdoor market in Deauville. They bought shirts and trousers for the men and tea dresses for the women. Then they set up an art studio in one of the Barrière Le Royal's ballrooms.

All day, Vanessa and Bunny painted the clothes in colors found in a painter's palette. Cadmium-red shirts and French ultramarine trousers. Tea dresses in viridian green, and a shade of blue that reminded Helen of Jack's aquamarine eyes.

When Helen tried on her blue tea dress—paired with a lemon-yellow straw hat—she felt a little bit brighter, as if the sun was finally peeking through the storm clouds. Perhaps Vanessa was right and a party was a good idea.

To eat, there were French cheese puffs and oysters in a mignonette sauce. Clive and Mary came with Angelica from London. Tommy returned from Cambridge. There were people Helen hadn't met: the owner of an art gallery in Paris who had shown Vanessa's paintings, a Parisian couple who had bought some of Bunny's furniture.

Halfway through the party, Sophie—radiant in a viridian-green dress that accentuated her green eyes and auburn curls—came up to Helen and said how sorry she was for everything that happened. Helen was tempted to escape back to her room, but she refused to let Sophie feel like she had won.

Edgar was there in an orange shirt that made his arms look brown and highlighted the sun streaks in his hair. She avoided talking to him altogether. Standing on the lawn beside him would remind her of the parties at Dumfries and Fieldstone Manor. They had said everything to each other in her room; there was nothing more to talk about.

The only person who was absent from the party was Jack. He sent a note from Paris saying he would try to return in time, but he wasn't sure if he could make the train.

Now it was late afternoon, and the celebration was winding down. Guests holding glasses of Loire Valley Sancerre strolled across the hotel lawn.

Vanessa hurried over to her. Her hat was missing, and her dark hair had escaped its bun.

"I have to go. Duncan is in the hospital in Deauville."

"Duncan?" Helen repeated.

Vanessa was frantic. "First, I have to get Angelica. She's in Clive and Mary's suite."

Helen put down her wineglass. "I'll come with you; we'll call a taxi."

They sat in the taxi with Angelica between them. Angelica wore a floral dress and clutched a stuffed Peter Rabbit.

Vanessa disappeared to talk to the doctor. Finally, she joined Helen in the waiting room. It was sparsely furnished with two worn chairs. There was a table with a pitcher of water and a small bunch of flowers.

"Duncan is going to be all right." Vanessa sunk onto a chair. "Angelica is with them; they're playing checkers. I whispered to Angelica that the fastest way for Duncan to get better is to let him win."

"I don't understand. What happened, and who else is with him?"

Helen realized that she hadn't seen Duncan since the day of the gunfire in Louis's room. She had been too swept up in everything to notice that he was gone.

"He took too much sleeping powder. The doctor said if he wasn't built like a horse, he would have died."

"But why?" Helen asked, puzzled.

Vanessa poured a glass of water.

"It was about Jack, of course." She sipped the water. "Jack and Duncan went to Paris together. They were lovers years ago, you know. Duncan broke Jack's heart."

Helen let out a gasp. It wasn't possible.

Helen had known Jack her whole life—she would have noticed if he liked men. She pictured garden parties at Dumfries. Jack always had a stunning girl on his arm: blondes in chiffon gowns and jeweled T-strap sandals, brunettes sporting newly bobbed hair and wearing drop-waisted dresses. They drank glass after glass of champagne and twirled around the dance floor.

The bachelor's life had been perfect for Jack. He could come and go between his apartment in Philadelphia and the pied-à-terre in New York. When he felt like painting, he could cancel his engagements and lock himself in his art studio. And he loved attending dinner parties. He was the perfect guest—every hostess on the Main Line clamored to have him at her table.

More important than anything, being single meant that Jack never belonged to anyone besides her and Daisy.

Now, Helen saw how selfish she had been. Jack had been there for her ever since she was a child. When she wanted a bigger horse instead of a pony, he convinced her parents that she wouldn't fall off. When she left Foxcroft and her mother wanted her to attend a Swiss finishing school, Jack begged Charlotte to let Helen stay home and work on the farm. The times Helen had come home from a party convinced that boys would never dance with her because she was too tall, he promised that the boys would grow. He hadn't reached his own six feet three inches until he was twenty.

Jack was charismatic and wealthy. He could have spent his life doing whatever he pleased: Traveling to Italy and being invited to grand palazzos. Joining an expedition to Mount Everest. Big-game hunting in Africa. Instead, he stayed in Philadelphia because he wanted to be close to Helen and Daisy. And yet, he had never confided in her. Not when she was a child, nor recently, when she had love problems of her own. She prided herself on their close relationship, but he didn't trust her enough to reveal his true self. Helen blamed herself. Jack knew how rigid and judgmental she could be. He had been afraid she wouldn't understand.

Helen pulled her mind from her thoughts. "But when?"

"It started years ago, when Clive brought Jack to Charleston Farmhouse," Vanessa said. "One could almost feel the attraction between Jack and Duncan. The two most beautiful men in the world, like the constellations Orion and Pegasus coming together."

Duncan and Bunny had broken up months earlier, and Vanessa was pregnant with Angelica. Somehow, she didn't mind Duncan and Jack being together. Duncan loved Jack and Vanessa in different ways; none of them were jealous.

"Duncan craved domesticity, but he had to be with a man. I accepted that. So many other things made me happy at that time. My sister Virginia and I were so close, and I couldn't have survived without painting. And I had my children. When you have children, your heart becomes so full.

"It was different for Jack. Jack put everything into his relationship with Duncan. They ate breakfast together, and painted together, and had picnics. At night, they played the phonograph or sat on the porch and looked at the stars. Jack bought Duncan a telescope. Once, I heard Jack say to Duncan that his wildest dream would be to discover another planet that they could live on."

Helen recalled the nights that she and Edgar sat by the swimming pool and gazed up at the stars. Had Jack somehow taught her that? Nothing was more beautiful or full of possibilities than the sky on a starry night.

"Then Duncan and Bunny got back together," Vanessa continued. "Bunny didn't want to share Duncan with Jack. They got into terrible fights, and eventually Jack went back to America. This is the first time we've seen him in years. When Duncan and Jack met again at the casino, it brought all the memories back."

Jack and Duncan had gone to Paris together.

"It was Duncan's idea, and Jack went along with it." She pointed down the hallway. "Jack is with him. He looks terrible, as if he took the rest of the sleeping powder himself."

Helen debated going into the hospital room, but it was better to wait for Jack to appear. An hour later, he came into the waiting room. He looked more haggard than she'd ever seen him. His eyes were hooded, and his skin was white and papery.

Vanessa stayed at the hospital with Duncan and Angelica. Helen and Jack took a taxi back to the hotel. They didn't talk until they reached Helen's room. She wanted to say so many things. Jack shouldn't have had to pretend for all those years with beautiful women on his arm. He should have been himself in front of his family.

"I'm sorry I missed the party," Jack said before she could begin. "Vanessa and Bunny throw the best parties. I'm sure it was a success."

"Vanessa told me about you and Duncan and Bunny," Helen blurted out. "Duncan insisted you go to Paris, and you agreed."

Jack took off his straw hat. He poured two glasses of brandy and handed one to Helen.

"He suggested it the first night at the casino." Jack nodded. "I explained that I was in Deauville to see you and Edgar, but he didn't believe me. He'd missed me so much and begged me to spend a few nights in Paris." Jack swirled the brandy. "I finally gave in. I could never win an argument with Duncan."

It was early evening. From the window, Helen could see couples strolling along the promenade. There was the put-put of a yacht's engine, and birds rested on the branches outside the window.

"We were supposed to leave for Paris right after the picnic. After what happened between Edgar and Louis, I wanted to cancel. But we already had our reservations, and Duncan knew I'd be leaving Deauville soon.

"The view from our hotel room was of the Place des Vosges. It's my favorite park in Paris. The hedges are immaculately groomed, and there's a rose garden and walking paths. The first day, I woke up early and bought croissants at a boulangerie. I brought them back to the room and we sat on the balcony, talking about everything that we had missed in the last twenty years." He stared out at the sea. "Duncan really is a good father. Every other sentence was about Angelica. He loves her more than anything. After breakfast, we visited an art gallery that used to show my work, and some furniture shops that carry Duncan and Bunny's furniture. We walked to Montmartre and climbed to the top of the hill to the Church of the Sacré-Coeur. At night, we treated ourselves to dinner at an elegant restaurant on the Champs-Élysées. Escargots in butter, duck l'orange, and lemon soufflé for dessert.

"The next couple of days were more of the same. Then we started fighting. Duncan drank too much wine at dinner and became maudlin. He blamed me for going back to America. He declared that he and Bunny aren't in love anymore; they only stay together because it's comfortable." Jack paced around the room. "He said he would have left Charleston Farmhouse ages ago if it wasn't for Angelica. That isn't true. You've seen him with his paintbrushes and his wheelbarrow. He's like so many British landowners, completely happy puttering around the grounds of his country manor."

Helen recalled the first time she saw Duncan from the window, pushing Angelica in the wheelbarrow. She often saw him standing on a ladder, patching a leak in the ceiling or touching up the wainscot.

"Duncan asked me to come back to Sussex," Jack was saying. "I refused. My home and family are in America."

Helen didn't know when she would return to the Main Line, and Daisy was in Portofino. Nothing was stopping Jack from staying at Charleston Farmhouse.

"Duncan wanted me to move there permanently." Jack ran his fingers over his glass. "Even if he and Bunny break up for a while, they'll get back together. And I couldn't do that to Vanessa and Angelica. They don't need more drama in their lives." He paused. "I don't belong there. I never really did. I was the bright, shiny American that Clive brought home from Paris. My hair was blonder than the others', I had a muscular physique and an American accent." He looked at Helen meditatively. "Duncan and Bunny and Vanessa share a connection. It's easier to stay in love with someone from the same background. You have a shorthand."

"If you're talking about Edgar and me, you can save your breath," Helen said crisply. "I'm filing for divorce when I leave for Paris. Nothing you can say will stop me."

"People make mistakes." Jack's tone was gentle. "I'm sure Edgar is suffering."

Helen wished she was like Vanessa, who was able to keep Duncan's love for Bunny in a separate compartment so that it didn't hurt her. Or Louis's wife, Christiane, who let him go on business trips when she must suspect that he saw other women. But she couldn't stay married to Edgar when he had lied and cheated.

They talked about the party and the doctor's prognosis for Duncan's recovery.

"I'm going to Greece for a while before I return to Philadelphia," Jack said. "I've always wanted to paint the Acropolis. You should come with me."

It would be lovely to explore another country, to share meals with Jack and see the sunsets over the Aegean Sea. But what if he met someone? She didn't want to get in the way.

"It's a lovely offer, but I've heard the Greek sun is very strong." Helen set her glass on the coffee table. "I don't want more freckles."

"Where will you go?" Jack asked.

Suddenly the idea came to her. She didn't want to say anything to Jack until she was sure it would work.

She kissed him on the cheek. "Paint me a landscape of Athens, and don't worry about me. I'll be fine."

Jack left, and all Helen wanted was to take a bath. She had to make a phone call first. She dialed the operator and gave him the number.

"Helen, this is a surprise," Daisy's voice came over the line. "We only got our phone working a little while ago. Is everything all right?"

Helen said that she was still in Deauville.

"I was thinking about coming to Portofino for a few weeks. I wondered if I could stay at the hotel. I'd pay for my room and board."

Daisy took a few moments to answer. Helen clutched the phone, waiting for her reply.

"The hotel isn't full, and we'd be happy to have you. Send a telegram with your arrival date."

Chapter Seventeen

Portofino, Italy, June 1928

Helen left for Portofino the following week. Duncan was out of the hospital, and he and Vanessa and the others returned to Charleston Farmhouse. Jack had taken the train to Greece. Edgar was going to stay in Paris for a while. She didn't ask what he was going to do afterward. As long as the divorce lawyer had his address, it didn't matter.

The train from Paris to Portofino took most of a day. When she arrived at the little station and the other travelers stepped out, wearing smart holiday clothes and directing the porters to their steamer trunks, she wished she hadn't come. She wasn't ready to enjoy herself; she only wanted some quiet. To stand at the edge of a cliff and see if the natural beauty—the riot of flowers, the green-blue of the Mediterranean that Jack had described—could quell the anxiousness that threatened to overcome her.

Then the taxi drove her up to the villa, and she began to feel better. The driver prattled on in a mix of Italian and English. By the time they arrived, she was quite sure he had invited her to dinner with his family. Jack said the Italians were the friendliest people, and he was right.

The villa was three stories, set among a grove of pine trees. It had a terra-cotta roof and circular balconies facing the sea. The shutters were painted orange, and there was an orange front door. Flowerpots were filled with geraniums, and bicycles lay in the driveway.

Inside, the tile entrance opened onto a living room. Faded velvet sofas were arranged around a wooden coffee table. There was a stone fireplace and a sitting area under the window. A tea set was set up on the sideboard.

"Look at you, you're so Italian," Helen said to Daisy.

Daisy wore a floral dress with a yellow scarf. Her cheeks were thinner and her skin had lost some of its youthful glow, but it suited her. She looked more mature.

"We were so busy during the winter getting the villa ready, sometimes I forgot to eat," Daisy admitted. "Now I'm gaining the weight back and more. Wait until you try the local fruits. The apricots are sweet as honey."

"Thank you for letting me come," Helen said. She felt awkward. She was grateful that Daisy let her stay at the villa, but she still didn't approve of her eloping, and she didn't know what to say.

"You don't have to thank me." Daisy walked to the desk. "We haven't been open long, so not all the rooms are full. We serve a continental breakfast, and there's always food in the pantry. We don't carry American newspapers, but there are books in the library."

Helen stopped her. "Daisy, I'm not just any guest." She smiled gently. "So many things have happened, I want to spend time together." She tried a different approach. "Jack thought it was a good idea when I told him. He loved being here."

Daisy bit her lip. When she looked up, her expression was guarded.

"I'm glad you're in Portofino, and so is Roland." Daisy pointed to a painting above the fireplace. "Jack was a wonderful guest. He painted this when he was here."

The painting was a watercolor of a horseshoe-shaped harbor. Outdoor tables were shaded by striped umbrellas. Fishing boats bobbed at the shore, and inlets held sailboats and a diving platform. The water was the clearest blue-green Helen had ever seen.

Helen wished Jack were there, beside her. She had been buoyed by his approval of her plan. Now she wasn't sure it had been the right thing to do. Daisy was cool toward her, and Helen couldn't blame her. If Jack were there, he would know how to patch up their quarrel.

"It's the view of the room he stayed in."

"Can I have the same room?" Helen asked.

For the first time since their argument in Daisy's bedroom at Dumfries, Daisy gave a real smile.

"I already prepared it for you. I'll take you there."

Helen spent the next few days exploring Portofino. She visited Castello Brown that was built in the fourteenth century. It had a cemetery and views of the coastline. One day, she hiked the Azure Trail that connected the five villages of the Cinq Terre. At night, she ate at the trattorias on the Piazza Martiri dell'Olivetta.

But she wasn't closer to figuring out her future. And she worried about her sister. Daisy and Roland seemed happy, but the villa couldn't be making much money. At breakfast, the dining room was only half-full. There were plenty of room keys on the board behind the desk.

The plumbing didn't work in her bathroom. When she told Roland, he fixed it himself. She wondered what Roland's father would say if he knew that his son, who had been at Harvard, was crawling under a sink.

Daisy showed Helen the room they had kept for themselves. In the closet, there were only a few cotton dresses and a knitted cardigan. Gone were the designer gowns—the Jean Patou with the butterfly sleeves, the Jeanne Lanvin "garçon-look" chemise evening gown that Daisy had fallen in love with in Paris.

Helen wondered if Daisy had sold them. She broached the subject with Daisy after breakfast one morning. The kitchen was empty. Roland had taken a few guests on an excursion to explore the fishing inlets. Daisy suggested that Helen accompany them, but Helen wanted to spend time together.

"I'll do the dishes," Helen offered. "I've grown quite good at it. Edgar did most of the cooking during our marriage, I did the cleaning up."

They worked silently, moving the plates and cups to the kitchen. Helen longed for the ease of their relationship before Daisy and Roland eloped. Then they always had so much to tell each other, their sentences overlapped.

Helen tried to think of something to say. "It must be hard to live in Portofino when the local people speak Italian. Even the hotel guests speak different languages. The couple next to me at breakfast only spoke German."

"Roland is good at languages, and I'm learning Italian." Daisy shrugged. "My favorite thing is talking in Italian to the vendors at the outdoor market. I know the names of many fruits and vegetables."

Helen was about to say their parents would be pleased—Charlotte spoke a little French, and Robert was quite good at German. But it was hard enough talking to Daisy; she didn't want to bring up their parents.

"Jack is in Greece," Helen said instead. "He promised to send some postcards."

"Roland is dying to visit Greece." Daisy screwed the lid on a jar of homemade jam. "Maybe next year if we save enough money, we can take a vacation."

"You work too hard." Helen frowned. "You wake up so early. When do you sleep?"

Daisy explained that she had to get up early. The eggs had to be collected from the chicken coop, and she had to make breakfast before the first guests came downstairs. Then the rooms had to be cleaned before guests returned from their daytime activities.

Helen couldn't imagine leading Daisy's life. Even when she spent all day working on the farm, she set her own hours and rested whenever she felt like it.

"Are you sure this is what you want?" Helen asked, stacking the plates in the sink. "You and Roland could come back to the Main Line. You could live at Dumfries for a while and go back to Bryn Mawr. Roland would think of something to do."

Daisy's eyes flared, and her cheeks became hot.

"You still don't think I'm grown-up enough to make my own decisions." She set the saltshaker on a shelf. "Our marriage is some kind of play-acting, like when you and I were children and made up stories with our dolls."

"I don't know what you mean," Helen said, puzzled.

"When you asked if you could stay at the villa, I thought you were sorry for what you said about our elopement," Daisy replied. "You haven't changed. I saw you looking through my closet and inspecting the tablecloths in the dining room. The villa might not be up to the standards of the Warwick Hotel, but Roland and I have put a lot of work into it."

"I was worried that you don't have pretty dresses," Helen defended herself.

"It's all right for you to wear slacks and boots on the farm, but you don't approve of my clothes," Daisy returned.

Helen wanted to say that was different. She had never liked clothes, but Daisy loved dressing up in beautiful evening gowns.

"I care about you. I want you to be happy," Helen said.

"Roland and I love each other. Eloping was the best thing I've ever done. And we love running the hotel. Until you can see that, there's nothing to talk about." Daisy stalked out of the kitchen. "You can finish the washing up since you volunteered. I have to check on the deliveries."

Helen rinsed the dishes and placed them on the counter to dry. She had handled everything poorly, and she and Daisy were no closer to making up. It was her fault, and she didn't know how to fix it. The best thing was to stay out of Daisy's way and try again later.

At lunchtime, Helen took a book and started down the path to the piazza. Her heel caught, and one of her sandals flew off as she tumbled to the ground.

"*Stai bene?*" a male voice called.

A man in his late twenties walked toward her. He had dark, wavy hair and wore a chambray shirt. He was holding her sandal.

Helen shook her head. "I'm sorry, I don't speak Italian."

"Are you all right?" he asked in accented English.

Helen dusted the pebbles from her knees. "I'm fine, thank you."

"You lost this." He examined the sandal. "The heel is broken."

She'd have to get it fixed in the piazza. She couldn't walk back up to the villa without a shoe.

"Is there a shoe repair in Portofino?" she asked.

The man nodded. "Yes, but it's closed between noon and two for siesta. I can fix the shoe for you."

Helen didn't want to give her shoe to a stranger.

"No, thank you." She took the shoe. She was about to limp away, when he stopped her.

"Are you sure?" he asked. "This is Italy. Sometimes the siesta lasts longer."

"Quite sure." She nodded. "Thank you for your help."

Helen studied the menu at the trattoria. The other tables were filled with couples eating steamed mussels and drinking Campari. She imagined what it would be like to be in Portofino with Edgar. They'd rent a little car and explore the different beaches to go swimming. At night, they'd get dressed up and have dinner on the villa's patio. Edgar would put a record on the phonograph, and they'd dance under the stars. Then they'd go to their room and make love with the breeze wafting through the open shutters.

She couldn't let herself think about Edgar.

"I'll have the linguini, and a salad with mozzarella," Helen said to the waiter.

"You can get linguini anywhere in Italy. The best mozzarella is in the south, in Naples," the waiter responded. "May I suggest the *trofie el pesto*. It's a pasta only found on the Ligurian Coast. And you must try the Ligurian flatbread. It was invented in the thirteenth century when a ship on its way to Genoa was shipwrecked. The only thing the sailors had to eat was chickpeas and flour mixed with seawater. They put it in the sun to dry out, and it was delicious."

The voice sounded familiar. She glanced up at the waiter.

"You're the man who wanted to fix my sandal."

"My name is Lorenzo." He made a small bow. "If you give me the sandal, it will be ready by the time you finish your meal."

"I'm Helen. You said the shoe repair closes for the siesta."

He smiled at her. Helen noticed his teeth were very white.

"The shoe repair is owned by my uncle. He's in the back of the trattoria, eating his lunch. He won't mind; he needs the extra money."

"Your uncle owns the shoe repair shop?"

"My other uncle and aunt own this trattoria, and my cousin has a souvenir shop," he explained. "My family has been in Portofino for a hundred years. They're very happy about the new tourists."

Helen had to laugh. It reminded her of her family's deep roots in Philadelphia.

"All right." She handed him the sandal. "Tell your uncle I'll pay him extra to work through lunch. And I'll take your advice and try the *trofie el pesto*."

After lunch, Helen put on her repaired sandal and strolled along the waterfront. She bought postcards and a bottle of eau de cologne for Daisy. She still felt terrible about their argument after breakfast. Perhaps she could mend things by giving her a small present. And she wanted Daisy to have something pretty for herself.

Later in the day, Helen took her book out to the villa's patio. The other guests were in their rooms, getting ready for dinner. A table was set up with a pitcher of lemonade and a bowl of grapes.

A taxi pulled into the driveway. The passengers stepped out and entered the villa. The taxi driver walked over to her. She recognized him—it was Lorenzo.

"Don't tell me you have another uncle who owns the taxi company," Helen said with a laugh.

"My neighbor owns the taxi company. I drive for him occasionally."

"Is there any business in town that your family isn't involved in?" It was nice to talk to someone. The only other hotel guests were a young couple on their honeymoon and two older women traveling together.

"A new restaurant opened on the piazza. The owner is from Florence." He looked at Helen. "Would you dine there with me tonight?"

Helen shook her head. "I'm sorry, I'm busy."

Lorenzo glanced at Helen's book.

"You don't look busy. My uncle is worried that it will be competition for the trattoria. If you are with me, we can try more dishes."

It was a lovely evening; the air smelled of lemons. And she was tired of eating alone.

"All right." She put down her book. "Let me go up and change."

The restaurant was named Raphael's. It was wedged between a bakery and a dress shop. Inside, a fishing net hung from the ceiling. The walls were lined with wine racks, and a painting of Portofino hung above the cash register.

Lorenzo ordered a bottle of Chianti and several dishes and told her about his family. His father was a fisherman; his mother worked at the Hotel Splendido. Helen had seen it on one of her walks. It sat high above Portofino and had a swimming pool and a tennis court. All the film stars stayed there. The previous week, Charlie Chaplin and Lionel Barrymore occupied suites on the same floor.

Lorenzo was saving money to buy the trattoria from his uncle.

"I couldn't be a fisherman like my father—I get seasick. My uncle is teaching me to cook—he makes the best *fritello di baccalla*—Italian fritters made with salted codfish—in Portofino."

Helen told him about Dumfries and the farm. All she ever wanted was to have her own dairy company.

"Then you have to try *focaccia di Recco con frammagio*." Lorenzo handed her a plate of flatbread filled with melted cheese.

The focaccia was famous—it was made in the neighboring town of Recco. The cheese was called *stracchino*, and it came from cows that lived in the Italian Alps.

"*Strach* means 'tired.' The cows get tired from being led up and down the Alps to graze, and tired cows produce richer milk."

The cheese was thick and tangy, but Helen thought Ayrshire cows' milk was creamier.

"You know so much about Portofino, you could be a historian," Helen said with a smile. For the first time since she arrived, she was enjoying herself. "I thought all Italians wanted to travel."

Lorenzo shrugged. "One of my cousins moved to Athens, and another wants to go to America, but I love it here." He waved out the window.

Outside, the stars glinted on the bay. The moon was silver-white, like the inside of an oyster shell.

"Why would I want to leave," Lorenzo said, "when I live under a sky with so many stars?"

When Helen arrived back at the villa, Daisy was dusting the furniture.

"I brought you some milk candy." Helen handed her a little package.

"You didn't need to get me anything," Daisy said stiffly. "I can afford to buy my own candy."

"I want to do something for you." Helen told her about her dinner with Lorenzo. "You were right this morning about Portofino. I can see why you want to stay. The people are so friendly, and I've never been anywhere so beautiful."

Daisy put down her dusting rag. Her expression was tentative.

"Sometimes, I'm so happy, I have to pinch myself. I stand at my window, and can't believe I'm looking out at the Mediterranean."

"I apologize for telling you how to live your life. I still think you're making a mistake, giving up everything on the Main Line. But we're sisters, and nothing is more important than family. I don't want to fight anymore," Helen said. "There's so much I want to tell you. I've made my own mistakes, and some of them I don't know how to fix."

Helen finally let it all come out. She told Daisy about seeing Edgar and Sophie kiss. About Charleston Farmhouse, and Duncan and Jack and Vanessa. The terrible scene in Louis Renault's suite, and Duncan taking sleeping powder and ending up in the hospital.

The only thing Helen was sure of was that she and Edgar had to get divorced.

"Edgar didn't do anything wrong with Sophie." Daisy frowned. "Perhaps he deserves another chance."

The hair on the back of Helen's neck prickled.

"He still lied and gambled. Even if she kissed him, he put himself in that position by going to her room. Anyway, it's no use. Edgar and I should never have gotten married. We'd find another reason to want to kill each other. I'm better off alone." She shook her head. "What if Edgar or Jack had been injured? And there are other things I'm ashamed of."

Helen told her about finding out that Jack preferred men.

"All those years, Jack felt like he had to pretend in front of us. I feel terrible that he didn't trust me enough to tell me the truth."

"We were young, we wouldn't have understood," Daisy said. "Jack told me when he was here. I'm sure he was going to tell you too."

Helen's head jerked up.

"He told you?"

"Roland and I saw him having dinner with a young man in the piazza." Daisy nodded. "He introduced us, and we had drinks together."

The air left Helen's lungs. Jack had trusted Daisy enough to show her who he really was. It hadn't been Jack who told Helen; it was Vanessa. Would Jack have said anything if Vanessa hadn't already told her about him and Duncan?

"Does anyone else know?" Helen asked.

"Mother has always known, and Jack's friends in New York."

"She never said anything," Helen said in disbelief.

"It wasn't her place to tell us." Daisy shrugged. "It doesn't matter now."

Helen had accused her mother and Daisy of behaving as if it were the nineteenth century when it came to men. But it was Helen who had acted as if she were in a Victorian novel. She told herself that she didn't care whom Jack fell in love with—the important thing was that he was happy. She would ask him more questions the next time she saw him.

About the first boy he had fallen in love with, and whether there was anyone in Philadelphia or New York. They were both adults, and Helen had been married. She knew all about sex. She'd be open to whatever he wanted to tell her and show him that she was deserving of his trust.

It had been foolish to come to Portofino. Helen wasn't like the other tourists, who sipped Campari at lunch and licked gelato cones while they walked. She'd never get tipsy in the middle of the day or risk getting ice cream on her blouse. The only person she'd ever be was Helen Hope Montgomery, the Philadelphia princess that Edgar wrote about in the piece in the *New Yorker*.

"What are you going to do?" Daisy asked.

She recalled nights sitting by the swimming pool at Dumfries, gazing up at the stars. Days spent riding and feeding the cows in the barn. The rustle of evening gowns at her parents' garden parties. Portofino might be the right place for Daisy and Roland, and for Lorenzo. And Jack might be happy painting landscapes in Greece. But Helen belonged on the Main Line. Maybe there, she could begin to make changes in herself and become the person she wanted to be.

"Do you remember when our parents brought me home from Foxcroft?" Helen asked Daisy. "I was so embarrassed. You'd know that I left because none of the girls wanted to be my friend."

"You tried to slink into your bedroom without saying hello," Daisy recalled. "But I'd been waiting at the window for ages."

Daisy had decorated Helen's room with balloons. There was a WELCOME HOME sign in the entry, and the staircase was covered by a red carpet.

"I had never been so happy to be home, with Mother always on the telephone in the living room and the delicious smells coming from the kitchen," Helen reflected.

She walked over to Daisy and gave her a hug. It felt good to put her arms around her sister.

"I'm going home. I belong at Dumfries. The only thing I wish is that you were going with me."

Chapter Eighteen

The Main Line, Philadelphia, August 1928

Helen arrived home at the beginning of August. She moved into the pool house behind the swimming pool. It was only one large room with a kitchenette, but she enjoyed the separation from the main house. She decorated it with a black-and-pink sofa she had purchased with Daisy at Syrie Maugham's furniture salon in New York. There was a Lucite desk where she kept her paperwork, and an art decor mirror shaped like a fan.

Edgar had taught her how to cook in Sussex, and she could prepare roast chicken and pots of spaghetti. She made her own porridge and coffee in the mornings before she went to the farm. It made her feel grown-up and independent.

Her parents had canceled their holiday to the South of France. Instead, her father was in South America, looking into investment opportunities for his clients. When her mother first told her, Helen was angry. It was an excuse for Robert to be away and become involved with another woman. But she read in the newspapers how American businessmen were making a fortune investing in gold and silver mines. She couldn't help but be proud of him. Instead of relying on the financial strategies used by his father and grandfather, he was trying something new.

And it was easier not having him at Dumfries. After everything that happened with Edgar and Sophie, she believed even more strongly in the importance of fidelity in marriage, and she still wasn't ready to forgive him.

With her father away, Helen and Charlotte spent more time together. Charlotte had learned to drive—she was a much better driver than Helen. She promised to teach her, but they were both so busy. Helen accompanied Charlotte to the Children's Aid Society and the New Century Club. Helen met with Thomas Danforth at the creamery and visited other dairy farms.

Jack was still in Greece. He had met someone and was going to spend the autumn there. Helen was at her happiest when she received his postcards, with their references to a man named Christos. She wondered what he looked like and whether Jack was in love. The important thing was that Jack felt comfortable enough to write his name on the postcard.

Helen sold the silverware set that she and Edgar had received as a wedding present and started a scholarship for girls at Foxcroft School. The remaining money she used to buy cows. She even sent a check to Lorenzo to help him buy his uncle's trattoria. She debated writing to Edgar in Paris and telling him, but the silverware had just been sitting there. If he had any problem with it, they'd work it out during the divorce proceedings.

Helen wrote to Daisy often. She kept her letters light—little stories about the new cows and a shopping trip that Helen and their mother took to Bergdorf Goodman in New York. She often included a bottle of perfume or a pretty scarf. Daisy didn't always reply right away. When she did, the letters were short—the hotel was almost fully booked for the summer, and the girl they hired to clean the rooms had quit. Helen opened each envelope eagerly and kept them in a box on her desk.

This evening, Helen was attending a garden party at Whitewood Hall. It was a fundraiser for one of April's charities. Tables were covered with black-and-silver tablecloths. There were tall vases of long-stemmed red roses and giant urns filled with dahlias. A bar was set up by the swimming pool, and there was a stage for an orchestra.

Helen stood on the terrace, holding a Tom Collins. It was her third cocktail for the evening, but she couldn't face making light conversation without something to drink. April walked toward her. She looked very pretty in a red Florrie Westwood evening gown and gold sandals.

"Everything looks so beautiful," Helen greeted April. "I can't believe you decorated the lawn yourself."

"I love throwing parties. I'm thinking about becoming an event planner. I'll be like Madame de Pompadour at King Louis XV's court," April said merrily. "She arranged parties for Marie Antoinette with costumes and themes and entertainment."

"Your clients would be lucky to have you," Helen said with a smile.

Since Helen returned from Portofino, she and April spent a lot of time together. April had known Jack for so long, she had known about his love affairs. It was only with April that Helen could admit she felt she had failed Jack. She was trying to become someone that he would be proud of.

April went to greet the other guests. Helen noticed a man in his late twenties crossing the lawn toward her. He wore one of the new tuxedo jackets over a soft collared shirt. A silver watch gleamed at his wrist, and he wasn't wearing a top hat. He had light brown hair and blue eyes.

"George Kitteridge." He held out his hand. "Can I offer you my plate of hors d'oeuvres?"

"No, thank you," Helen replied.

"I just moved to the Main Line." He picked up a deviled egg. "I must say, I never thought that a plate of deviled eggs and oysters could set me back twenty dollars."

"If you're referring to the cost of the fundraiser, it's for a good cause," Helen said.

"I'm a big believer in supporting charities," George agreed. "In fact, I wrote April a check for fifty dollars."

"Well, you did really want to come." She arched her eyebrows.

"I had to." He looked at her levelly. "I wanted to meet you."

Helen gulped her Tom Collins. She wasn't ready to talk to men. But the fundraiser was important to April, and she wanted to be polite.

"I read that piece about you in the *New Yorker*. 'The Philadelphia Princess,'" George continued. "You like to ride, and you're good at games, and you're an excellent swimmer."

"That piece was written ages ago. What if I've changed?"

George shook his head. "People don't change."

Helen's mind went to her father and Edgar. "I suppose not. Well, then, now that you've found me, what do you plan to do?"

"Ask you to dinner, of course. Isn't that what most men do when they want a first date?"

Helen had only been trying to make conversation. She didn't expect him to take her seriously. "Why would I go to dinner with you? I don't know anything about you except your name."

"I can think of a number of reasons." He ticked them off his fingers. "I own one of the largest construction companies in Philadelphia. I just bought the Duponts' estate in Radnor, and I'm building a summer home in Newport. I like rowing, and I'm quite fond of art."

There was something about the way he carried himself and how he dressed that made Helen think he would be different from other men. But he sounded like all the boys she had grown up with.

"Let me guess, you inherited the construction company from your father. The Vanderbilts told you which piece of land to buy in Newport because your families have been close for years. You learned to row at Harvard or possibly Princeton, and you studied art during a semester in Florence."

George sipped his Tom Collins.

"My father was Irish. He was one of eight children; four of them died in childhood. He never went to school; he started working in a shipyard when he was twelve."

George continued his story. When he was a boy, he often went with his father to the shipyard. He built his own rowboat and learned to row on the Delaware River. His father died when he was fifteen, and George worked as a bricklayer. He spent any free time rowing and made the 1920 US Olympic team. He won two silver medals but he still didn't have any money, so he returned to Philadelphia and worked for a construction company. He put his wages back into his own projects and built his company from scratch.

"I never wanted to go to the Olympics to begin with—there was no money in it," George reflected. "I applied to race at the Henley Royal Regatta in England. It's the most prestigious event in rowing. My application was accepted, and I spent the rest of my money on my ticket. At the last minute, they rejected me." His brow furrowed. "They said it was a scheduling problem, but the real reason was they found out that I had done manual labor. The regatta only accepts gentlemen."

"I'm sure that's not the reason," Helen said.

George kept talking. "I used the boat ticket to go to Antwerp and compete in the Olympics instead. I still row on the weekends. I'll take you out on my boat sometime."

"You're very presumptuous, Mr. Kitteridge." She nursed her glass. "What makes you think I'll go anywhere with you?"

George looked at her for a long time. His eyes seemed even bluer, like the center of a topaz.

"Please call me George. Two reasons. The first is your husband. He made such a mess of your marriage, you wonder if you can ever trust a man again."

"How do you know anything about my marriage?" Helen interjected.

"My lawyer works at the Philadelphia office of the firm that is handling your divorce. I heard him talking on the phone. Don't worry, I would never say anything to anyone."

"I still don't see what that has to do with you."

"Someone has to show you that all men aren't lazy and arrogant and impossible to live with," he said. "I've been working since I was a kid. I'm the perfect candidate."

"How do you know my husband was those things?"

George swallowed his deviled egg. His mouth crinkled up at the corners.

"You named them in the divorce proceedings."

Helen didn't want the lawyer to write that Edgar had been unfaithful, but she had to tell him something in order to get the divorce.

Compared to husbands who worked at an office from eight to five, Edgar did seem lazy. And he could be arrogant about his work. But she knew that wasn't quite true. He was only arrogant about his work when he was defending it to himself. Edgar was usually the one who made dinner and did the dishes. And how many nights had he sat at the typewriter long after she went to bed?

The only part that was accurate was that they couldn't get along. She wondered why she still missed him.

"Well, I'm not looking for a replacement," Helen said to George. "It was nice to talk to you, but April needs me."

After dinner and dancing, the party moved to the ballroom. Rows of chairs were assembled in the middle of the floor. A small podium stood next to the window.

April stood at the podium and addressed the guests.

"Thank you all for coming," she began. "The Philadelphia Orphan Society wouldn't exist without your donations. Tonight, I'm making it easier for people to write their checks. It isn't with more whiskey or a faster pen." April's hazel eyes danced. "Instead, we're auctioning some of the paintings of Jack Tyler." She searched the crowd. "Now, who will be the first bidder?"

It had been Helen's idea to auction the paintings that Jack had given her over the years. He was so talented, his work deserved to be displayed in the living rooms of important collectors on the Main Line. When she wrote to him and told him her idea, he had agreed. Now, seeing the still lifes with Jack's scrawled signature, she missed him even more. If he were there, he and Helen and April would have gone to the Warwick Hotel afterward to celebrate the money that was raised. She slipped out of the ballroom and walked to the driveway.

Helen didn't trust herself to drive at night, so she had asked the Dumfries's chauffeur to wait for her.

She climbed into the back of the car. "Home please, Donald."

~

201

The next morning, she sat at her desk in the pool house, going over the farm's expenses.

"I have a delivery for you, Mrs. Scott." A young man stood at the door.

Helen wondered if the man she met at the fundraiser had sent flowers.

"Thank you. Please leave them on the table," she said without looking up.

"They're too big for the table. They're almost too big for this room."

Helen put down her pen. "I don't understand."

The man turned to the door and grinned. "Wait here, you'll see."

A few minutes later, he returned with a dozen paintings in gold frames.

"Where did these come from?" she asked in shock. They were the paintings from the auction.

"There was no card." He glanced around the room. "Whoever sent them has never been here. You're going to need more walls."

Helen was so surprised, she couldn't return to work. She tried calling April, but there was no answer. An hour later, her phone rang.

She snatched it up. "This is Helen."

"George Kitteridge," the voice came over the line. "I wonder if you got my delivery."

Helen paced up and down with the receiver. "I don't know if this is some kind of joke, Mr. Kitteridge. If I wanted Jack's paintings, I would have kept them. Now, please ask the deliveryman to return them to Whitewood Hall."

"Why would I do that?"

"You obviously convinced April not to sell them. Well, for your information, I gave the sale a lot of thought. The Philadelphia Orphan Society is one of my uncle's favorite charities. He wants them to have the money."

"Of course I bought them," George insisted. "You can see my checkbook."

"You bought all of them?" Helen gasped.

"Isn't that the point of holding an auction?"

There had been over fifty people at the fundraiser. To outbid them all, George must have spent a fortune.

"You'll have to give some of them back to April. I'm sure she'll return your check," Helen said impatiently. "I live in the pool house of my parents' estate. There isn't room on the walls."

George was silent for a moment.

"I have a better idea. Are you free for lunch?"

"What does lunch have to do with this?"

"You'll see. I'll pick you up in thirty minutes."

George pulled up in a late-model Chrysler convertible. It had white wheels and a jump seat in the back.

"My other car is bigger, but this one will do," he said, appraising the framed pictures spread around the pool house.

"This one will do for what? And why do you own two cars?" Helen asked.

She didn't know anyone with two cars. Even her father and mother shared the car with the Dumfries chauffeur.

"I can't drive a shiny yellow convertible to a construction site. What will my workers think?"

On the drive, George told her about the estate he bought in Radnor. He was remodeling the grounds. There would be an indoor tennis court and an Olympic-size swimming pool.

"Physical fitness is important for mental health," George said. "I learned that when I was a boy. Whenever I felt frustrated or unhappy, I'd go out and row. A few laps on the river and I'd feel better."

The car stopped in front of a building in Germantown. The street contained a few dilapidated mansions separated by paddocks. Helen had never been to that part of Philadelphia. It was on the outskirts of the city, far from the fashionable areas like Rittenhouse Square.

"Where are we having lunch?" Helen glanced around for a restaurant.

"That's the funny thing about wealthy people," George reflected. He picked up the paintings. "They never see the places where they send their money. This is the Philadelphia Private Orphanage."

George had decided that the best place to hang the paintings was the orphanage where the children could appreciate them. Helen agreed it was a wonderful idea.

"How did you know about this place?" Helen asked, after George had given the paintings to the woman in charge.

"My mother told me about it," George said.

The rooms were dark and old-fashioned. There was an odd smell, like mothballs mixed with laundry soap.

"Does she volunteer here?"

George paused. "No, she lived here until she was sixteen."

George's mother lost her parents to smallpox. She was treated quite well at the orphanage, but when she was eleven, she was sent out to work as a laundress. She attended school only a few weeks a year. At the age of sixteen, she took the bit of money she had saved and enrolled in secretarial school.

"Then she married my father and had me and my three younger sisters," George continued. "After my father died, she went back to work in an office. But every night she was home to give us dinner and supervise our homework."

"She must be quite something," Helen said in awe.

They entered a room with two long tables.

"Being raised at the orphanage taught her that you get out of life what you put into it." George's tone was serious. "I apply that to my construction company. I work as many hours as my laborers. And I'd never send them to do a job that I wouldn't feel safe doing myself."

George pulled out a chair for Helen and sat opposite her.

"I'm glad you brought me here," Helen said. "And I'm sorry for anything I said earlier. You're doing a wonderful thing. I'm happy to be a part of it."

The somber look in George's eyes disappeared.

"That's what impressed me in the piece in the *New Yorker*. Helen Hope Montgomery is a Philadelphia princess because of the acts of kindness she does for others. Buying a puppy for the stable hand or giving small presents to the maid and the cook at Dumfries," George quoted from Edgar's article.

Helen was surprised that he remembered the article so clearly. It had appeared in the *New Yorker* nearly a year ago.

She changed the subject. "You still haven't told me where we're having lunch."

The door to the garden opened. A group of children ran into the room.

"Right here in the cafeteria," he said, introducing the children. "This is Paul and Joan and Jeremy."

Helen learned from the children that George was a regular visitor. He often took them out for ice cream, and on weekends he coached the boys in baseball.

After lunch, they drove back to the Main Line. George pulled up in front of Dumfries. He opened Helen's car door and walked with her to the pool house.

"I had a wonderful time," Helen said.

"You were a hit." George nodded. "Joan wants to wear her hair the way you have yours. And Paul wants you to teach him how to swim."

Perhaps Helen could do more for the children. Bring them to the farm and show them how to make butter. Hire an art teacher and encourage talented girls to apply for the scholarship to Foxcroft School.

George had inspired her. He would know what the children loved to do.

Helen took the key out of her purse. "I was wondering if you'd still like to have dinner with me."

George slipped his hands in his pockets. He whistled a short tune. "I was hoping you'd ask. There's nothing I'd like more."

Chapter Nineteen

Helen spent the next month preparing her first order of butter and cheese for Mr. Danforth. She still needed a loan to buy modern equipment, but she had enough saved to create the first shipment. Seeing the butter wrapped in wax paper stamped with Dumfries' logo—a cow with a large D—was one of Helen's happiest moments.

And she went out to dinner several times with George. He was the most considerate man she'd ever met. Before every date, he sent the menu of the restaurant to make sure she approved. The first time, when she received the dinner menu from a French restaurant that was impossible to get a reservation for, she called George in disbelief.

The chef, Luc, was a friend of George's. They'd met during a summer when George worked at the docks. George gave Luc money to find a place to stay. Now Luc was one of the most celebrated chefs in Philadelphia, and he never forgot George's kindness.

It was the same everywhere they went. At the Warwick Hotel, the orchestra played all George's favorite songs. When Helen asked why, George explained that he lent money to the trumpet player so he could get his trumpet out of a pawnshop. They were treated to drinks at a nightclub on South Broad Street. George had financed the nightclub himself because he didn't want his friend becoming involved with the Mafia.

Sometimes, Helen accompanied George to the charities he supported. He donated shoes to Saint Joseph's House for Homeless, Industrious Boys. The boys had beds and enough to eat, but they were always growing out of their shoes. Another day, they visited the Home for Training Girls in Housewifery and Sewing. Afterward, they sat in George's convertible and talked about the girls Helen met. It was wonderful that the girls were taught domestic skills, but George believed they should be taught to do things that could lead to a proper profession.

Today she was going to speak to the bank manager, Mr. Fairbanks, about a loan. First, she was meeting George for lunch at Wanamaker's. He had something to discuss with her. She wondered if he was going to say that he had feelings for her.

"There you are," George greeted her at the entrance of the restaurant. "We're already sitting in the booth."

George hadn't mentioned they were dining with anyone.

A woman of about fifty sat at the table. She had faded blonde hair and George's blue eyes. She wore a blue crepe suit with white gloves. A gold brooch was fastened to her collar, and she wore a cloche hat.

"You must be Helen." The woman held out her hand. "I'm Alice, George's mother. George told me so much about you, I feel as if we've already met."

George never said they were going to have lunch with his mother.

"I mentioned that I was meeting you today." George turned to Helen. "Mother insisted she join us. I hope you don't mind."

"It's wonderful," Helen said to Alice. "George told me everything about you too."

"George is so good to me," Alice gushed. "I never owned a brooch before." She pointed to the piece of jewelry. "And my only gloves were the ones I knitted myself."

"Mother and I did a little shopping this morning," George admitted. He picked up the menu. "What shall we eat?"

George ordered tomato soup and club sandwiches for the table. They talked about Helen's dairy products and the house George was building in Newport.

"George loves real estate. He says why would anyone keep their wealth in a safe deposit box when it can be used to build apartments that families can live in," Alice reflected. "He has so many wonderful ideas. I'm glad he's running for office. Now many people will benefit from them."

Helen glanced at George in surprise.

"George never said anything about going into politics."

"That's because there's nothing yet to say," George said. He was obviously embarrassed.

"Of course there is." Alice tasted her soup. "He's going to announce his candidacy for state congressman next month."

Helen didn't know anyone in politics. It wasn't the kind of thing that boys who grew up on the Main Line did. Politicians had their photos in the tabloid newspapers, and people offered them money and gifts in exchange for favors.

"I've been passionate about politics for years." George buttered a bread roll. "Nothing is going to change until someone changes it."

George wanted to create a law that prevented orphans from being sent to work at a young age. He promised the orphanage that he'd hire any boy who wanted a job, as long as he attended school until he was eighteen. And he wanted to pass a law that demanded equal pay for men and women doing the same job.

George didn't want to be a politician for the money and the fame. He truly wanted to help people.

"Last year, George and I visited the Lincoln Memorial in Washington," Alice said. "Lincoln's statue is eighteen feet tall. In real life, Lincoln was six foot four inches, one inch taller than George. I told George it's not a man's height that casts the longest shadow, it's what he does with his life. Lincoln believed in freedom and dignity for all people. I raised George to be the same."

After lunch, Alice left to do more shopping. Helen and George sat at the table, finishing their coffee.

"Your mother is lovely," Helen commented.

"She talks about me too much." George chuckled. "I suppose all mothers are the same."

Helen changed the subject. "You wanted to discuss something?"

"It's about the Radnor Hunt next month."

Helen guessed that George wanted her to sponsor his membership to the hunt club. It was almost impossible to become a member unless one was related to the founders.

She busied herself with her coffee cup so George wouldn't see her expression. She had thought he was interested in her as a woman, but he only wanted her connections. She didn't know why it bothered her. The Radnor Hunt needed bright young men like George.

"I can write to my father in South America," Helen suggested. "He's good friends with William Leverton on the board."

"I'm already a member," George cut in. "I helped Horace Hare build the new racetrack."

Horace Hare was the club's Master and Huntsman of Radnor. He had spearheaded a committee to build a new racetrack in Chesterbrook.

"Then what did you want to talk about?"

George glanced up from his cup.

"I don't know how to ride a horse."

Helen almost burst out laughing. She didn't know anyone who couldn't ride a horse.

"I've been on a horse a few times. But after a couple of minutes, I fall off," George admitted. "I could hire an instructor, but I thought . . ." He looked at her, and there was something new in his eyes. "Well, I thought it would be a good way to spend more together . . . if you want to spend time together."

Helen's eyes met his. For the first time, she felt something stir inside her, like a pinprick when she was being fitted for a dress.

"I'd be happy to teach you to ride a horse."

~

Helen sat in Mr. Fairbanks's office. Her file lay on his desk.

He sat opposite her. "It's nice to see you again, Helen. I'm sorry about your divorce. Your finances are in order, and we'd be happy to extend a small loan." He collected the paperwork. "In fact, Edgar was here this morning."

Helen's eyes widened in astonishment. She hadn't known that Edgar was in Philadelphia.

"Edgar was at the bank?" she repeated.

"He cleared up his overdraft." Mr. Fairbanks pointed to a paperweight shaped like the Eiffel Tower. "He seemed in very good spirits. He gave me a paperweight from Paris to apologize for overdrawing his account."

Helen thought about the last time she had seen Edgar, at Vanessa's party at the Barrière Le Royal Hotel in Deauville. There had been circles under his eyes, he hadn't been eating, and his clothes hung on him. He couldn't have ended up with Sophie—Vanessa had written that Sophie and Tommy were engaged. She wondered if he'd met someone new in Paris.

"I'm glad Edgar's feeling well. That's the wonderful thing about him," Helen said darkly. She stood up and shook Mr. Fairbanks's hand. "Edgar always lands on his feet."

~

When Helen arrived at Dumfries, her mother was arranging flowers in the living room. Helen sat on the divan.

"Aren't these beautiful? Gardenias are my favorite." Charlotte set the vase on the coffee table. "You'll never guess who brought them."

Helen had a sinking feeling in her stomach. "I'll take a stab at it. It was Edgar."

Charlotte glanced at Helen in surprise. "How did you know? He arrived yesterday, from Paris. He gave me this Jean Patou scarf. It's from Patou's latest collection."

She wondered again why Edgar was there. It couldn't have anything to do with the divorce. Edgar had received the papers weeks ago.

"You shouldn't accept gifts from Edgar."

"Why not? Just because you two are fighting doesn't mean Edgar and I can't be friends."

Helen hadn't told her mother that she had seen Edgar kissing Sophie outside her hotel room. There didn't seem to be a point. Instead, she said that she had been innocently sitting in Louis's suite and Edgar burst in and got the wrong idea.

"We're not in a fight; we're getting a divorce," Helen reminded her.

Charlotte stepped back from the vase.

"Are you sure that's what you want? What you and Edgar went through was horrible, but it wasn't anyone's fault."

"The divorce isn't only because of what happened with Louis. It's because of everything." Helen sat on the sofa. "Edgar and I should never have gotten married."

Charlotte shook her head. "I disagree. You're both so strong-minded. Even though your father and I insisted you get married, you wouldn't have chosen Edgar unless you loved him. And he loves you." Her voice softened. "I saw it in his eyes on your wedding day."

"Perhaps he was looking into the sun," Helen snapped. "I don't want to talk about Edgar. He didn't tell me he was in Philadelphia, so he obviously didn't come home to see me."

"He did ask how you were," Charlotte said carefully. "I thought it would be nice to have him to dinner."

"Please tell me you didn't invite him without asking me!"

"Of course not," Charlotte said. "He's only here for a few days, then he's going back to Europe. He's meeting with publishers in New York about his book." She pointed to a bound set of papers. "It comes out in England next year. He brought me the manuscript in case I want to read it."

So, Edgar had finished his novel! There was a small tug at her heart. Edgar had worked so hard, it would have been wonderful to celebrate together. Perhaps she'd send him a note when it was published.

"Well, I'm glad you asked me first." Helen leaned against the cushions. "Anyway, I'm having dinner with George."

"You've been seeing a lot of George lately," Charlotte commented.

"You say that as if you don't approve. You must like George. He's handsome and charming, and he supports all the same charities." She looked at her mother archly. "Unless you're being a snob, and it's because of his upbringing."

"I do like George. I just wonder if you have enough in common," Charlotte answered. "Sometimes having the same upbringing makes things easier. Your father and I understand each other. It's as though we share a language. It's funny, I feel it even more since his affair. Perhaps it wouldn't have been so easy if we came from different backgrounds. As it is, it's been like slipping back into an old jacket that was kept in the garden shed."

Helen was shocked. Charlotte treated everyone who worked at Dumfries the same as the guests at her dinner parties. She taught Helen and Daisy to do the same. And Helen didn't believe that her mother was completely healed from her father's affair. It had to be difficult for Charlotte to be around him and not be reminded of Rosalee. Helen thought her mother had blossomed since Robert was in South America.

"That sounds like a snob to me," Helen remarked. "George can't help that his mother was raised in an orphanage and that he worked as a bricklayer. And you can't tell me that you haven't been happy while Father has been away."

"I have enjoyed your father being gone," Charlotte acknowledged. "I'm free to do the things I enjoy. But the point of being married and having children is caring for other people. Otherwise, life can become empty."

"Are you saying I need to get married?" Helen asked impatiently.

"I'm saying you should open yourself up to love." Charlotte went back to her flowers. "If you're falling in love with George, then I'm happy. If you aren't, there's no reason to be together."

Helen went to the kitchen for a glass of water. Inwardly, she was fuming. Edgar had a way of making trouble even when he wasn't there. She wondered what Edgar would think of George.

When she returned to the living room, her mother was gone. The manuscript lay on the table. She picked it up and took it to the pool house. Her mother wouldn't read it—she only liked romance novels. And Helen was curious. She had read the first dozen chapters so many times, she wanted to see how it ended.

~

The next morning, Helen went to Dumfries to borrow a bowl of sugar. She had stayed up most of the night reading Edgar's book. She went through an entire box of tissue. It was sure to be a bestseller.

Her mother appeared in the kitchen.

"There you are," Charlotte said. "Edgar was here earlier. He picked up a few things to take to Daisy."

"To take to Daisy?" Helen repeated.

"He's going to visit Daisy and Roland in Portofino. He wants to set his next novel in Italy."

"I'm glad he's on such good terms with everyone in the family," Helen said dryly. "I have to go. I'm meeting George to go riding."

"Edgar left something for you," Charlotte said. "It's in the driveway."

Edgar's Model T Ford was parked near the garage.

"He left me his car!" she exclaimed in disbelief.

"He wrote a note." Her mother handed her a piece of paper. "He was going to deliver it himself, but he didn't want to disturb you."

Helen unfolded the letter.

> Dear Helen,
> I thought you should have the car in the divorce. I'm sure you can find someone to teach you to drive it. Try not to run into any egg trucks. Once the eggs crack, no matter how hard you try, it's impossible to piece them back together.
> Edgar

Helen climbed into the driver's seat. She could call Edgar and thank him, but there wasn't a point. He was leaving in a few days.

She put the key in the ignition and turned on the engine. George would teach her how to drive.

Chapter Twenty

The next few weeks passed in a flurry of activity at the farm and teaching George how to ride.

She used the check from the bank to buy a new milking machine called the Surge Milker. It was more efficient than milking the cows by hand. And she bought a Babcock tester to measure the amount of butterfat in the milk from each cow. Nellie's milk was often the richest. Helen rewarded her by spending extra time brushing her back.

In the late afternoons, she and George met at the stables. The first time, Helen couldn't believe her eyes. George's outfit was obviously brand new. His Chester coat was made of the finest shantung silk. He wore gabardine jodhpurs, and his boots were Russian calf leather.

The members of the Radnor Hunt didn't buy their clothes at fine equestrian stores. Instead, they dug them out of their fathers' closets and wore the same breeches and boots for years. She didn't have the heart to say anything. George didn't have a father, and he was only trying to fit in.

Once she had taught him the most important thing—to show the horse that he trusted it—he became an excellent rider. She loved riding together through Dumfries's paddocks. A few times, they rode to the Merion Cricket Club for cocktails. The foliage was the golden-green of autumn, the leaves were a rust-colored orange. They sat on the club's veranda drinking gin rickeys, and Helen experienced a moment of complete happiness.

Most evenings, George took her to dinner and dancing. He taught her the Texas Tommy and the black bottom. One night, when she was quite drunk, she asked how he knew all the current dances. He admitted that he hired a dance instructor. Helen could tell that he was embarrassed, so she didn't mention it again.

On the weekends, they took long drives in the countryside. It was different from the drives she had taken with Edgar. She and Edgar never ran out of things to talk about. Even their silences felt complete. With George, they stayed on the same few subjects. When there was a pause, she desperately tried to fill it. She told herself that was normal. It would take a while to get to know each other.

They finally kissed at the end of an evening that started with cocktails at the Green Room bar of the Hotel Du Pont. From there, George had taken her to Dante & Luigi's for spaghetti Bolognese. After that they went dancing, and by the time George pulled up at Dumfries, Helen felt high from champagne.

George was too much of a gentleman to make a move. So she interrupted him midsentence and kissed him. He was so surprised, he pulled back. But then he wrapped his arms around her and kissed her. She was glad she had kissed him. It took away any awkwardness between them.

∼

Helen was in the pool house with April, choosing which dress to wear to the Radnor Hunt ball.

April held up a red Molyneux gown with a low-cut back. Helen had worn it to the casino in Deauville.

Helen shook her head. "I can't wear that—it's too risqué for the Main Line."

April raised her eyebrows. "You're not going to wear yards of white chiffon like some innocent debutante."

"There's nothing wrong with chiffon." Helen held up an ivory Norman Hartnell gown with a high collar.

"You're giving George the wrong signals," April reflected. "He's not going to propose if he thinks you want to become a nun."

Helen turned to April in surprise.

"Who says I want George to propose?"

"You're always together." April made a mock pout. "I'm beginning to feel neglected."

She had been spending all her time with George. At first, it was because she somehow felt protective of him. He was trying so hard to fit in to local society. But the more time they spent together, the more she believed in what he was doing. He had announced his run for state congress, and he had so many wonderful ideas.

"At least George isn't like most young men on the Main Line, who either take over their grandfather's businesses or think they can have a career in the arts."

April glanced at Helen. "Don't tell me you still think about Edgar."

"Of course not. I'm glad Edgar can devote his life to writing." She shook her head. "But George has so many plans. He's building afford-able housing so the poor won't have to live in tenements. And he's fund-ing a program to provide childcare for children up to the age of twelve."

"That all sounds noble, but are you in love with him?"

"You sound like my mother. I'm not ready to fall in love."

Helen didn't want to live in the pool house forever, and she didn't want to end up alone. Someday, she wanted a husband and children.

"How about sex? Marriage has to include good sex."

"I'm not interested in sex." Helen blushed.

"Everyone is interested in sex," April replied. "Don't tell anyone, but I have a lover."

Helen gasped. "Why didn't you tell me?"

"At first, it was too soon after Alistair died." April shrugged. "Then I didn't think you'd approve."

"Don't tell me he's married!" As much as Helen adored April, she couldn't stay friends with her if she was involved with a married man.

"Of course not. I'd never hurt anyone." April fiddled with her necklace. "His family doesn't know about me. He's a Quaker."

There were many Quaker communities in the Lehigh Valley. Quakers weren't allowed to marry outside their faith.

"Our relationship is perfect for us. Ethan is an artist; he doesn't want children. And I've already started my event planning business. Margaret Coe hired me to plan her Halloween ball." April took a green Paul Poiret gown from the closet. "At least wear this one. And when George proposes, you have to let me plan the wedding."

George arrived with a pink orchid corsage for Helen and a bunch of tulips for her mother. He wore the traditional black tie and tails and a top hat with a black silk sash.

He adjusted the hat's brim. "My tailor suggested the top hat. He thinks it looks very debonair."

"I didn't know you had a tailor," Helen remarked.

The men of her father's generation still used tailors, but many young men bought their clothes at department stores. Edgar refused to go to a tailor. He said standing around while someone took his measurements with a piece of white chalk was a terrible waste of time.

"I never had a tailor before," George explained. "But I need one if I want to get elected."

Helen didn't say anything, but it seemed strange. George was running for office because he wanted to see change.

"I even sold my watch and bought this one instead." He showed her the Piaget watch on his wrist. "Horace Hare wears the same watch. He inherited his from his father."

~

Helen stood on the terrace at the Radnor Hunt clubhouse. The night was cool, and a fur stole was draped around her shoulders. It had been a successful evening for George. Howard Pew invited him to tour his stables, and Edward Beale and his wife asked George and Helen to make up a tennis foursome. Helen had to smile at George's enthusiasm. Each time a member introduced himself, George shook his hand as if he were meeting the US president.

George joined her at the railing. He handed her a glass of champagne.

"Andrew Mellon asked me to play squash at his private club." George couldn't keep the excitement out of his voice.

Andrew Mellon was one of the wealthiest financiers in the country. He was serving his third term as secretary of the Treasury.

"Anyone Andrew Mellon supports is bound to get elected." He glanced at Helen. "I knew from the moment we met that you and I would make a wonderful team."

Helen sipped her champagne. "I don't know what you mean."

"With your pedigree and my ideas, we can go all the way to the White House." His eyes were bright as fireflies. "Not immediately, of course. I wouldn't mind living abroad. Perhaps he'd recommend me to be the American ambassador in London. You already know people there. We'd live in Mayfair and throw grand dinner parties."

Helen gave a small smile. She pictured Vanessa and Duncan showing up at an elegant dinner party dressed in their hand-painted clothes and hats.

"Is that why you want to spend time with me?" Helen wondered. "Because of my wealth and my mother's family tree?"

"That's one reason," George said matter-of-factly. "There's nothing wrong with that. It makes you who you are."

Helen turned to George curiously. "And who am I?"

"You're a young woman who's never had to think twice about how the rack of lamb or lobster bisque ends up on her plate," George continued. "That isn't a crime. In fact, it's the reverse. Money and pedigree free you up to achieve the important things: going after your own dreams, and making the world a better place for others."

"I hadn't thought about it like that," Helen said. She turned George's words over in her mind. She remembered her fights with Edgar. "Some people think I'm spoiled."

"Well, I don't agree. The children at the orphanage loved you, and I've seen how kind you are to the gardeners and the stable hands. I wouldn't ask you the next question, if all you cared about were pretty dresses and shopping."

"What question?" Helen asked.

Helen thought she knew what George was going to say. She had been ready to turn him down. It was too soon after her divorce. They should get to know each other better. But George's words inspired her. As long as she had the farm and her dairy products, she was happy to help George pursue his career.

George took a velvet box out of his trouser pocket.

"Many men want their bachelor days to last forever, but I've been waiting for this moment since I was a boy." He took Helen's hand. "Helen, you're everything I could ask for in a woman. Would you do me the honor of becoming my wife?"

Inside the box was a large emerald, flanked by two diamonds.

"I had it made at Harry Winston." George took out the ring. "Your father told me that you love emeralds."

"My father!" Helen's eyes darted up from the ring.

"I had to call and ask his approval," George said. "I told him I'd pay for the wedding. We can hold it at Fox Hill Manor at Thanksgiving. It will be an excellent time for the local constituents to see it."

Helen didn't need her father's approval. She didn't even know if she wanted a proper wedding. It would be better to get married in front of a judge, followed by a family luncheon.

"It's too soon for a big wedding. We should wait until next summer."

"We'll be campaigning next summer," George urged. He paused before adding, "And you can't expect me to wait that long. I'm in love with you. I want to be married now."

She wondered if Jack would like George. Jack was so carefree and easygoing, it was hard to imagine them together. She had written and told him about George, but it was difficult to put her feelings in a letter. Jack had decided to stay in Greece for a couple more months, so there wasn't time to get his opinion.

Jack and George were so different. Jack never had to worry about money. Having George around would be good for all of them. Her mother would stop being a snob, and George might even encourage her father to be faithful. George was honorable; he would never cheat on his wife.

"You're in love with me?" Helen gulped.

George hadn't said anything about love before.

"Of course I am." He squeezed her hand. "I'd never propose if I wasn't. You make me feel like I can do anything. Think how much we can accomplish together."

Helen felt her excuses slip away. "I suppose we could get married this Thanksgiving."

George slipped the ring on her finger. He leaned forward and kissed her.

"I knew you'd say yes." He placed her hand on his arm. "Let's go inside and tell everyone."

~

A week later, Helen and George sat in the living room at Dumfries, going over the wedding plans. She couldn't believe they were getting married in less than two months. Whenever she was going to say they weren't ready, or she was going to be busy at the farm, or George was launching his campaign, she stopped herself. It was best to let George handle things. He was so clear about their future.

Helen's mother wanted the wedding to be at Dumfries. She and George finally compromised. The ceremony would be at the church in Villanova, and the reception would be held at Dumfries. The night before, there would be a pre-wedding ball at Fox Hill Manor. Helen wanted to say that guests would be hungover, so one party was enough. But she didn't have the heart to argue. She was fine with whatever they decided.

"I told April she could help with the decor," Helen said to George. "I'll be busy at the farm, and it's too much for my mother to do alone."

"I wanted to talk about that," George said. "It's better if you stopped working until after the election."

Helen almost dropped her coffee cup.

"You want me to stop working at the farm!"

"Only until I'm in office," he said. "I'm afraid the voters on the Main Line wouldn't approve. The wives might support women working, but they vote with their husbands. The men expect women to stay home and raise the children."

"We don't have children." Helen jumped up. She walked to the sideboard and picked up her cigarette case.

"And you should probably stop smoking, at least in public. It gives the wrong impression."

Helen put the cigarette case down. She had been trying to quit, but strangely since she started dating George, she had been smoking more.

"I can stop smoking, but I won't give up the farm."

George walked over to her. He placed his arms around her. "I know it's a lot to ask, but think how much good we'll do once I'm elected. You have years to grow the dairy business. It's only a few months."

George's request wasn't unreasonable. And he was right—most men on the Main Line, including her father, treated women's interests as if they were hobbies. But she couldn't stop now. The bank had given her a loan. Mr. Danforth was waiting for the next shipment.

"I don't think I can." She shook her head. "Maybe we should have a long engagement. Get married a year from Christmas instead."

A scowl crossed George's lips.

"You can't be serious!" he said. "We couldn't even travel on the campaign together. People might start to talk. They'll say that you only want to marry me if I win."

"That's absurd," Helen countered. She was about to argue, when her mother entered the room. Her eyes were wide, and she was clutching a piece of paper.

"I just received a cable from a hospital in Buenos Aires. Your father had a heart attack."

Helen gasped. She strode over to her mother and took the piece of paper.

"Is there a phone number that we can call?"

"Let me call." George took the paper from Helen. "I have a business associate in Buenos Aires. He'll be able to help."

George spent the next several hours on the phone, while Helen fed her mother cups of tea laced with bourbon.

Finally, George appeared in the doorway.

"Robert has been transferred to a private hospital. My friend Carlos went to see him. There's nothing to worry about. Robert is under the care of the most respected heart surgeon in Argentina."

"Will he be all right?" Charlotte asked urgently. Her cheeks were drawn, and her skin was the color of paper.

"The doctor assured me that he'll be as good as new in a few weeks," George promised. He turned to Helen with a smile. "I told your father that the wedding is scheduled for Thanksgiving. He said to tell you that he can't wait to dance the father and daughter dance."

Chapter Twenty-One

Helen's father arrived at Dumfries in early October. George insisted on paying for a nurse for the first month. By the beginning of November, he was much better. He still took most of his meals in the study, but he walked for half an hour each day and often joined Charlotte in the living room after dinner.

Helen returned the loan to the bank and told Mr. Danforth that the next shipment would be delayed until next summer. Writing the check to the bank was the hardest thing she had ever done. She told herself it was for the best. There wouldn't be time to work at the farm. Between planning the wedding and accompanying George to campaign events, she had never been busier.

But she couldn't give up the farm entirely. A few times, when George was preoccupied in the morning room where he had set up his campaign headquarters, Helen said she was going riding. She threw on a pair of breeches and boots and rode down to the barn instead. She brushed Essie's fur and cleaned Nellie's stall and mixed Clara's feed the way she liked it. Afterward, she stood against the barn door, smoking a cigarette, and wondered if she was doing the right thing.

She wondered what Jack would say if she told him that she was hiding things from George. She never had any secrets with Edgar. But Jack kept his own subterfuge for years. He sent a telegram from the RMS

Mauretania, saying that it would dock in Southampton the morning of the wedding. By then it would be too late to question her decision. Even now, the bridal flowers had been ordered, and she'd already had two dress fittings. Besides, she had given George her word.

The wedding was the following Saturday. The ceremony would be at the church in Villanova. Silver bows would festoon the pews, and there would be an arch decorated with pink and white chrysanthemums at the altar. After the ceremony, the guests would drive to Dumfries for the reception. Cocktails would be served in the living room, followed by dinner in the grand ballroom. There, the colors would be bolder than at the church. Long tables with teal tablecloths and black-and-white hexagon china. Peacock feathers in tinted vases, and a blue-and-gold-trimmed wedding cake.

Helen studied each sketch that April handed her and merely nodded in agreement. She couldn't help thinking about her and Edgar's wedding. How she had stood in front of the mirror in the bathroom of their honeymoon suite and worried whether the marriage had been a mistake.

She hadn't heard from Edgar since he gave her the car. There was nothing left for them to say. But she couldn't help but wonder what he would think of her marrying George so soon after their divorce.

Helen and George sat together in the morning room going over their social engagements.

"I hired Addison Huntwell's firm to redesign the bedrooms at Fox Hill Manor. He wants to meet with us after the honeymoon." George glanced up from a stack of papers. "William Patterson invited us to the holiday ball at Gray Craig the second week of December."

"The Pattersons are terribly frugal. They always dilute the punch," Helen said without thinking.

"William Patterson owns the largest paper company in Philadelphia," George countered. "If he likes me, he'll tell all his managers to vote for me."

Helen felt bad for not mirroring George's enthusiasm. He received each social invitation as if it were a letter from Santa Claus.

"The Pattersons will love you." Helen smiled. "I have to go to Philadelphia this afternoon. I'm going to donate some of our wedding presents to the Philadelphia Orphan Society. They always need things, and we have plenty of linens and housewares."

"I'll go with you. I want to pick up some albums for your father. Listening to music after dinner takes his mind off not being able to smoke cigars."

George and her father had grown quite close. Helen often heard them in the study talking about George's construction projects and Robert's plans for the firm. They listened to Josephine Baker on the radio and were planning a fishing trip for the following spring.

"There's one other thing." George collected his papers. "I had a call from the editor at *Town Topics*. They want to cover the wedding for the magazine."

"I hope you told them no."

"They want to send a journalist and a photographer out today. Have them cover the whole week so they get to know us. Helen Hope Montgomery, the wealthy society heiress, marrying the rising young star in Pennsylvania politics."

The last thing they needed was a reporter hanging around the house.

"It's out of the question," Helen said firmly.

"Actually, I think it's a good idea," George replied. "*Town Topics* isn't some trashy tabloid newspaper; it only covers high society. We couldn't pay for better campaign publicity. Every household on the Main Line reads it."

"You know what reporters are like." She frowned. "They'll make up things just so they have a story."

"I told the editor I want to read the piece first," George said. "If we don't like anything, we'll take it out. And I asked him to send his best team. It won't be some young kid trying to make a name for himself."

"You already agreed?" Helen asked in disbelief. "What will my mother and father say?"

George should at least have told the editor that they would discuss it.

"Your father agrees that it will be good for my image. It will benefit him too. There will be photos of Dumfries and a story on Robert being the head of Philadelphia's oldest investment firm."

Helen's father seldom read *Town Topics*. And Helen never told him about the article Edgar had written about Rosalee.

"I'll bet he did," Helen said under her breath. "I wish you had asked me first."

"The editor needed an answer right away." George apologized. He took her hand. "I do think this is important. Don't worry, they'll love you. How could they resist the most spirited young woman on the Main Line?"

~

Later that afternoon, Helen dropped George off at Fox Hill Manor. She parked her car in front of Dumfries and went into the living room.

Her mother was standing near the fireplace, reading a letter.

"We got a letter from Daisy," Charlotte said. "She wrote it before she left Portofino. She and Roland are on the ship; they're going to be at the wedding."

Helen had written to Daisy soon after she was engaged and begged her to come to the wedding. At first Daisy wasn't sure they could afford it. Then George insisted on sending a check. Helen was relieved that Daisy was coming. She missed her sister very much.

"Did she say anything else?" Helen asked.

"The hotel is doing much better. They have bookings for next season," Charlotte read. "And she said to tell you that Edgar had been in Portofino. He was disappointed not to receive his own wedding invitation."

"Edgar was still in Portofino?" Helen repeated in surprise.

"He stayed for two months." She turned the page. "He and Roland fixed the roof and put new shutters in the bedrooms."

Helen tried to imagine Edgar hammering shutters and crawling onto a roof.

"I doubt Edgar ever held a tool before in his life," Helen remarked. "And he's my ex-husband. Of course I wouldn't invite him to the wedding."

"We did invite Edgar's parents," Charlotte reminded her. "Your father and I have known them socially for years."

"No matter how we start our conversations, they always turn to Edgar," Helen snapped. "Please remember that I'm marrying George."

Charlotte opened her mouth as if she were about to say something. But Helen interrupted.

"Anyway, we have more important things to worry about." Helen told her mother about the journalist and photographer who were coming to write about the wedding.

"I don't know what George was thinking," Helen grumbled. "Where will we put them for a whole week? I'm staying in the pool house."

"I'll make up two guest rooms," Charlotte said. "I think it's a nice idea. The house will look so beautiful."

"They're not here to take photos of Dumfries decorated for the holidays. What if they find out about Father's affair? I never told George—it didn't seem relevant."

"You worry too much. That's all behind us," Charlotte counseled. "They can't write something they don't know. It will be good for your father. Men love to see their name in print. It makes them feel important."

Helen handed her mother a parcel. "George bought some new albums. I'm going to take a bath before our visitors arrive."

~

An older Model T Ford pulled into the driveway as Helen was walking back to the main house. It was early evening, and George was coming over soon for cocktails.

Two men stepped out of the car. The driver was in his midtwenties. He was quite short and had dark, thinning hair. The other man was tall and thin as a scarecrow. He wore a badly fitting suit; a camera was draped around his neck.

"Good evening, gentlemen," she greeted them. "Would you like to come inside?"

"We can come back later if you're going out," the shorter man suggested.

"What makes you think I'm going out?" Helen wondered.

The tall man waved at her evening gown. "That dress, and the stole. Like you're going to the opera."

"My mother likes us to dress for dinner." She led them into the living room. "And I have to walk over from the pool house. I get cold easily at night."

"My mother never dresses like that." The tall man whistled. "That stole must cost more than she earned in her whole life."

"Well, now you know what it's like living on the Main Line," Helen said before she could stop herself. "Isn't that why you're both here? To dig up some dirt on our lives."

She knew she should be polite. But she was still angry. George should never have agreed to this without asking her. And her parents shouldn't be supporting him.

"We're here to cover your wedding," the shorter man corrected. "I'm Philip Barry, and this is Conrad Edwards."

"Pardon my comment. I'm not used to being around such elegantly dressed women." Conrad held out his hand. "And congratulations to the groom. He couldn't have picked a more beautiful bride."

Helen shook their hands. She walked over to the sideboard and poured three Tom Collins. Conrad reminded her of Jack. He had a warm expression and clear blue eyes. She wished Jack were there. Jack would tell her to calm down. The only person she could hurt with her behavior was herself.

"Apology accepted. I'm sorry if I was rude." She handed them each a cocktail. "I've never spoken to a magazine writer before."

"You have nothing to worry about." Philip accepted the glass. "Our readers fall into two categories. Either they're members of high society, although if we publish something scandalous about people they know, they'll never buy *Town Topics* again. Our other readers dream of living in mansions like this one. They want to keep the people we write about on pedestals."

"That's very astute." Helen nodded. "You must be very smart."

Philip let out a laugh. "My fiancée doesn't think so. She won't marry me until I give up writing and join my father's menswear business."

"And you, Mr. Edwards." Helen turned to Conrad. Despite Philip's assurances, he made her nervous. Conrad seemed easier to talk to. "Are you engaged or married?"

"Completely single." He took a sip of his drink. "It's hard to find a woman to date on a photographer's salary. Unless she's partial to egg salad sandwiches."

"Egg salad sandwiches?" Helen repeated, puzzled.

"I make them myself," Conrad said proudly. "They're very inexpensive. I buy day-old bread and mayonnaise in bulk."

They talked about Philip's childhood in Rochester and Conrad's family business in Baltimore.

"My mother is getting ready." Helen was running out of things to talk about. "And my fiancé, George, will be here any minute."

"So, tell me about George, Helen." Philip nursed his glass.

George was easy to talk about. She told him about George's humble beginnings and how much of his life now was devoted to charity.

"You see, Mr. Barry," she finished, "not all of us on the Main Line only care about traveling to Europe or owning the latest-model cars. Some of us want to do something important."

"I'm impressed," Philip said smoothly. "It must be such a difference from your first husband."

"My first husband?" Helen repeated.

"Edgar Scott," Philip prompted. He took a folded newspaper from his pocket. A photo of Edgar stared back at her. He was seated in a booth in an ornate dining room. He looked incredibly handsome in a topcoat and tails.

Under the photo was the caption: "Soon-to-be-published author Edgar Scott enjoying a lobster dinner."

No matter what she did, Edgar seemed destined to haunt her.

"You're right, Mr. Barry. George couldn't be more different from Edgar."

Chapter Twenty-Two

The following day was spent showing Philip and Conrad around Dumfries and the Main Line. George gave them a tour of Fox Hill Manor, and Helen and George took them to dinner at the Merion Cricket Club.

George loved having them there. He posed for Conrad in his riding clothes and staged a photo with Helen in front of Fox Hill Manor's newly completed swimming pool. Conrad took photos of Helen and her mother picking flowers in the greenhouse, and Philip spent an hour with Robert in his study, learning about the investment firm.

Now it was Tuesday; the wedding was in five days. Helen woke early and couldn't go back to sleep. Finally, she did the only thing that calmed her nerves. She threw on a sweater and a pair of boots and rode her bicycle down to the barn.

"Isn't it a little cold to be outside so early in the morning?" a male voice asked.

Helen leaned the bicycle against the barn door.

"Well, good morning, Mr. Edwards," she greeted him. "What are you doing up so early?"

"Please, call me Conrad. I'll call you Helen, if that's all right." Conrad stood beside her. "I had an early-morning paper route for years. It ruined me forever; I can never sleep past five a.m."

"I hope your room is comfortable. Mother gave you the best guest rooms."

"Your mother didn't have to go to so much trouble," Conrad offered. "Philip and I could have shared a room at a local hotel."

"There aren't any hotels on the Main Line." Helen shook her head. "And Mother loves to have company."

"Your mother is very gracious. I can see where you get your beauty." Helen opened the barn door.

"You don't have to flirt with me just because you're staying with us." She gave a short smile. "I'm hardly beautiful, and I don't look anything like my mother."

"You may not resemble her exactly, but you have the same grace and elegance." Conrad studied Helen thoughtfully. "And I never flirt. My sisters told me it was a waste of time. I'm too tall and thin for a woman to be interested in me." He pointed to his neck. "And I have this Adam's apple, see. I can't do anything about it."

Helen let out a laugh. For the first time since Philip and Conrad arrived at Dumfries, she relaxed.

"I've always thought my long neck makes me resemble a giraffe," she confided. "You seem too nice to work at *Town Topics*. How did you come to be a magazine photographer?"

Conrad took a pack of cigarettes from his pocket and offered one to Helen.

She shook her head. "No, thank you. I'm trying to quit."

Conrad's mouth crinkled into a smile. He was almost attractive when he smiled, like a slightly mangy dog who needed to be groomed.

"I try to quit at least once a month. It never lasts." He lit a cigarette and handed it to her. "Go on, I won't say anything to Philip. It will be our secret."

Helen accepted the cigarette. She inhaled, the familiar smoke filling her lungs.

"Why are you partners with him?" she asked. "I get the feeling that under his smooth demeanor, there's a cobra waiting to strike."

"Philip is intense when he's working on a story, but he's all right." Conrad lit his cigarette. "I wanted to be a wedding photographer. It's decent money, and people are actually grateful to have you record their special day."

Helen recalled her parents' wedding album. Her mother had been young and beautiful. And her father had looked so handsome. Helen had stashed her own wedding photos in a box in the attic. She never wanted to see them again.

"I wasn't completely honest about never having dated," Conrad admitted. "I was engaged once. Her name was Betty; she was in nursing school." He took a long drag of his cigarette. "After she graduated, I was going to start a wedding photography business. She fell in love with a doctor and called off the engagement. I'd used up my savings to pay for her nursing school, so I had to take whatever job I could find."

"I'm terribly sorry."

Conrad shrugged. "At least *Town Topics* isn't the *New York Post*. And I get to meet interesting people. I have the feeling that you're more special than you give yourself credit for."

Helen glanced at Conrad curiously. He didn't seem to be flirting with her. It was almost as if he were a big brother.

"I don't know what you mean."

"I've only been around you for a few days, and you've let George do most of the talking." He shrugged. "But you seem deeper than other women I've met. Something hurt you, and you don't know how to heal the pain."

The smile went out of Helen's expression.

"I doubt you're qualified to judge." Her voice was tight. "I'm getting married in five days. There's no happier time in a woman's life than before her wedding."

"I'm sorry, I didn't mean to overstep," Conrad apologized.

Helen thought again that Conrad reminded her of Jack. She longed for Jack fiercely. He would tell her if she was doing the right thing.

There was no point in taking her anxiety out on Conrad.

"I'm going to say good morning to the cows, then why don't we go back to the house," Helen suggested. "On Tuesdays, Mary makes the best pancakes."

~

Conrad went to his room to change his clothes. Helen entered the dining room alone.

The room was empty except for someone sitting at the head of the table. A newspaper was open in front of him. He put the newspaper down.

"Hello, Helen." Edgar smiled broadly. "I was wondering when you'd wake up from your beauty sleep."

Helen's mouth dropped open. Edgar had lost his summer tan; otherwise he looked the same. He wore a V-neck sweater over a blue shirt. His gold watchband was strapped around his wrist.

"I understand this is a shock." He jumped up and pulled out her chair. "Sit down, and I'll fix you a plate of pancakes. I'd forgotten how good Mary's pancakes are."

Helen tried to pour a cup of coffee, but her hands were shaking. She didn't trust herself to speak.

"You should get someone to check out that tremor." Edgar frowned. "I hear that George knows all the best doctors."

"How dare you sit at the breakfast table as if you live here!" Helen let the words tumble out. "What are you doing here anyway? The last I heard, you were eating lobster bisque in some fancy dining room."

Edgar beamed. "You saw that photo? It was taken at the captain's table on board the RMS *Majestic*. I'm not even a published author yet, and I'm already in demand."

Edgar explained that after he left Paris, he traveled to Rome and Venice. He spent two months in Portofino, helping Roland around the villa and working on his new novel. When Daisy received the wedding invitation, he had to come home. He was staying with his parents at Fieldstone Manor.

"What do you mean you had to come home?" Helen fumed. "You're not invited to the wedding."

"Even if I'm not invited, you're giving up my name and taking George's." Edgar cut his pancake. "I had to make sure that I approved. It's almost as if George and I are going to be related."

If Helen wasn't so furious, she would have laughed.

She told him about George's construction company, and his different charities. His political goals, and the things they would accomplish together.

"That's all very admirable," Edgar replied when she finished. "You didn't say anything about love."

"You never mentioned love when you proposed to me in my father's study," Helen blurted out.

"Is that all you remember?" Edgar asked. His voice was thick. "I remember other things. Your mouth under mine during our kiss. Getting angry at myself for not kissing you longer."

Helen pushed back her chair. She didn't need to sit there and listen to Edgar.

But before she could leave, George appeared in the doorway. He wore a full-length racoon coat.

Edgar jumped up. He reached his hand over the table and introduced himself. "You must be George. I'm Edgar. Helen was telling me all about you. She didn't mention that you were a Harvard man, or is it Yale? I need to dig my racoon coat out of the closet."

Helen shot Edgar a look. She had just told him that George hadn't attended college.

George looked puzzled. He shook hands tentatively.

"So, you're the ex-husband."

"I prefer 'former' husband," Edgar said smoothly. "Ex sounds so permanent."

Helen told a small white lie. "Edgar brought over some Scottish yellow roses from his mother's greenhouse. Mother thought they would look nice at the wedding."

"Helen is very big on her Scottish ancestry," Edgar addressed George. "I'm sure she's shown you photos of the Ayrshire cows her grandfather imported from Scotland." He turned to Helen. "How is Clara, the new calf? You'll have to take me down to the barn."

"Helen hasn't shown me any photos of cows." George turned to Helen.

Helen darted Edgar another look. Now he had gone too far.

"I don't have time to take you to the barn," she said sweetly. "George and I have the whole day planned. We're going to pick up our wedding rings. Then we're having lunch with Father at the Warwick Hotel."

"Actually, about that," George said to Helen. "Your father and I thought it would be a good time to take photos of the investment firm. Afterwards, he and I are going to take Conrad and Philip to the Philadelphia Club for lunch."

Helen let his words sink in. "Are you saying you don't want me to come?"

"We thought it's best if you weren't seen in the private dining room. Women are allowed as guests, but some of the members don't like it."

"I'll take Helen to pick up the wedding rings," Edgar volunteered. "I have to go to Philadelphia to pick up a new suit."

"That's out of the question." Helen shook her head.

"It's not a bad idea." George rubbed his forehead. "Someone needs to get the rings. And my car is in the shop. I thought I could use yours."

"See, it works out splendidly." Edgar sat back down. "Now let's all have some pancakes, and George and I can get to know each other better."

~

Edgar was driving his father's brown model T Ford. It had a walnut dashboard and leather interior. It was cold outside, so the top was up and Helen draped a blanket over her lap.

It felt strange to be sitting in the car with Edgar. They talked about her first shipment to the creamery and Edgar's new publisher in New

York. There had been an auction, and an editor at Doubleday beat out Max Perkins at Scribner to publish the novel.

Helen thanked Edgar for paying off his overdraft and for giving her the car. It was only when they skirted around other subjects—Charleston Farmhouse, Sophie and Tommy, Vanessa and Duncan—that she felt as if the road they were driving on was filled with dangerous potholes.

When they arrived at Wanamaker's, Edgar insisted that he try the suit on. It was a pin-striped gray morning suit with a gray vest. A yellow handkerchief peeked out of the breast pocket.

"I needed a new suit. I get invited to so many weddings in London." Edgar adjusted the collar.

Edgar had taken a flat in Belgravia. He was going to stay in London for a while, editing the new novel with Malcolm. The book was set in Portofino. It was about a young man who falls in love with a beautiful American tourist.

"She's completely wrong for him," Edgar told her. "She has a fiery temper and almost pushes him off a cliff. But he can't give her up."

After they picked up the rings, they walked past Jack's apartment. Helen recalled the morning after she threw the vase at Edgar, when she found Edgar hunched over a brandy snifter. She wished Jack were at his apartment now. Jack would mix a pitcher of old-fashioneds, and they'd talk about paintings and books and farming. She was counting the hours until Jack returned; he would help her sort out her feelings. But he wasn't arriving until the day of the wedding. She'd be so busy, they wouldn't have a chance to talk.

Edgar cut into her thoughts. "Do you remember your first dinner date with Harold? I ran into Harold in London. They celebrated their first wedding anniversary. Jane is pregnant."

"I'm glad." Helen nodded.

"Marriage is easy for people like them," Edgar mused. "Jane's criteria for a husband is someone who is attractive and gives her a generous allowance. Harold is similar," he reflected. "Marriage gets difficult when you really care about the other person. That's when you hurt each other." He paused. "Don't worry, you won't have that problem with George."

"I don't know what you mean."

"George is in love with himself. You want to be in love with him, but it won't last."

Helen turned to Edgar angrily.

"If you say one more word about George, I'll never speak to you again," she warned. "You're one to talk. I never came first with you; it was always your writing. And helping women. You thought you had to be a knight in shining armor for all women. George treats me like an equal. We're going to do good together."

Helen had never put her feelings into words. It felt good to say them out loud.

Edgar was completely quiet. He slipped his hands in his pockets and kept walking.

"I need to stop at the library, then I'll take you home," he volunteered.

Edgar had brought advance copies of his novel to give to the library. He dropped one off at the front desk and took a stack to the offices on the third floor.

Helen picked up the copy while she waited. Inside, there was an inscription.

> *This book is dedicated to Helen Montgomery Scott. Most of us only get one chance at love. If we're smart, we hang on to that love forever. Even if we make mistakes and lose it, our lives are richer for having experienced it.*

Helen's eyes filled with tears. There was a lump in her throat. She closed the book and placed it on the counter. Maybe she had misjudged Edgar. What if she gave him another chance? As quickly as the thought crossed her mind, she dismissed it. She and Edgar had plenty of chances—at Jack's house in Sussex, and at the Barrière Le Royal Hotel in Deauville. Something would always happen to start a new argument. Besides, she was with George. They complemented each other, and he was helping her to become a better person.

They were quiet on the drive back to the Main Line. Edgar pulled into the driveway.

"I'm sorry if I said anything to upset you." Edgar turned off the engine.

"I should have expected it," Helen returned. "We could never be in the same room for long without trying to hurt each other."

"I don't agree." Edgar shook his head. "We had a wonderful time. Making spaghetti in the cottage, dancing at the Warwick Hotel." He paused. "I didn't come to Philadelphia just to check out George. I came to—"

Suddenly another car pulled into the driveway. Daisy hopped out. She looked incredibly pretty in a red overcoat. Her blonde hair was in curls, and she wore a red cloche hat.

Helen had never been so glad to see her. She jumped out of the car and hugged her.

Daisy hugged her back. She poked her head into the car and then turned to Helen. "What's Edgar doing here? I was hoping to meet George."

Helen put her arm through Daisy's. Suddenly she felt more like herself. She wasn't going to sit with Edgar and reminisce about the past. Her sister was here, and in five days she was getting married.

"You will meet George; he's with Father. And Edgar was just leaving."

Chapter Twenty-Three

The day before the wedding, Helen spent an hour packing her suitcase for the honeymoon. They were going to spend a week at the Breakers Hotel in Palm Beach. It had been completely rebuilt after it was damaged by a fire three years earlier. George read the newspaper clippings that described the Venetian glass chandeliers, the ceilings hand-painted by Florentine artists. All of Philadelphia society vacationed there. He had already made dinner plans with the Carnegies and the Goulds.

Since the night Daisy and Roland arrived, Edgar had been strangely absent. Helen blamed herself. She had been too hard on him. But she resolved to put Edgar out of her mind. This was the last time she was going to be a bride; she was determined to enjoy herself.

Her days were spent going over last-minute details with her mother and April. In the evenings, Helen and George went to dinner with Daisy and Roland. George insisted on paying for both couples. One night, they drove to New York to see the musical *The New Moon* on Broadway. George booked a table at Sardi's, and they met members of the cast.

Roland and George got along well, and Helen could tell that Daisy liked him. George wanted to hear everything about the villa. He announced that they would visit next winter after the election. Then he squeezed Helen's hand and said Portofino would be a perfect place to try to start a family.

George was so sweet to her. Every morning, he called to tell her that he couldn't wait to be married. When she came downstairs for breakfast, there was always a new bouquet of flowers. They were accompanied by a note and a gift. A silver evening gown to wear on their honeymoon, sapphire earrings from Tiffany's. The previous day, there was a box with a diamond-and-ruby bracelet. Her father had brought the rubies back from South America, and George had them made into a bracelet.

After Helen finished packing, she walked over to the main house. Philip sat in the living room. A coffee cup was on the table next to a plate of scones.

Helen had avoided being alone with Philip. But it would be rude to walk by without saying hello.

"Good morning, Mr. Barry."

Philip glanced up from his notebook. He wore a brown sweater and camel-colored slacks.

"Please call me Philip." He motioned for her to sit down. "Join me for a cup of coffee. Mary is quite a cook. Every morning there are fresh pastries."

"Mother will never let her go. She's practically part of the family." Helen poured a cup of coffee and sat opposite him.

"You're an interesting woman," Philip said. "I can't figure you out."

Helen shifted uncomfortably against the cushions. "I don't know what you mean."

"Most people I write about can't wait to talk to me." He set aside his notebook. "I did a piece on Mary Pickford for *Vogue*. She gave me a tour of her estate in Hollywood, and she let me hold her Oscar statue. Even the queen of England wanted to introduce me to her husband's, the king's, beloved Labradors."

"I'm not a Hollywood actress, and I don't have any pets," Helen remarked.

"We all have something we want the world to know about. It makes us feel important."

"What makes you think I want to feel important?" Helen questioned.

"It's like that from the moment we're born. Babies cry before they learn to talk because they want everyone to hear them." Philip ran his fingers over his cup. "That's why people get married. They want to feel as important to someone else as they do to themselves."

"Neither of us are equipped to talk about marriage," Helen said sharply. "You're only engaged, and my marriage didn't last."

Philip and Conrad hadn't met Edgar, but everyone on the Main Line knew that they had been married.

"I still think it's odd." Philip rubbed his forehead. "You live in this grand house, and you've been raised with everything, and you don't want to show it off."

"Some people are more private." She sipped her coffee. "You wouldn't know anything about that. You write for a magazine."

"People like what I write." He shrugged. "By the way, I was leafing through the magazines your mother receives in the mail. There was an envelope addressed to you. I set it aside."

He picked up an envelope from the coffee table. Helen read the return address.

Rosalee Watson
Chateau-Sur-Mer, Oyster Bay, New York

Her hands started shaking. Her cheeks turned white with rage.

"How dare you go through the mail! And what do you know about Rosalee?" she exclaimed.

"I told you, I was looking for a magazine," Philip said calmly. "Of course, I know about Rosalee. I'm a reporter; it's my job to research my subjects. Don't worry, I won't say anything."

Helen didn't believe him. Her father's affair would make for a much richer story.

Philip set down his coffee cup. His expression was serious.

"This might be hard for you to understand, but I believe in what George is doing. I wouldn't write anything that jeopardized his run for office."

"Are you sure that's the reason?" she demanded. "Or are you going to ask George for a new car if you promise not to print any scandal about our family."

"I have a perfectly good car." Philip waved toward the driveway. "And there are enough zeros in my bank account to keep me happy. But I've seen what it's like for people who didn't grow up with my opportunities. Children who started working in my father's factory when they were twelve. Women who stand in the production line for hours even though they're nine months pregnant. We need young politicians like George instead of the old guard who make decisions over gin fizzes at their private clubs."

Maybe Helen had been wrong about Philip. Lately, she realized she had been wrong about several things. Daisy had been right in following Roland to Italy—they were the happiest couple she knew. And her mother and father were closer than ever. Charlotte seemed so relieved since Robert returned from South America. And Robert was more attentive to her. Often, Helen caught them holding hands when she came down for breakfast. They even passed notes to each other when they all sat together listening to music in the living room. Helen had seen one the other night by accident. It had been in her father's handwriting and read:

I'm going up to bed. Please join me as soon as you can, darling. I'll wait up for you.

Helen turned her attention back to Philip.

"I still don't know what you need from me. George loves talking about his plans."

Philip took a bite of his scone. He studied Helen thoughtfully.

"You and George are getting married. You can tell a lot about someone from the people they keep around them."

~

Later in the day, Helen sat on the sofa in the pool house. She read Rosalee's note.

Dear Helen,

I read the wedding announcement in the New York Times and wanted to congratulate you. I still remember your kindness. Because of you, I started my own theater company, and I give free acting lessons to girls who can't afford them. I also met a producer who wants to marry me. I told him I'd think about it. For now I'm happy living alone.

Best wishes,
Rosalee

Helen slipped the letter back in the envelope. A glimmer of tears filled her eyes. She told herself it didn't mean anything. All brides got emotional before their wedding.

Her eyes were still damp when Daisy appeared. Helen tucked the envelope into a drawer. Daisy never knew that she had gone to see Rosalee.

"I was just deciding what jewelry to wear tonight." Helen walked to her dressing table. "Where's Roland?"

"He and Edgar went riding."

"Roland and Edgar?" Helen raised her eyebrows.

"They grew quite close in Portofino." Daisy perched on an armchair in the seating area.

"Well, try to remember that I'm marrying George," Helen said briskly. She plumped the cushions on the sofa and arranged the magazines on the coffee table.

"That's what I want to talk about," Daisy ventured. "Are you sure that you want to marry him?"

Helen stopped what she was doing. She turned to Daisy.

"Of course I'm sure! You've seen how wonderful he is," Helen exclaimed. "Look at this bracelet." She picked up the jewelry box. "George had it custom made. There isn't another one like it on the Main Line."

"You never wanted jewelry except your pearls," Daisy commented. "I like George, but you don't have much in common. You're not interested in politics, and he doesn't know anything about the farm."

"Edgar read books by authors I'd never heard of, and he could barely tell a cow from a bull," Helen said stormily.

Sometimes, Daisy and her mother infuriated her. They assumed they knew what was best for her.

"Those things don't matter if you're in love," Daisy agreed. "You talk about all the good that George does, but you haven't said that you're in love with him."

"Love isn't something one talks about."

"Of course it is," Daisy protested. "I used to bore you for days talking about the boys I was in love with. And I can still talk about Roland for hours."

Helen gave a little smile. She remembered all the times that Daisy would crawl into her bed and tell her why she was in love with a certain boy. And when Daisy started seeing Roland, Helen learned everything about him.

"We're all grown up. We're not sixteen and seventeen anymore."

"I just think you should think about it."

Helen couldn't admit her feelings to Daisy. Daisy believed love was the most important thing in the world. Helen remembered the pain of seeing Edgar and Sophie kissing. If she and Edgar hadn't been arguing, the terrible scene in Louis's hotel suite wouldn't have happened. She might not feel that heady excitement when she was with George, but that didn't mean she wasn't in love with him.

"I know exactly what I'm doing." Helen glanced at the clock on the side table. She gave Daisy a small hug. "I have to get ready. George wants me to come to Fox Hill Manor early."

~

Fox Hill Manor had been built twenty years earlier in the Italian Renaissance style. It was three stories with a tile roof and overhanging, bracketed leaves. The house faced a stone forecourt, and there were wide porch arcades and porticos.

The interior had a marble entrance hall and double sweeping staircases. There was a large reception room and a dining room that could seat one hundred guests. A music room held a Steinway piano, and the picture gallery contained paintings from George's growing collection.

The ballroom where Helen stood now was the largest room in the house. There was no furniture except for upholstered armchairs scattered around the edge of the floor. Chandeliers hung from the ceiling, and crystal light fixtures were placed on the walls next to large mirrors. There was a raised stage for the musicians and doors leading out to the terrace.

Helen had drunk two glasses of champagne, and she felt quite lightheaded. Edgar walked toward her. She grabbed a fresh glass of champagne from the bar. She hadn't expected him to be there.

Edgar joined her. "You should get married more often. You always look radiant the night before your wedding."

"What are you doing here? You weren't invited."

"I assumed that was an oversight," Edgar said easily. "Anyway, my parents were invited, and my father hurt his back. You know how my mother hates attending these things alone." He took a glass of champagne. "What are you doing standing all alone at your own ball?"

Edgar looked particularly handsome. His light brown hair was brushed to the side, and his cheeks were smooth with aftershave. He wore a gold tie clip, and his vest had pearl buttons.

"George is giving a tour of the sports pavilion to some guests."

"Fox Hill Manor is huge." Edgar whistled. "I almost got lost coming from the dining room. I took a wrong turn and ended up in George's private study."

"George had the swimming pool built, and he's going to put in tennis courts," Helen said proudly.

"Personally, I don't see why you need such a large swimming pool unless you plan on hosting the US Olympic team. But the estate suits you." He nursed his glass. "Perhaps if our house had been finished, you would have been happy."

"The house had nothing to do with our divorce. I was happy living at the cottage."

Edgar smiled as if he had tricked her.

"So was I." He moved closer. "I miss preparing your coffee in the mornings. You always appeared in the kitchen like an angel sent down from heaven."

The color rose to Helen's cheeks.

"Go away, Edgar. There are plenty of young women you can talk to."

"I'd rather talk to you," he persisted. "George shouldn't have left you alone."

"George and I are getting married tomorrow," she reminded him. "In case you hadn't heard, marriage is about trust."

Edgar's eyes seemed greener than she had ever seen them.

"So he won't mind if I ask you to dance?"

"I don't need George's permission to dance with anyone."

Edgar took her champagne glass and set it next to his own on the bar.

"Then dance with me. Just one dance, I promise; then I'll leave you alone."

The dance floor was filled with couples. Even Helen's parents were dancing. And she had hardly danced all night.

"All right, one dance," she relented. "But then you have to find someone else to bother."

As he took her hand, the song changed from a fast-paced jazz number to "Tonight You Belong to Me." Helen remembered dancing to it with Edgar on the ship's crossing to England.

Edgar kept his hand firmly around her waist. She let herself be swept away. Her head fit under his chin, and he smelled exactly as she remembered—of Acqua di Parma men's cologne he discovered the year he lived in Italy. They had always danced so well together. And her dress—a floor-length crepe gown with a tiered skirt—was perfect for skimming across the dance floor.

There was a tap on his shoulder.

"Do you mind if I cut in. I haven't danced with the bride-to-be."

It was Philip Barry. He wore one of the new tuxedo jackets and a black bow tie.

"Helen, this is my old friend Philip Barry," Edgar introduced them. "We studied journalism together at Harvard."

Helen glanced from one man to the other. Suddenly it all fell into place. Philip was the reporter for *Town Topics* who had put a word in for Edgar with his editor. Edgar must have put him up to writing the article about her family.

"I already know Philip." Her voice was cold as ice. "He's staying with us. He's writing a piece for *Town Topics* about the wedding."

Edgar's face lit up in a smile.

"You don't say." He whistled softly. "That should be interesting. I can't wait to read it."

Helen's cheeks turned hot. She faced Edgar angrily.

"This is all your fault. You told Philip to come and bring his photographer because you were intent on ruining my wedding. Well, it's not going to work. George and I love each other, and tomorrow we're getting married. Just because we weren't happy together, you never want me to be happy again."

Helen picked up her skirt and ran from the dance floor. She slipped out the door and almost collided with a man coming out of the powder room.

"Are you all right?" the man asked. It was Conrad. He wore a dark suit and scuffed black shoes. The sleeves on the jacket were too short, and the shirt was badly creased.

Tears filled Helen's eyes, but she blinked them away. "It's nothing. I'm thirsty, I need a drink."

Conrad studied her carefully. "I just came from the ballroom; there's a full bar. It's something else."

More than anything, Helen wanted to get away from Edgar. But George was with the other guests, and she was too tipsy to drive.

"What I'd really like is to go home."

"Then I'll drive you." Conrad took her arm. "That's the beauty of serving so much excellent champagne. By this time of the night, everyone is too drunk to notice who leaves."

~

When they arrived at Dumfries, the house was quiet. Her parents and Daisy and Roland were still at the party.

"If you show me where Mary keeps the coffee, I'll make a pot," Conrad offered.

Helen didn't want coffee, and she didn't want to sober up. She marched into her father's study and took the bottle of brandy from the sideboard.

Conrad followed her. He watched her fill a glass.

"Are you sure that's a good idea? You're getting married tomorrow; you don't want to be hungover at your own wedding."

Helen poured another glass and handed it to Conrad.

"The ceremony isn't until five o'clock. Anyway, I never get hangovers. Didn't you read Edgar's article about me in the *New Yorker*?"

"You're not making sense." Conrad accepted the glass.

Helen let it all come out. That she had always been faulted for having high standards. At Foxcroft, the other girls made fun of her because she turned her assignments in on time and because her bed and desk were neat and organized. Her family thought she was too rigid, and the only man she had dated before Edgar broke up with her because she had too many opinions.

"Then Edgar wrote that piece saying I was a Philadelphia princess. I thought Edgar was different. But once we were married, we couldn't be in the same room together without wanting to throw things at each other." She set down her glass. "Men want wives who are soft and forgiving. They don't want a society princess who never gets hungover and always says what she thinks."

Helen poured another glass of brandy. She took a long sip and placed it on the sideboard.

"I've been trying to change and become more accepting of others," she continued. "I don't mind anymore that my mother wants to stay with my father, and I'm happy that Daisy and Roland are running their hotel in Portofino. I've even put up with Edgar even though sometimes I can't stand the sight of him. No matter how I try, it's not enough. My own family still sees me as an ice princess. And I don't have any friends besides April. Young women in our social circle don't have the same interests."

Conrad gulped his brandy.

"On the contrary, I've been looking at photos of you in the dark room all week. You're much more than that. You're a beautiful young woman who cares more about other people than anyone I've met."

"I don't understand." Helen frowned.

"The way you try to include George in everything. And how you join your parents for dinner even when you don't feel like it. You say you're spoiled, but you walk around the house in breeches instead of fancy clothes, and you treat the cook as if she was your friend." He gave a small smile. "And don't forget about the farm. Cows have good instincts; they know when someone is genuine."

Helen let out a sigh. If only George would allow her to work at the farm. She hated sneaking around, but she missed Essie and Nellie and Clara.

"I do love the cows." She suddenly remembered whom she was talking to. "You don't have to be nice to me. I won't stop Philip from writing his story. George thinks it will help his run for office."

"I wasn't being nice, I was telling the truth." Conrad set down his glass. "If someone like me had the chance to marry you, I'd do it in a minute. But I'd have too much competition. There were already two men who wanted to marry you at the pre-wedding ball."

"What do you mean two men?" Helen asked, puzzled.

"There's George, of course, but there was also Edgar." Conrad paced around the room. "I'm trained to notice people's expressions. When Edgar danced with you, he was John Barrymore making love to Dolores Costello in a movie."

"Edgar drank too much champagne, and so did I." Helen waved her hand. "I don't want to talk about Edgar. It's because of him that Philip's piece is going to run in *Town Topics*."

"All I'm saying is if I had taken a photo of the two of you dancing, it wouldn't have been the type of thing you would have shared with George," Conrad replied.

Helen recalled the way it felt to have Edgar's arms around her before Philip interrupted them. She had always loved dancing with Edgar. They couldn't argue when they were on the dance floor, and they fit so well together. Like interlocking pieces in a puzzle. But she couldn't give in to those emotions. Edgar had shown again with Philip that he couldn't be trusted.

"Well, there is no photo, and I don't want to talk to Edgar again," Helen said fiercely.

"Then forget what I said." Conrad shrugged. He gave a wide smile. "I want there to be a wedding tomorrow. If there isn't, I won't get paid."

Helen's mind went to the satin bows that April had ordered for the church pews. Her wedding dress was hanging in her bedroom, and her suitcase was packed and ready in the hallway.

If she was determined not to be an ice princess, she had to start now. Their marriage might be rocky in the beginning while she and George learned to care about each other. But many couples began the same way.

Conrad stopped pacing. He picked up his brandy.

"Why don't you get some sleep. It might sound like a corny line from a movie, but everything will be clearer in the morning," he suggested.

Helen walked to the door. She turned and smiled at Conrad.

"Thank you for tonight. I'll never forget it. You've helped me more than you'll ever know."

Chapter Twenty-Four

The next morning, Helen lay on the sofa in the pool house. A wet cloth was spread across her forehead, and a bottle of Bayer aspirin sat on the side table.

In eight hours, Helen was getting married. She wondered why she wasn't more excited.

She replayed the events of the previous night. George disappearing to give a tour of the estate to some guests. Drinking champagne and Edgar asking her to dance. Feeling light and happy in Edgar's arms until Philip cut in. Then the realization that Philip's presence at Dumfries was all Edgar's fault.

She wanted to blame her mood on the three glasses of champagne she drank and her current hangover, but that wasn't the only reason. She had been dismayed by what Conrad said about Edgar. Of course, Edgar wasn't in love with her, and she wasn't in love with him. They shared one slow dance before she was reminded that she and Edgar always brought out the worst in each other.

The florists and the caterers would be there soon. She'd run down to the barn and spend some time with the cows.

Before she could move, there was a tap at the door.

It was Jack, looking more handsome than she had ever seen him. His cheeks were bronze from the Greek sun, and his thighs were strong from walking. He wore a long navy overcoat and black boots.

She practically flew off the sofa and into his arms.

"I've never been so happy to see anyone in my life," she said, hugging him tightly.

"Slow down, I'm not going anywhere," he laughed. "From the pharmaceutical selection on the side table, it looks like you should avoid any sudden moves."

Helen groaned and fell back on the sofa. She picked up the wet cloth.

"You should be the one getting married, not me," she said. "You have a wonderful tan, and I look like death warmed over."

"Most of the guests who were at the ball probably have the same splitting headache." Jack sat opposite her. "And even at this time of year, one can't avoid a tan in Greece. You and George should go there on your honeymoon."

The mention of their honeymoon made her head throb even harder.

"George planned our honeymoon. We're going to Palm Beach. He's already made dinner plans with half of Main Line society." Helen set down the cloth. "I can't wait for you to meet George. You're going to love him."

"I did meet him. He was at the gatekeeper's cottage when I arrived." Jack frowned. "He was saying something to Abe about wearing a uniform for the wedding."

Abe had been the gatekeeper at Dumfries since before Helen was born. His arthritis was bad, so he no longer walked around the grounds. George thought it would be nice if he left the gatehouse to greet each guest. He bought a pair of herringbone slacks with a matching vest and cap for the occasion.

"I'll talk to George about Abe," Helen said. "You'll meet George officially soon."

"First, I want to talk to you." Jack leaned forward. "It was a shock when you wrote and said you were engaged. I thought you'd take more time."

Something in Jack's tone made Helen wary.

"Don't tell me you've been talking to Mother or Daisy," she said irritably. "Everyone is telling me what to do."

Jack's eyes crinkled up at the corners.

"I would never tell you what to do. You proved in Deauville that you were perfectly capable of taking care of yourself."

Helen argued that he was wrong. She let her jealousy about Sophie almost get Edgar and Jack killed.

"That wasn't your fault. Both men acted as if they were in a swash-buckling novel." Jack chuckled. "It was afterwards. You visited Daisy even though you didn't know how she'd receive you. Then you came back to Philadelphia without Edgar. That couldn't have been easy."

Most of the gossip had died down by the time she returned to Dumfries. And she was glad she had gone to Portofino. She had been miserable without Daisy, and they finally made up.

"I brought you a wedding present. It's in the car; I'll get it."

Jack returned with a painting in a silver frame. It was a portrait of a man with dark hair and eyes. He was standing on a cliff. Below him were bursts of flowers and a green-blue sea. It was Christos in front of the cottage they had rented on the island of Mykonos. Mykonos was nothing like Deauville with its promenade and elegant hotels. It had only recently been discovered by tourists, and most of the visitors were from Athens. Christos came on an archaeological dig and loved it so much, he stayed.

"It's wonderful," Helen said. "But you should keep it for yourself."

"I painted more like it. I want you to have it," Jack said. "If it wasn't for you, I would never have painted a portrait or fallen in love again."

When Jack had left Sussex twenty years earlier, he never wanted to get close enough to someone to paint their portrait, and he felt the same about falling in love. Then he visited Helen and Edgar in Deauville and ran into Duncan. Their time in Paris convinced him that he wasn't in love with Duncan anymore, so he was free to fall for someone new.

Christos was going to spend the winter in Mykonos on an archae-ological dig. After that, Jack would go back to Greece in the spring, or Christos might come to Philadelphia.

"If he does, I'd love to meet him." Helen smiled.

She had done something good for Jack, and the revelation made her happy.

Jack propped the painting against the wall. "Tell me more about George."

Helen repeated some of the things she had written to Jack in her letters. George's charity work and the changes he was going to make if he won the election. Somehow, she couldn't gather her usual enthusi-asm. It was because of her headache and the aspirin. Aspirin made her stomach upset, and it was hard to concentrate.

"I have a breakfast appointment, but I'll be back shortly," Jack said when she finished. "I'll ask Mary to make a batch of pancakes and a pot of coffee on my way out. Black coffee is a much better cure for a headache than aspirin."

~

After Jack left, Helen grabbed her coat and bicycled down to the barn. She had expected the barn to be empty, but her father stood in Essie's stall.

"What are you doing here?" Helen asked. "It's freezing outside. You'll get sick again."

Robert looked much better than when he returned from Argentina. His color had come back, and he had put back some weight.

"I've never been healthier. Your mother has me on a strict diet. She even made me give up my nightcap." Robert chuckled. "I fought her like a child, but of course she was right."

"It still doesn't explain why you're at the barn." Helen picked up Essie's brush.

"I wanted to see you. I figured you'd come down here. It's where I spent the morning of our wedding."

"You did?" Helen questioned.

Suddenly she missed the close camaraderie she'd once had with her father. If they had been on speaking terms, she would have come to him with her problems. He would have helped her sort out her feelings about George and the farm.

"You and I are the same that way," he remarked. "Where else would we go when we're nervous?"

"Who says I'm nervous?" Helen asked.

"I can tell by the way you're frowning." He pointed to her forehead. "You almost never frown. Daisy read in a magazine that frowning gives you wrinkles before you're thirty."

Helen remembered the summer that Daisy started reading their mother's magazines. Daisy made a list of the things that a young woman should do to maintain her looks. Balance a stack of books on her head when she walked to improve her posture. Use lemon juice on her skin to get rid of freckles, and coat her cheeks with foundation at night to keep them soft.

Daisy insisted on doing all of them, and she made Helen promise to do the same.

A lump formed in Helen's throat. She changed the subject. "Why did you want to see me?"

"I saw you dancing with Edgar last night."

All the anger boiled up inside her. She told her father that Edgar asked Philip to write the piece for *Town Topics*. Edgar was trying to stir up trouble—he didn't care about their family.

"It's my fault. I should never have talked to Edgar again," she finished.

Robert fiddled with a piece of straw. "Actually, it's my fault. I invited Philip to come to Dumfries and write the article."

Robert explained that he and Philip had met at a dinner party in Buenos Aires. Philip was in Argentina on an assignment and happened to mention that he went to journalism school with Edgar. It was just before Helen and George were engaged.

"I don't understand." Helen was puzzled.

"I told Philip everything about Rosalee. Of course, he promised not to write about it," Robert continued. "The article was going to be about you. Since you were a child, you dreamed of having your own dairy company. It didn't matter that you were a girl or that you were brought up on the Main Line. I wanted to show how proud I am of you. I'm lucky to be your father."

Helen didn't know what to say.

"But I'm not doing anything about the company now," she finally said. "George doesn't even know I'm at the barn."

"That's what I wanted to talk to you about. I admire George; he's almost the son I never had. But that doesn't mean you should marry him."

Helens stopped brushing Essie's back. "I don't know what you mean."

"Ever since I was a boy, my life was planned out for me. I was expected to take over my grandfather's business, and inherit Dumfries, and marry the right girl," Robert said thoughtfully. "I suppose that's why I took up with Rosalee. I wanted to see what it was like to live a different life. It turned out, I wanted the life I was expected to have. Not because I needed a grand estate or a summer house in Maine but because I fell in love with a girl who understood me.

"You may think you have to marry George because he's got plans to change the world. But the only reason to get married is for love."

"You think I'm still in love with Edgar?" she asked incredulously.

"All I'm saying is you don't want to make a mistake," Robert reflected. "I learned the hard way that it's easy to lose the people you love." His eyes turned watery. "Once you do, it's almost impossible to win them back."

Before she could stop herself, Helen hugged him.

"You haven't lost me," she sobbed into his neck.

Robert hugged her back. When he spoke, his voice was choked with tears. "I'm sorry for everything I did. I love you and Daisy and your mother so much. All I want is for you to be happy."

Her father went back up to the house. Helen brushed Clara and Nellie. She mixed their feed and swept out the stalls.

When she walked back to the house, George was in the living room.

"George, I've been wondering where you were," she greeted him. "Jack was here. He said that you met."

"I came early to talk to Abe. You disappeared last night. I came back from giving a tour and you were gone."

Helen was about to tell him that after the honeymoon, she wanted to work on the farm. The idea came to her when she was crossing the fields to the house. Being with the cows made her happy; she couldn't give them up. And she was so close to being able to distribute their dairy products. She would show voters that a woman could do what she loved and take care of her husband and family at the same time.

"There are some things I want to talk about," she ventured.

A car pulled into the driveway. George walked back to the window.

"Can it wait? Reverend Brown is here to discuss the ceremony. We need to stand at the altar so the photographer gets the best angle of our faces."

George was so excited. The *New York Times* was sending their own photographer. The ceremony was going to be featured in the *Times*'s wedding section.

Helen crossed the lawn to the pool house. She'd take a bath and then talk to George.

When she entered the pool house, Edgar was hunched on the sofa. A bottle of brandy sat on the coffee table.

"Well, you're not acting like a bride." Edgar glanced at her breeches and boots. "I expected to find you sitting here, fussing with your hair and makeup. Instead, you've obviously been at the barn. Does George know? He might not approve of you spending your wedding morning getting comfort from the cows."

Had George noticed that she'd been at the barn? She doubted it. He was too preoccupied.

"Everyone thinks I'm so nervous," she replied. "For your information, I'm perfectly calm. That's what happens when I know I'm marrying the right man."

"Well, then I'm nervous for both of us." Edgar held up his glass. "I hope you don't mind. I helped myself to a glass of your brandy."

"What are you doing here, Edgar?" She sat opposite him.

Edgar gulped the brandy. He set the glass on the coffee table.

"I need to talk to you about something. It can't wait until after the wedding."

"If it's about Philip, I already know."

She explained everything that her father had told her.

"I'm sorry I didn't believe you," she finished.

Edgar's face broke into a smile.

"It's worth it to hear you apologize." He beamed. "Philip Barry is a good guy. He won't write anything to hurt you." He picked up the glass. "That's not why I'm here. It's about George. You can't marry him."

Helen paced around the room.

"You're the second person today who's tried to tell me what to do," she fumed. "Of course I'm going to marry George. Daisy will be here in a few hours; we're going to get our hair done. Then the photographer will take photos with my parents at the church. After that, guests will arrive, and pre-wedding champagne will be served. The violinist and cellist will play Schubert's 'Ave Maria,' and the ceremony will begin."

"I don't care if you've hired the entire Philadelphia Orchestra." Edgar's eyes flashed. "George is a crook, and you can't marry him."

"What are you talking about?"

"I'm a journalist. I did some research of my own," Edgar said. "Good old George has been involved in some nasty business practices."

Helen listened while Edgar told her about the flaws that George's construction workers built into their projects. Windows that didn't open properly, brick chimneys that restricted the airflow. When the new owners complained, he immediately sent out a crew to fix it. He blamed the supplier for the problem and didn't charge the owners for the extra work.

"The owners were so indebted to him, they gave him their future projects," Edgar finished. "An article about it was going to come out in the *Philadelphia Inquirer*. George paid the reporter five thousand dollars not to publish it."

Helen didn't believe him. George was the most honorable man she knew.

"You know better than anyone that newspapers make things up all the time," she reminded him. "Look at what you wrote about Rosalee."

"The reporter is a friend of mine." Edgar sipped the brandy. "He showed me the letters between George and him."

Helen felt a little dizzy. She sunk onto the sofa.

"There must be an explanation," she said staunchly. "I'll go ask George about it right now."

Edgar took an envelope out of his pocket.

"There's another reason you can't marry George." He handed it to Helen.

Helen unfolded the papers. It was their divorce agreement.

"I never signed it," Edgar explained.

Helen's signature was on the bottom of the last page. The line above Edgar's name was empty.

"I don't understand. You received this months ago."

"I never sent it back." Edgar shrugged. "At first, I was too angry. I told you that nothing happened between Sophie and me, but you wouldn't believe me. Then I started to miss you. It wasn't bad at first. I had my writing, and I enjoyed Paris. Then I finished the book, and I got so lonely. For weeks, I kept the divorce papers under my pillow. As long as they were there, you were still part of me." His voice was thick. "I'm still in love with you, Helen."

Helen took a deep breath. It would be so easy to listen to her father and Edgar. To call off the wedding and go back to the way things were.

But she had given George her word. And it was more than that. She and George wanted the same things: to help others, and to have a home and family.

And it would never work with Edgar. They'd never stop fighting.

"I don't love you, Edgar. So you better sign it. Or I'll have you thrown in jail for obstructing the divorce."

"You wouldn't dare!" Edgar jumped up. "Think about the scandal if the newspapers found out that you threw your ex-husband in jail on your wedding day."

"I have been thinking. I'm done with worrying about what people say. And I'm finished having men tell me what to do." She reached for the phone. "Sign it right now, or I'll call my attorney."

Edgar picked up the papers and stopped.

"First, talk to George," he offered in compromise. "If I'm wrong about what I heard, then I'll sign it and walk out of your life forever."

Helen made Edgar go outside while she changed into a sweater and skirt. Then she walked back to the main house and waited until George finished speaking with the reverend.

"Helen, there you are," George greeted her. "Reverend Brown was so accommodating. I suggested we face the guests when we exchange rings, and he agreed. Then the photographer will be able to catch our expressions."

Helen didn't want to face the guests. She wanted to look only at George. But there were more important things to discuss.

She told him what Edgar had said about the construction company.

"I don't know what you're doing talking to Edgar on our wedding day," George said brusquely. "The reporter's name is Harvey Peterson; he was a scholarship student at Harvard on the crew team. He was jealous of me because I took his spot at the Olympics." He rubbed his chin. "He never had any proof. He made the whole thing up to blackmail me."

"Why did you give him the money if it wasn't true?"

"Harvey said he needed it because his sister was very ill. I felt sorry for him." George shrugged. "It was easier to just give him the money. If someone I loved was sick, I'd do anything to make her better."

What George said made sense. It was easy to believe him. He was so kind and generous.

"What about the letters?" she questioned.

"I should have asked him for the letters," George agreed, "but I didn't think of it. I had four projects going, and I was coaching baseball at the orphanage on the weekends. Harvey promised that he wouldn't write about it, and that was enough for me."

Helen was about to tell George that she had reconsidered her decision not to work on the farm until after the election. She would make a better campaign wife if she spoke from the heart. Other wives and even their husbands would respond to her.

Before she could begin, George continued talking.

"Edgar put these ideas about Harvey into your head, but I guess that's to be expected," George fumed. "He's a terrible influence. He's never had to work for anything in his life."

"What do you mean?"

"Do you think you'd marry me if I was a bricklayer?" George demanded. "I worked sixteen hours a day since I was fourteen to get where I am today." He waved at the sofa. "You and Edgar are divorced, but he lounges around as if he's a member of the family. Edgar thinks he can have anything he wants just because he grew up on the Main Line."

George had it all wrong. Of course she'd marry him if he was a bricklayer, as long as they were in love. And Edgar had worked hard on his novel. George could say the same things about Helen. But she was willing to do anything to have her own dairy company.

She opened her mouth to answer, but George moved closer and took her hand.

"In a few hours, we're getting married," he said, stopping her. "Let's stop talking about Edgar and put the past behind us."

Helen didn't want to argue anymore. There would be time to talk about the farm during the honeymoon.

She gave a small smile.

"You're right, of course. I'll see you at the church."

~

Helen walked back to the pool house. Edgar was sitting on the sofa reading a magazine.

She told him everything that George had said.

"Sign the divorce papers, Edgar." She handed him the agreement. "And please don't show up at the ceremony. George wouldn't like it."

Edgar took a pen out of his shirt pocket. It was the same pen that he had used to correct the pages of his novel.

Helen remembered all the days in Sussex when the novel was going well. Edgar would bring her flowers from Vanessa's hothouse, and they'd make the farmhouse feel bright and sunny. She recalled nights at the casino in Deauville. How they'd return to their hotel room, slightly tipsy from kir royales and Gauloises, and make love.

Edgar hadn't meant to shoot Louis. But he found Helen in his hotel suite. He had been jealous because he was in love with Helen.

Jack believed in love. He was finally allowing himself another chance to be happy. And he wasn't afraid to be his true self. Helen had to love herself before she could truly love someone else.

She remembered what Robert had said in the barn. Just because she and Edgar fought didn't mean they weren't meant for each other. Love wasn't easy, but Helen had never backed down from a challenge.

It was one thing to have high standards, but it was another to never allow people to make mistakes. What her father did with Rosalee was terrible, but it had brought him and Charlotte closer together. And Roland should never have cheated on his exams, but it led Daisy and Roland to find a life that was better suited for them.

The worst mistake Helen could make would be not admitting that she was still in love with Edgar.

She and Edgar could accomplish some of the things that she was going to do with George. Edgar could write a children's book and give part of the proceeds to the orphanage. Once the dairy products turned a profit, she could donate part of it to charity.

She took the divorce papers and walked out to the swimming pool. Then she tore them into shreds and tossed the pieces in the water.

Edgar followed her. He gaped at her in astonishment.

"What are you doing?"

She walked back into the pool house. "I lied to you earlier. I said I didn't love you." She took a gulp of air. "It wasn't true. I've loved you since the beginning. I never stopped."

Edgar was silent. She waited for him to say something. What if he had a chance to think while she had been with George and changed his mind?

Edgar got down on his knee. He took the engagement ring from Helen's finger and placed it on the coffee table.

"Helen Montgomery Scott, will you marry me?" he asked.

Helen let out a laugh. "I can't marry you—we're not divorced."

"None of the guests know that," he said eagerly. "You can tell George there's been a change in the grooms; then the whole thing can proceed."

"You want to get married today?" Helen asked in disbelief.

"Why not? Your mother and April would be disappointed if we canceled the wedding." Edgar's eyes were bright. "And you and I deserve a good party. We've been through a lot."

Helen thought about it. April had worked so hard on the decor; she was going to use the wedding to get more clients for her business. And her mother was so excited. She hadn't thrown a big party at Dumfries since Helen's debutante ball.

"All right, why not?" she agreed. "You better go."

"I thought I wouldn't leave quite yet." He stood up and wrapped his arms around her. "We still have a few hours, and we have a lot of catching up to do."

Helen kissed him. Then she moved away and laughed.

"If you think I'm going to make love to you before we're officially remarried, you're wrong." Her eyes danced. "Anyway, you have to leave. It's bad luck for the groom to see the bride before the wedding."

Edgar kissed her one more time. "I don't need any luck. I have you."

Chapter Twenty-Five

The first person that Helen had to tell was George.

She dreaded it, but there was no easy way to go about it. It was like when her mother pulled a splinter from her finger as a child. It always seemed to hurt Charlotte as much as it hurt Helen.

George was still in the living room at Dumfries. A stack of papers sat on the coffee table next to a plate of scones and jam.

George looked up. "You should be at the church," he said. "The *New York Times* photographer is already there. We can't keep him waiting; he gave up a wedding at the Rockefeller mansion to cover our wedding."

"I won't be late for the church." Helen sat opposite him. "But I'm not going to marry you today."

George frowned. "You're talking in circles."

Helen had an idea. She picked up a pencil.

"Not in circles, it's more like a hexagon." Helen drew on the back of one of George's papers. "Here's me, and this point is you, and there's Edgar. This point represents Nellie and Essie and Clara. Over there is Thomas Danforth's creamery, and Mr. Fairbanks at the bank."

George leaned forward. His face had a puzzled expression.

"Geometry was my favorite class at Foxcroft," she continued. "If these points can't exist happily together, the hexagon will break apart. I do love you in a way, but I love Edgar too. And I can't function if I don't spend time with the cows. Thomas Danforth is going to distribute my dairy products, and I can only achieve my goals if the bank gives me a loan." She sat back. "I don't think you'll be happy with these people in our lives, so it's best if we part now."

"Did you say you're in love with Edgar?" George demanded.

Helen put down the pencil.

"I didn't realize it until a few minutes ago. It was just before I tore up the divorce agreement and threw the pieces in the swimming pool."

George looked as startled as a rabbit during the Radnor Hunt.

"You're going to marry Edgar today!"

"It would save money, and the guests are probably on the way to the church," she said. "I hope you don't mind if we use Reverend Brown. He's known me since I was a baby. He officiated at my christening."

There was a lump in Helen's throat. She didn't want to be insensitive, but a rush of adrenaline filled her, and she couldn't calm down. She reached out and touched George's hand.

"I'm very sorry. You've been so good to me," she offered. "I'm trying to become someone new, but being in love with Edgar is the one thing I can't change."

George stared down at his papers for a long time. Then he stood up and walked to the door.

"I'll get my things from the house and stables later." He turned around. "I'll survive. There's plenty of pretty young women who would be happy to marry the Main Line's most promising political candidate. I'm only sorry for my mother. She was counting on telling her friends that her daughter-in-law's ancestors came over on the *Mayflower*. Maybe I got out at the right time. The world will keep moving forward, while you and Edgar will be stuck in your cow pastures and libraries."

Helen stayed silent. The previous months had taught her many things. The kindest thing she could do for George was to allow him the last word.

~

Jack returned from his appointment, and Helen told him everything that happened. He drove her to the church in the same red Roadster they had driven to meet Rosalee in Oyster Bay. Life was unpredictable. Then, Helen had been so miserable; now she couldn't be happier.

Jack told the guests of the change in grooms, while Helen rushed into the anteroom to get ready. She felt odd putting on the wedding gown she had planned on wearing with George. But George had never seen it. The dress was stunning. Oyster-colored crepe de chine with a tiered skirt and a silver sash. A wreath of her mother's yellow roses adorned her hair, and she wore a gold bracelet that had been a birthday gift from Jack.

After the guests' initial surprise, the ceremony went off perfectly.

Edgar looked handsome in high-waisted gray-and-black-striped pants and a cravat tie. He carried white gloves, and a white pocket square fanned out in his vest pocket.

April supplied the wedding rings. She kept a whole box of "emergency products" for the wedding day. A needle and thread in case there was a tear in the dress. A bottle of Phillips' Milk of Magnesia for stomachaches. She even had a small flask of one hundred proof whiskey in case the bride or groom needed extra courage to walk down the aisle.

The only difficult moment was when the reverend said George's name by accident during the reading. Edgar quickly announced that Reverend Brown officiated at so many weddings, it was a wonder he didn't mix up names all the time. Everyone laughed, and George's name wasn't mentioned again.

Now the reception was in full swing. Helen stood next to the dance floor, while Edgar went to get plates of hors d'oeuvres.

Philip Barry approached her. He held a plate of caviar and lobster tails.

"You people on the Main Line know how to throw a party." He whistled, scooping caviar onto a silver spoon.

"We know how to do a lot of things," Helen replied. "My father told me why he asked you to write the article. I'd be happy to sit down and tell you my plans for the dairy company. You might want to interview Edgar too. He can tell you how hard it is to get a novel published."

"That sounds terrific, though George might not like it," Philip said. "He was counting on the piece to help him get elected."

"Lots of reporters would love to write about George," Helen remarked. "A man named Harvey Peterson would be happy to write about his run for office."

Philip took in what she was saying. He smiled at her approvingly.

"I told you that you were an interesting woman. It feels good to know that I was right. It makes me trust my instincts."

Philip wandered off. Conrad walked over to her. He wore the same badly fitting jacket and scuffed black shoes that he had worn the previous night.

"It was a beautiful ceremony; I cried in three places." He stood beside her. "April wants to hire me to be the photographer at weddings and house parties. The pay is much better than shooting for magazines."

"April's clients will be thrilled to have you." Helen nodded. She felt light and happy. "You have to promise me one thing. With the first check, you buy yourself a new suit."

Helen's mother crossed the room. She looked particularly lovely in a pale pink full-waisted evening gown. A strand of pink pearls hung around her neck.

"You're the most beautiful bride." Charlotte hugged her. "I always knew you'd stay married to Edgar."

"You did?" Helen said in surprise.

"George is very nice, but you and Edgar love each other." Charlotte sipped her champagne. "Your father and I are going to spend a year in Italy. It will be nice to be close to Daisy and Roland, and the doctor says it will be good for his health. When we return, we're going to find a smaller house. We wanted to know if you and Edgar would take over Dumfries."

"You want us to live at Dumfries forever?" Helen asked in shock. She had expected her parents to live there for years.

"Dumfries needs a young family, and you'd be closer to the barn," Charlotte said.

"I'll have to ask Edgar, but I can't think of anything we'd like more."

Charlotte went to join Robert. Helen walked over to Daisy's table.

Helen had hardly seen Daisy all day. Daisy was late to help Helen get ready. When she did appear in the pool house, she complained of a terrible headache. Now she looked awful. Her skin was as pale as Helen's dress.

"You look like you're coming down with something." Helen sat next to her. "April has milk of magnesia for your stomach. Or aspirin if you think it's the flu."

Daisy sipped a glass of water. "It's neither of those things. I didn't want to tell you until after the wedding. I'm pregnant. The baby is due in June."

Helen thought of how hard Daisy and Roland had worked on the villa.

"Are you happy?" she asked cautiously.

"Roland is petrified, of course, and I feel sick all the time." Daisy gave a little laugh. "But we're both over the moon."

"Then I'm thrilled. You're going to be the best parents."

Daisy's large blue eyes were thoughtful.

"If it's a boy, we're going to name him Robert Jack. And if it's a girl we'll call her Roberta."

Helen's heart constricted. Her father had made mistakes. He almost made them lose Dumfries. But he apologized and proved how much he loved his family. In a way, she had him to thank for bringing her and Edgar together.

"Those are wonderful names. I might use one when we have a baby," Helen said to Daisy. "I have to go. Father and I are about to dance the first dance."

After the first dance, there were speeches and the cake cutting. It was the first time that Helen had been at a ball and not seen Jack with a beautiful woman on his arm. He danced three dances with Helen and the rest with Daisy and Charlotte.

Now it was getting late. Helen was tired, and she needed some air. She stepped onto the balcony.

"What are you doing out here?" Edgar joined her. "You'll freeze to death."

"The ballroom was so crowded. I needed some fresh air."

"We haven't talked about the honeymoon." Edgar leaned against the railing. "I thought we could go to Sussex. Vanessa would love to have us, and I can meet with Malcolm to tell him that I'm coming back to America. We'll have to edit the book by post."

Helen told Edgar about Dumfries.

"I'd love to live at Dumfries." Edgar was pleased. "I have an idea for a novel set on the Main Line. It's about a young heiress who surprises everyone by what she accomplishes."

She laughed. "It sounds like a bestseller."

Helen remembered their first wedding night, when she sat on the bathroom floor of the honeymoon suite and worried whether getting married was the right decision. Now, she didn't have any of those concerns. Marrying Edgar was the best thing she had ever done.

She could hear the orchestra. They were playing "Tonight You Belong to Me."

"I'm ready to go back inside." She took Edgar's arm. Together, they entered the ballroom.

Acknowledgments

Thank you to my wonderful agent, Johanna Castillo, for her unfailing wisdom and support, and to my editor, Alicia Clancy, for her editorial brilliance. Thank you to the team at Lake Union, including Danielle Marshall and Gabriella Dumpit. And thank you to my readers.

Book Club Questions

1. When Helen discovers that her father is having an affair with Rosalee, she is confident that her mother would want to know the truth. Helen's sister, Daisy, disagrees, and the sisters argue about it. Who do you think is right?

2. Helen agrees to her parents' wishes that she marry a man who will save her father's firm because she is afraid of losing the farm and the cows. This is an interesting perspective for a young society woman of the 1920s. Are times different now? Would her actions shock you if the story was set in the present day? Why or why not?

3. Describe Helen's relationship with her mother. Does their relationship change after Charlotte tells Helen that she's going to stay with Robert even though he had an affair with Rosalee?

4. Who is your favorite secondary character in the book and why?

5. Do you think Daisy is correct in supporting Roland, even though he cheated and was expelled from Harvard? Would you have done the same thing in her position?

6. Helen is considered to be an "ice princess" because she holds everyone, including herself, to such high standards. How does she change throughout the book, and which events cause the changes in her?

7. What are your feelings toward Jack, and which scenes in the book influenced the way you see him?

8. Do you think Helen was justified in going up to Louis's suite because she saw Edgar with Sophie? Or should she have confronted Edgar first?

9. Describe Edgar and Helen's relationship. Do you think they are meant for each other? Can a couple fight and really love each other?

10. Of the different locations in the book—the Main Line in Philadelphia, Sussex in England, Deauville in France, Portofino in Italy—which stays with you the longest and why?

About the Author

Photo © 2019 David Perry

Anita Abriel is the internationally bestselling author of *The Life She Wanted*, *The Light After the War*, and *Lana's War*. She received a BA in English literature with a minor in creative writing from Bard College. Born in Sydney, Australia, Anita lives in California with her family. Her hobbies include walking on the beach, seeing classic movies, reading, and traveling. For more information, visit anitaabriel.com.